The Cornish Village School –
Summer Love

KITTY WILSON

The Cornish Village School

SUMMER LOVE

CANELO

First published in the United Kingdom in 2019 by Canelo

This edition published in the United Kingdom in 2019 by

Canelo Digital Publishing Limited
57 Shepherds Lane
Beaconsfield, Bucks HP9 2DU
United Kingdom

A CIP catalogue record for this book is available from the British Library.

Print ISBN 978 1 78863 577 6
Ebook ISBN 978 1 78863 334 5

Look for more great books at www.canelo.co

Printed and bound in Great Britain by Clays Ltd, Elcograf S.p.A.

For my mother – You are an inspirational woman and I thank you for it. I love you very much.

Chapter One

The crocus-yellow sunshine peeked through the clouds in the early April sky as Pippa snuck out the side entrance of the school. She skipped down the three granite steps into the playground and through a gated arch, revelling in the warmth of the new season.

Springtime in Cornwall meant colour, scents and sounds were flooding the county, bringing it back to life after dormant winter. Even the school car park was alive right now with the sound of birdsong and the sight of the green and pink pride-of-Fowey pushing its way out of the dry-stone walls, stretching towards the sunshine, its flowers clamouring for attention.

She had to be quick. She didn't want to be seen by the children; it would spoil the magic if she were spotted. She was fairly noticeable, dressed from neck to toe in grey fun-fur complete with paws and a big white fluffy tummy. But hopefully she'd be a lot quicker without the giant head, long floppy bunny ears, whiskers and caricature teeth that she had left upon the staffroom table.

Safe now she was in the car park, she tried (and failed) to cross it without hopping or raising her paws upwards as she went. It was so difficult not acting the role of rabbit when dressed as one. Actually, it was next to impossible:

her feet felt extra bouncy and her taste buds were craving raw carrot, most unusual.

Reaching her car, she spied the bag stuffed full of chocolate eggs that she had come to fetch. They were her donation to the Easter Egg hunt this afternoon, and had been topped up by her brother and sister, who wanted to contribute, the Easter egg hunt being one of the Penmenna traditions they had all loved as children. Although she suspected her brother, Pete, was motivated more by whether the eggs would make it out of her car in one piece and on time, rather than natural generosity.

He said some mean things about her car.

Nearly all of them right.

Pippa looked through the window at the bag of eggs nestling on a pile of hangers in the back seat, next to a box of books she had been meaning to take to the charity shop for about eight months now. She could do it tomorrow.

She peeked back in again. Was that the embroidered smocked top she had been looking for? How had that got in there? She was sure she had lost that in the back of the shop, she may have even blamed Lottie for throwing it out. Whoops. She needed to clean this car out, but her priority now was that chocolate.

Putting the basket down, it took her a further ten seconds to realise that rummaging in a handbag for one's keys whilst wearing over-sized bunny paws was not the best way to do things. Like her 1940's vintage mittens, they may be warm and look cute but practical they were not.

She was aware of someone else coming through the gateway but didn't look up, being too busy rifling in her bag and trying not to swear loudly in a primary school car park.

A-ha. She finally managed to get her paw onto her set of keys. If she could just wiggle them up the side of her bag, she could maybe catch onto the keyring as it reached the curl of the top with her teeth. She was fairly sure humans had been using teeth as a tool for years, and this was perfectly normal.

Grasping the keys in her teeth, she let her handbag fall to the ground and then used her free hands to grab onto the keyring, her big furry covered thumb pushing down on the unlock button as hard as she could with a layer of thick fur between her fingers and the mechanism.

Ha! Success. The car flashed its lights to confirm it was now unlocked and she wrenched open the back door to grab the carrier bag of chocolate. If she hadn't come back to get it she knew full well it would be forgotten and she would one day find a huge puddle of chocolate in the foot of the car, swirling with all sorts of lost treasures.

This weekend she would clean this car out until it was the shiniest-looking vehicle in the village so every time she got into it, it would practically squeak at her, the smell of pine or lemon or something desperately clean wafting over as she drove. She could picture the car smiling at her in return, its little lights flickering as eyes in a thank you. Pete and her father would be so shocked they would be rendered speechless, which would be a huge bonus. Oh, although… she did have that Vintage Easter Fayre to work this weekend in Penzance; it would have to be next weekend instead, but she would definitely get around to it.

She pulled the bag out of the car, trying not to get tangled as she did so, and then placed it inside the basket she had been carrying, hoisting it up to her elbow, since it wasn't going any further past the fur. That's when she spied another three large boxed chocolate eggs on the other side of the car. For goodness sake! She had told her mum she didn't need any more but the woman couldn't help herself. She supposed she should be grateful there wasn't a Tupperware container balanced atop the eggs and rammed with Easter biscuits shaped as rabbits and lambs.

Her mother was an all-round wonder-woman but one obsessed with baking novelty-shaped biscuits, all of which were delicious and seriously contributed to Pippa's curves. She had found a pile of almond and raspberry flower biscuits next to her bed the other day.

She hadn't lived at home for at least eight years.

Her mother had ninja burglary skills as well. Or the opposite of burglary, whatever word meant breaking into people's houses and leaving stuff.

Pippa returned to the job in hand. She could try and balance the boxes in a tower and hope she could go back inside without bumping into anything or dropping them sixteen times. She could do that. She hadn't won last summer's It's-A-Knockout at Penmenna Feast Week without having some skills.

Hearing the car door slam next to her, she briefly took a look just in case it was someone who could help. But it was no one she recognised, not that she got a proper look but Pippa knew all the staff cars by sight, and a lot of the parents as well. It was probably one of the interviewees for Lynne's maternity cover. Rosy was holding the last day of interviews today.

Picking up her handbag, she managed to hook that on her shoulder, keep the chocolate egg basket on her elbow, pile up the three Easter eggs her mother had added, and shut and lock the car doors (her chin working the key fob this time). She was just taking one, two, three deep breaths before waddling across the car park and back into the school building when she heard the car next to her start.

Or rather fail to start. The corner of her eye caught sight of a man inside turning the key, repeatedly trying the ignition and having no luck. Maybe she should help? She had jump leads in the back under the clothes hangers; she knew she did.

She'd just have to put these boxes down again and…

The car next to her flashed its lights a couple of times.

She slid the boxes onto the roof of her car, took the basket off her arm and turned to see the back of a man's head as he came out of the car, popped open the bonnet and secured it.

Hmm, a male primary school teacher, if that was what he was. They were rare indeed. Interesting.

She wandered over to him and coughed.

'Would you like me to take a look?'

She saw from the back that he had jet black hair, and despite leaning over the car, appeared tall and well dressed. But then if you couldn't be well-dressed on interview day, something was wrong. She did have a bit of a thing for a man in a suit. People expected her to be all about beard-sporting hipsters or men with dreadlocks and piercings, but actually a well-cut suit or a sniff of tweed and she got dizzy.

The man in front of her turned around and she took a step back. His eyes were deep puddles of the darkest brown and fringed so beautifully with triple the number of eyelashes people normally had. That just wasn't fair! She tried not to stare. Or fall in love. It was difficult.

'Ah, the half-woman, half-rabbit I spotted juggling boxes as I was getting in the car.'

Oh shit, she had forgotten she was dressed like a rabbit. Of course she was. Perfect. She'd have to brazen it out.

'Us half-women, half woodland creatures are pretty good with cars.' She grinned at him, praying she hadn't smudged her lipstick with the key fob.

'Really?'

'Oh yes, especially ones like me who hang around in car parks. Known for it. Although, you are running the risk that I'm fibbing and I am a cunningly disguised car thief.'

'Ha, well in that case, perhaps I shouldn't let you near my car.'

'Could be wise. But now you'll never know if I could have helped.' Pippa turned as if to go, pretending to pout as she did so.

'Don't be a cross bunny, a hot...'

'Don't make that joke. That's an awful joke, and once out you'll never be able to take it back.' She didn't turn around as she spoke, delivering the words with her back to him, arms folded and trying to keep a giggle from tumbling out.

'Ha, okay, fair point. Stay and help, please, you have to know more than me. If you've got a minute that is. I'm really rubbish with cars, and haven't a clue what I'm doing. It's a miracle I know how to clip the seatbelt in, let alone change gears.'

Pippa turned and the man beamed. A grin that not just reached his eyes but made them flash at her as well.

For goodness sake!

He wasn't madly good-looking, not in a traditional sense – his nose was just a smudge too crooked, his lips weren't entirely symmetrical and his face was round, very round and really smiley – but there was something about him that was pulling Pippa right in. Something more complex than a well-cut suit, crazily beautiful come-to-bed eyes and a daft sense of humour akin to hers. Something she couldn't quite put her finger on.

Naturally, the first attractive man she had seen in ages would find her in a car park, dressed as a rabbit. He had probably seen her pulling her keys out with her teeth and clunking the button with her chin as well, fully high-lighting the quadruple chin thing that she blamed her father for. She wouldn't be surprised to discover there was a huge neon arrow hovering somewhere above her head saying 'Little bit odd. Best avoided.'

If she accepted right now that he wasn't feeling the same immediate effect in her presence as she seemed to in his, she could take a look at his car, then flee back to the safety of the school, eggs and all, before she made more of a fool of herself.

'Right, okay, what's the problem?' She used her most sensible voice, trying to be brusque and business like. 'What have you noticed? It won't start presumably?'

'Yep, and I thought it might be the battery, but the lights all light up okay and the radio is on.'

'Yeah, I saw you flash the lights. I'd gamble the battery is fine. It could be a couple of things. I can take a look if you'd like.'

'Are you sure? Under the bonnet? Here?'

'Yeah, I've got a couple of minutes before they send a search party. Hang on.'

Pippa wished she was a super siren that could unzip the top half of her rabbit costume and hold eye contact with the man in front of her as she did so, maybe waving her hair at the same time before turning around and fixing his car in three moves, dripping effortless glamour as she did so.

But this was a school car park and, Pippa reminded herself as she shrugged the costume down and tied the sleeves around her waist, she was always going to be way more Bugs Bunny than she would ever be Jessica Rabbit.

Chapter Two

Kam's head was spinning a little. His interview had gone really well; he liked the head here and you could pick up on the feel of a school as soon as you walked through the door and this one felt good. But then after the interview he had been jumped upon by a very thin woman who appeared to have henchwomen who stood behind her as she looked at him rapaciously whilst asking how he felt about the promoting of the school Christmas Fayre as a Winter Wonder celebration instead. It was the fourth of April.

And then when he had come into the car park he had seen a woman with the blondest bob singing as she skipped across the car park. Actually skipping, and armed with a wicker basket. Not only that, but she was dressed in some kind of furry costume from the neck down.

He couldn't tell whether he really wanted this job or should run a mile.

And now, his car being a bugger and refusing to start meant that the Easter Bunny was standing in front of him, bright red slash of lipstick forming itself into that weird shape that mechanics make with their mouths before shaking their heads while examining your car.

Next, said woman had unzipped the front of the bunny costume, pulled her arms out of the sleeves, and was rolling the top of her costume down and tying the sleeves around her waist, as if they were overalls and she was utterly used to this. Out of costume it was revealed that she wore a deep green blouse with a ginormous bow tied at the side. It was unusual and at the same time it seemed utterly fitting with the woman in front of him, her platinum bob and red lips, making her look like she had just walked straight off a film set during the golden age of Hollywood. And not at all like she worked with small children in the twenty-first century in Cornwall. Or like she was blessed with innate mechanical knowledge.

'Right.' She beamed the cheeriest smile at him, and then came and budged him out of the way with her hip. 'Okay then, let's have a look.' The intimacy of her movement surprised him, but he had to admit he kind of liked it. Cornwall was so good for this. People were relaxed here. You bumped someone back home, and it was considered an aggressive action to be received with a snarl.

She was confident moving around the engine and, as he watched her somewhat in awe, she made an 'oh' noise, as if whatever she'd seen in there was the most obvious thing in the world.

'Easy. Okay, give me a second.' She leaned in and started wiggling a wire. 'Jump back in and try and see if it turns over now.'

'Okay.' Kam jumped into the front seat, leaving the door open as he turned the key.

The engine roared into life, and he left it idling as he got out and came around the front again.

'How did you do that?'

'It was easy: your wire to the starter motor is loose. If it doesn't start again, just try giving it a wiggle.'

'A wiggle? Is that a mechanical term?'

'It is actually. But you will need it looked at sooner rather than later to stop it going all together.'

'I've just moved to the area. I'm staying with my friend in Newquay for the time being. I'll see who he uses.'

'Good plan, or I could give you my dad's number. He's the mechanic in the village and can be totally trusted. If you drive out from here, just by the church is a sharp right hand turn down a lane. Go down there and it'll look like you shouldn't be driving any further but do. Have faith and keep going. You'll find him right at the bottom. Penmenna's best kept secret. He'll see you okay. He's not one of those "kick your tyres and shake his head" kinda guys who then whack you with a quote the equivalent of a small mortgage.'

'Oh, I know the look. You mean this one.' Kam pursed his lips up and shook his head slightly, hoping he was managing to convey a look of abject alarm and not just like he was sucking lemons. The one he knew he had seen on her face but minutes earlier.

She laughed. He had made rabbit girl laugh. People didn't often laugh at his jokes. They tended to look at him pityingly instead.

'Yes, that exact one.'

'Ah, I thought so, the one you were doing as you first looked at my car.'

'I did not!'

'Well, where else would I have learnt it? You so did.'

'Okay well, then it's genetic. Like my chin. Blame my father.' Kam looked at her, She had a rather nice chin he thought, rounded and at the end of her face, where it should be.

'Is your dad likely to look at it today? Newquay is a bit of a trek so it would be sensible to get it looked at as soon as possible, I guess.'

'My dad is always busy, but I expect if you tell him I sent you and if I ask him to pop you to the front of the queue then he probably will. I'll send him a text now. It's not a large job if it's just this loose wire. If it's the starter motor itself that's a few hours work but he'll be best placed to tell you.'

'Okay, thank you. Should I just say I'm a friend of your daughter, sir, the one who dresses as a rabbit?'

'Ha. No, that could be either of us. Best say you're a friend of Pippa's or a colleague, you know, in case you get the job I'm guessing you're here for. Actually, if you say that, he and my brother will interrogate you…'

'Oh, I'm used to family interrogations.'

'Maybe, but not this one. You'll know you're in trouble when they haul my mum in. Best just say Pippa sent you and keep it vague. He'll still bump you up the queue but won't invite you over for dinner or ask what your father does. I hope.' She started to pull up her costume again, struggling to get her hands into her paws and then fumbling over the zip. 'Right, I best get back to school.'

'Are you alright there?' Kam wanted to offer to help, but felt zipping her up may well breach the rules on touching in social situations. He didn't really know what to do with his hands; they suddenly felt awkward and unnecessary. They couldn't fix cars, and he was unsure about the appropriateness of them zipping up rabbits. He also quite liked the idea of being invited to dinner by the mechanic. He was interested to see what Pippa was like in a family situation. And whether all the family were larger than life as she was.

'Paws are the worst. I am so glad I'm not actually an animal. Having paws is even harder than long nails. I shall never take my hands for granted again.'

'Probably a good plan. Here let me help you back to school with the chocolate.'

'Oh, you're fine. I can do it. You don't want to leave the car like that. Penmenna may not be a criminal hotspot but there is such a thing as taking the mickey and you leaving this car with the engine running would be it. Here, if you just help load me up that would be grand.'

'Hmm, that doesn't seem very gentlemanly…'

'No, but it does sound very sensible. Now, are you going to let me go in or stand here arguing with me?'

'Fair point, but let me introduce myself first. I know you're Pippa so it's only polite to tell you my name: I'm Kam.'

'Hi, Kam. Pleasure to meet you. She reached out her paw and raised her eyebrow. Kam laughed out loud and shook her fur-clad hand.

'That's the first time I've ever shook hands with the Easter Bunny.'

'Well, make the most of it. I suspect you won't get the chance again in a hurry.'

'Ha, no. probably not. It's been an absolute pleasure meeting you, Pippa. You are a fun-fur-clad superhero and I can't thank you enough.'

'No worries, glad to be of help.'

'You've put a spring in my step.'

'Really? That's bad.'

'Not as bad as a receding *hare* line.'

'Just stop!'

'I know, I'd best *hop* to it.'

'Seriously. I help you and this is how you repay me?'

'It's been an *egg-citing* morning so far. I *carrot* wait to see how the rest of the day pans out.'

'Get out of this car park before I call security.'

'Is that the scary looking woman I met earlier?'

'Oh, we have many. Prison-guard facial expression, scrapped–back hair and trouser suit, or predatory yummy-mummy wearing ladybirds? Oh shit. I shouldn't have said any of those things. Forgive me. Oh and forget – please forget – I said that as well. Most unprofessional.'

'I'll keep your secret seeing as you fixed my car. Although, I'm half tempted to go back inside for another explore. But I guess it would be sensible to get to your dad's and keep my fingers crossed that it is just the wire thing.'

'Good plan. Nice to meet you, Kam.'

'And you too. I owe you one. Here.' He balanced the last egg box on top of the other two. 'It feels wrong not helping you carry this. Are you sure you can make it back inside?'

'Of course I am. Now stop your chitchat or I won't be back in time and we'll have some very sad children.'

'Okay, go. And thank you.' Kam headed back into the car but couldn't help but watch her and really hope he got the job. 'Oh!' he wound down the window and shouted out 'Remember, don't worry, be hoppy!'

Chapter Three

Pippa entered the infant playground, with a broad grin on her face. Kam had been a bit of a departure from the regular school day and she hoped he got the job.

'Ah good. We wondered where you had got to. Can't have our Easter Bunny disappearing today. Although you do seem to have lost your head.' The head of the PTA greeted her in her characteristic tone – faux politeness barely veiling constant criticism. The faux politeness usually being fairly quickly dropped.

Pippa loved her job as a teaching assistant but this woman, Marion Marksharp, and her fawning and freakily identical acolytes, drove her scatty and she was fairly sure she wasn't paid enough to deal with the levels of stress the head of the PTA brought with her. Any more than three minutes of talking to the woman and Pippa started to panic she would develop a rash. Following Marion around as she marched from playground to playground barking commands and shoving over-excited pupils out of the way was not Pippa's idea of a happy springtime celebration.

However, she was at work, so breathed deep, counted to three and then answered the woman standing in front of her, shaking with righteous organisation.

'It's in the staffroom, Marion, I'll just...'

'No need. Sarah, get the rabbit head from the staffroom, and bring it to the infant playground. Thank you.' Marion issued the command into her walkie-talkie.

'Now, let's just run through everything one more time. Eggs spread out fairly amongst both playgrounds: check?'

'Actually, Marion, I've got some extra. That's where I was. I had to fetch them from the car.'

'For goodness sake, all Easter Eggs were supposed to be collected by lunchtime and hidden by half past one. What on earth were you doing?'

'Working in the classroom, Marion, and then covering lunch duty.' Pippa felt her eyes roll as she answered back. This woman made her feel like she was thirteen again: deeply resentful and full of sass.

'I suppose it can't be helped.' Marion looked like she distinctly thought it could have and should have been, before pulling her walkie talkie to her mouth again. 'Code red, code red. Miss Parkin has forgotten to hand in her eggs, more eggs to come. I repeat more eggs. Could I please have someone from each playground to come and get the extras. Right, are all the teachers informed of and aware of the times we need the classes outside by?' The woman didn't stop for breath. Maybe she didn't need to. In fact, if she was not actually human and breathing normally wasn't a thing she had to do, quite a lot of things would make sense. Pippa found herself looking at her to see if she could spot signs of the paranormal, but even with all the squinting in the world, she couldn't spot a pair of horns or ghostly aura. She just looked like Marion Marksharp in full steam mode.

'Yes, Marion, Class One and Class Three will be in their playgrounds by thirteen forty-five and Classes Two and Four will come out at fourteen-thirty. That gives us time to hide the second tranche of eggs,' Jenny, Marion's deputy and possible twin, responded in the same military tone.

'Right, excellent. Here comes Sarah with your head, Miss Parkin. Now if you could kindly keep it on, that would be much appreciated.'

'I'll do my best.'

'Well, dear, it shouldn't be that hard. I'm sure you're more than capable. But if you feel it requires it, I shall be more than happy to staple you in.' Marion narrowed her eyes, tilted her head and fake-smiled before racing across the playground as something, or someone, caught her eye.

Pippa wondered if it would result in immediate dismissal if she rammed the PTA's walkie-talkie where the sun didn't shine.

'Hello, how you doing? Do I see steam coming out of those bunny ears?' Sylvie, the specialist PE teaching assistant slid next to her, and Pippa could see Sylvie grinning at her through her little bunny eye holes.

'I might have to kill her.'

'You'd be fairly easy to pick out from a line up – the suspect fled the scene wearing head to toe grey fur and a pair of whiskers.'

'Ha-ha, very funny. I don't know how you bear her.' Sylvie had joined the staff team last year during the September term and, like their headmistress, Rosy Winter, she was one of the few members of the school community who didn't seem to think Marion was the devil incarnate. Pippa respected Rosy endlessly and was very fond of Sylvie but for the life of her could not see why they were so forgiving of this tyrannical monster with her tautly stretched skin, bird prints and power heels.

'She's not that bad once you scratch the surface.'

'Hmm, scratching her I could get behind, but I dread to think what I'd find under my nails if I tried. It would probably generate some weird kind of organism that sprung to life after midnight, roaming the village with a walkie-talkie and an iPad, screeching at anyone she passes.'

'I like her. Well, I loathed her, but then I got to know her. Turns out she means well, really she does. And her boys adore her. That has to be indicative of something.'

'Stockholm syndrome?'

'Mrs Marksharp.' Sylvie called over to Pippa's nemesis, currently hauling a PTA member out of the bushes and shrieking abuse at her.

'Not in the bushes, for goodness sake! Has everyone here actually been lobotomised? I was quite clear. Miss Winter has requested we don't send the children into the bushes this year, what is the mat… oh hello, Sylvie dear.' Marion spun as she heard Sylvie calling.

Pippa felt herself sigh and roll her eyes again. Much more time spent around Marion and her eyes were going to spin right out of their sockets. She knew Sylvie, an ex-ballerina, was on Marion Marksharp's 'People I Value' list, but so bright were the beams now heading in their direction she felt like flopping her ears over her eyes for protection.

'Oh hello, darling, how are you? And the lovely Alex? And the children of course?' Monster Marksharp stalked her way over to them, having dropped Ashleigh's mum, Alison, on the playground floor, and grinning the most frightening grin since The Joker.

'We're all fine thanks, Marion. Alex has just got home from South Sudan, so we're all enjoying having him back. Give him a few days and we'll catch up. Richard and the boys?'

Pippa spotted a flash of something indecipherable cross Marion's face.

'Yes, yes. The boys and I are off to Bordeaux for the holiday. Chateau break, they're very excited.'

Pippa was amazed 'the boys' got through passport control. She fully expected Rafe, the eldest, to top Interpol's Most Wanted within the decade.

'Sounds nice. Harmony has sent me out to see if you're ready for us yet?'

Harmony Rivers was the Class Three teacher and known as Hippy-Dippy Harmony by the less kind members of the school community. She was on a personal crusade at the moment to raise everyone's awareness of the plight of the school hamster and had her class designing escape plans to set him free. Apparently, it was to help teach critical thinking skills.

Harmony spent her holidays fighting injustice wherever she saw it, waving placards and singlehandedly trying to stop global corruption. Interestingly, whilst she seemed to have no problem facing down dictators, it was no secret throughout Penmenna that she was absolutely terrified of Marion. Sending Sylvie was a sensible call. Pippa wished it were an option for her.

'I don't know how that woman is a teacher. Can she not tell the time? It's not even like she has to try and decode the Victorian school clocks on the wall. The world is digital these days and yet she still struggles.'

'I don't think she has a mobile phone, Marion.'

'Of course she doesn't. She probably relies on some method involving slugs and a cartwheel at home. She's got five minutes. And you can tell her that Miss Winter has said there's to be none of that stupid sharing of the eggs in her class later. Dividing the spoils is downright communist and there's no place for that sort of nonsense inside this school.' Marion grinned her biggest crocodile grin as she delivered this news and Pippa did a double take.

The classes had been sharing the eggs out for years now. She couldn't imagine that Rosy Winter would have changed the practice and she wouldn't know about it. Pippa was the teaching assistant in Rosy and Lynne's class for a start.

'You are so naughty, Marion. You know that's not true; you're just trying to wind her up. I'm not telling her that.' Sylvie had no truck with Marion's suggestion but sent her a warm grin all the same.

'Tut, you're no fun. Tell her three minutes. We need her here in three minutes.' And Marion formed a moue complete with downcast glance, as if Sylvie had stolen her favourite toy.

As Sylvie turned to leave, they heard the creaking of the door the other side of the playground and the sound of twenty four and five-year-olds spilling out into the play-ground with frenzied grins of anticipation and hunting for chocolate.

Marion looked up and quickly reverted to type. The walkie talkie was back in hand.

'Time minus zero and go. I repeat, time minus zero and go. What on earth are you still doing here? Go, go, go!' she barked at Pippa. Her words bounced around the playground, amplified by the walkie talkie welded to her lips.

'Hop to it. Do hurry up! Idiots and incompetents, the lot of you!'

Chapter Four

It had almost been a full week since the start of the Easter holidays and Pippa hadn't stopped to relax for a minute of it. The holidays were normally jam-packed with events where she could sell her vintage clothing, as tourists descended upon the county en masse. This one had been no different. Meaning that she raced through the front door of her parent's house only just in time for family dinner, a weekly event where everyone was expected to attend or they'd face the wrath of their mother. Wrath that may take the shape of sad face biscuits for the next week or all the washing done without the use of any fabric conditioner, both options considered nuclear by the Parkin family's matriarch.

The fact that neither Pippa, Polly or Pete asked their mother to wash their clothes was of no consequence. The fact that she broke into both Pippa and Pete's houses every few days to collect their laundry was an argument they had all tried and failed, both individually and collectively, to win. Pippa was the oldest and had begged and begged her mother not to keep coming around and letting herself in. But her mother protested she always knocked first and was only being helpful.

Pete had claimed that they could move to three different parts of the world and she'd still find a way to do the washing and expect them to turn up without fail every Thursday. Polly reckoned she'd invent either a hoverboard or zappy device so she could continue to come and visit them randomly, let herself in, take the laundry, and fill the cupboards with bleach and carpet cleaner.

However much the three moaned – and they did – about how their mother had her ever-loving fingers all over their lives, they did all enjoy Thursday dinner. It was always full of laughter and what they had known forever.

'Hey mum.'

'Hey love.' Her mum, Jan, uncurled herself from crouching by the oven where she was swooshing the potatoes from side to side, all fluffed up and covered with garlic and slabs of butter and smelling like heaven.

'I'll lay the table. Are the others here yet?'

'Yes, Pete is in the shed with your father and Polly is upstairs in her room. Apparently, she can't come out again until June. These exams will be the death of her and she's sitting up there with a cling film wrapped around her hair and a bottle's worth of ketchup squished on underneath.'

'She's doing what? Ketchup?' Pippa washed her hands and then grabbed the cutlery from the draw.

'What can I say? She's seen it on the internet. She dyed her hair emerald green yesterday and woke up this morning hating it. Says it makes her look dead. Then the internet told her… it told her' – Jan seemed to think the internet followed you around the house speaking to you, rather like she did – 'that the red in the ketchup would balance out the green in her hair. A natural colour wheel it said. Have you ever heard anything so stupid? I tried to tell her. Now I'm leaving it up to her. I've bought some hair dye remover and left it in the bathroom cupboard, and

23

when she decides she doesn't like smelling like a burger van then she might use it.'

'Oh, I'll nip up and see her.'

'No, she's in a foul mood. Save yourself and stay here and lay the table. We're starting a bit later tonight; we've got the Carpenters coming.'

'Oh, okay then, table for seven then?'

Pippa grabbed some extra knives and forks and headed into the dining room. The Carpenters had been family friends since forever and they all ate together every major holiday.

'No, eight.' Her mother's answer made Pippa pause.

'Eight?'

'Yes, eight. James is home so he'll be coming too. It's nice for Karen as he hasn't been back in years. Talking of beautiful young men—'

'I wasn't aware that we were.'

As ever, Jan ignored that which she didn't want to hear. 'I was most disappointed when you wouldn't tell us anything about that lovely young man you sent to Dad's. Nothing at all. And he was so cute. Dad showed me on the CCTV. Lovely young man. You need to accept that time is getting on; I had had both you and Peter by the time I was your age.'

Pippa smiled: Kam *had* been cute. Those beautifully fringed eyes, and those awful jokes. She had been attracted to him immediately – *boom!* – out of nowhere. She wasn't letting her mother anywhere near him! Plus, she didn't want children yet. What was so hard for her mother to understand? Pippa was nowhere near ready for the whole happily-ever-after that her Mum and Dad had. Surely that much was obvious. Plus, these days you were no longer considered a failure if you hadn't popped two children out by the age of twenty-five (a milestone she had long passed). Unless, it seemed, you were a Parkin.

'But not to worry. Like I say, the Carpenters have James visiting for the week. You remember James. You two were like two bugs in a rug when you were small. I'm sure there is more than a little romantic potential there. He's doing very well for himself now, you know? He's working in the City, making a fortune by all accounts...'

Pippa tuned her mother out. James Carpenter. Wow. She smiled a smile to herself, one so nostalgic and full of fondness it made her tummy feel warm. James who used to bake her bread and bring it into school for her, who put his coat over a puddle for her after they had learned about the Tudors. Fancy. Mind you, they had caught up about ten years ago, the last time he had been home, and he hadn't been quite so gentle then!

Tonight was going to be interesting.

She wandered back into the kitchen to grab the additional place setting as her father and Pete came back in from the garden.

'Hey, what do you think you're doing?' Her mother slapped Pete away from the oven as he tried to open the door and pinch a roast potato.

'It's only a potato, love.' Pippa's dad stuck up for Pete.

'*Pfft!* We've got lots for dinner tonight, and I've counted. He'll mess my numbers up.' Just as she turned to whip her husband with a tea-towel, Pete took advantage, wrenched the oven door open and rammed a potato in his mouth.

'Owww!' He hopped up and down as the potato took its revenge.

'Serves you righ—' Jan's retort was cut short as Jim plopped a kiss on her lips in an attempt to divert her. He followed up the kiss with a series of smacking noises.

'*Hmpf*, get off me. You're such an oaf.' Her mother tried flapping her husband off to no avail. They were still so cute. When Pippa found that, *that* was when she'd know she was ready. Relationship goals, right there. However, there was no way she was going to tell them that.

'It's no wonder Polly hides in her bedroom. She's the most normal out of all of you,' she said instead.

'Us, out of us. Don't think you're off the hook for not being weird. Your clothes are what, seventy years old?' Pete weighed in.

'You're not so old I still can't take you!'

Ding dong.

'Quick, Pippa, go get the door.' Jan spat on her hand and tried to smooth Pippa's hair down.

'*Urgh*, will you get off me? That is not okay.' Pippa flapped her hands in a futile attempt at self-protection.

Ding dong.

Chapter Five

James had grown up gorgeous, all blond floppy hair and sun-kissed biceps. He may work in the City but clearly spent all his downtime on the best beaches in the world. Pippa had a hard time not dribbling into her supper.

Dinner had been fun, James also was in full charm offensive mode and didn't bat an eyelid at Polly coming down the stairs still with her ketchup cling film wrap on and (almost) convincing everyone that what she was doing was rational. He had kept up a steady stream of conversation with Pippa's family, whilst his own family bathed in the golden light of reflected glory.

He managed to talk to Dad about how things were doing at the garage, and got Jan to talk about what it was she loved about her volunteer work at the hospice. Pete, he engaged in conversation about the Liverpool game the night before, and Polly was charmed as he discussed the summer festival circuit and her plans to fit as many as possible in. He mentioned that he may be able to get her a couple of VIP passes to two of them and her whole face lit up, flushing the same colour as the ketchup in the glow of his attention.

The only person he didn't address directly was Pippa, although he would include her in little asides, collaboratively, as if they were an established team, and she supposed they were. She just wasn't entirely sure what sort.

He really was very beautiful, like a warrior lion king, made of an odd mix of masculinity and sunshine, holding court, dazzling all present.

Their first course finished, James jumped up to help clear the table only to be firmly put back in his chair by Jan coquettishly pushing his shoulders back down until he was sat back in his original position. Her eyelashes practically took flight she was batting them so furiously. 'No, you're the guest and a much valued one. We can't have you doing chores. You sit here and talk to Pippa. You'll have all sorts to catch up on. Why, you can't have seen each other since you were Polly's age.'

And she was right, they hadn't, and her comment naturally meant that their very last meeting popped into Pippa's head where she had been battling to keep it out of all evening.

As children the two had been inseparable, making mud pies and sandcastles, rock-pooling and den building on Penmenna bay, years of being each other's ultimate confidante, partner in crime and all-round bestie.

Secondary School rolled around, its presence inevitable, and the two were split into different student cohorts. As they matured they drifted apart: Pippa spent her time with the artsy creative set, a little bit too much eyeliner and lots of talking about feelings and the meaning of life interspersed with drunken high-pitched shrieking. James, on the other hand, spent his time discussing coding and Firefly with his friends, the slightly geekier kids, the chess club clique, Pippa and he now only coming together when their families did. And even then, James would find himself spending time with Pete, who would constantly be talking cars. Even if the two did hang out together on holiday, Pippa knew she was guilty of racing back to her other friends as soon as term time returned.

She also knew James had then had more than a little crush on her. It wasn't that she didn't fancy him back then… actually, that was exactly what it was. She didn't fancy him. His conversations were way too complex to follow and he didn't really wash often enough. He was intense and competitive, and she much preferred the easy-going banter of her own friends to the soulful puppy eyes and waves of body odour emitting from her once best friend. As her life became a mad social whirl from the age of thirteen, more and more space grew between them.

That wasn't the last time she had seen him though.

Oh no.

The Christmas after he had first left Penmenna for university, left the idyllic coastal charms behind for fast-paced urban ones, he had returned home a different person. Bags of confidence had shone from him then, bright as tinsel and just as captivating. That and the fact that he had clearly ramped up the importance placed on personal grooming. Hair product and deodorant seemed to be one of the many new habits he had picked up from one term in Manchester.

Pippa wasn't sure what had triggered such a remarkable change, but it was a James who Pippa was interested in and could relate to. A James far more sophisticated than the boys who had stayed behind in Cornwall. Pippa didn't consider herself to be particularly shallow but at eighteen her head had been turned very easily and that Christmas they spent every day together, the core friendship they had so deeply buried not so far from the surface.

A friendship that turned to romance very quickly as James took her to dinner and verbalised that which she already knew: that all through his gawky youth he had always had a huge crush on her. He had spent their camping holidays in France as teens, biting back the jealousy as she skipped off with boys of all nationalities, whilst Pete would try and get him to understand why the Ford Cortina was due a come-back. Pippa would have the most wondrous holiday romances accompanied by tears, flouncing and petulance on the journey home, whereas James would be begging to return to the safety of his bedroom where his unrequited crush wouldn't be so blatantly rubbed in and he didn't have to hear about the merits of T-Cut.

That Christmas, he held her hand over the dinner table and Pippa had been dazzled by his brilliance, and cross that she hadn't seen his appeal sooner.

That Christmas, Pippa lost her virginity to her best and oldest friend. Was he going to be her forever partner? The one she could settle down with and build a relationship as strong as the one her Mum and Dad had?

Apparently not. In the new year, she heard nothing from him, nothing, not a jot until this evening.

The Carpenters had still been regular visitors to the Parkin household, just minus their son. They would talk at great length at the amazing things that he was achieving, how he was a huge name in banking, his understanding of computing systems having seamlessly transformed into massive success in playing the financial markets, and Pippa felt stupid every time. He had ghosted her before it was a thing that even had a name.

And now here he was in her dining room, charming everyone and somehow making her push her own doubts to the back of her mind as she witnessed what a glorious man he had become.

So glorious that achieving a First and building a glittering career meant that he couldn't operate a phone, visit his parents or respond to messages on social media.

It wasn't until her mother's very boozy berry trifle had been served and the table had been cleared that James made her the focus of his conversation. But not by actually engaging with her.

'Jan, that was absolutely delicious, but I'll never keep myself in shape if I keep eating like this. I can't remember ever having such a delightful meal. Would you mind if Pippa and I took Tatters for a walk? We'll do the washing up when we get back.'

Pippa shot a look at him: firstly his mother was also a great cook and looking a little put out, and secondly, she didn't want to go on a walk. She'd had a madly busy day and wanted to escape home straight after dinner to fall into bed and binge watch a few episodes of her favourite show. Plus, she was fairly sure it was Pete's turn to wash the dishes this week.

As intrigued as she had been to see him again and as impressed as she was about the way he was interacting with her family, she could feel her eyes narrow as she shot James her best killer-ray death glare. Alas, it appeared to bounce right back as he failed to notice it. Probably because he was too busy being bathed in looks of adoration from her mother and sister.

'Oh, that would be wonderful. Tatters does love an after-dinner walk, but there's no way you'll be doing the dishes, young man. You're our guest. I wouldn't hear of it.' Jan gushed so much she was beginning to provide some serious competition to Niagara Falls.

'Hardly a guest Jan. I like to think of myself as family, if it's not too much of an imposition.'

Pippa's eyes rolled so hard she could feel them practically bouncing out of her skull. Silence for thirteen years and *now* he was family!

James shook his golden mane as he let out a deep chuckle, secure in his belief that he was universally loved. Pippa watched her whole family simper as she began to wonder if he was a little too polished, a little... fake. The man was clearly emitting some kind of brainwashing pheromone. Even her dad looked a little starry-eyed!

She didn't want to go on a poxy walk and she wasn't sure she wanted to be forced into spending more time with James than she already had. She was willing to accept that life got in the way sometimes, and had no intention of holding a grudge against him because he hadn't been in touch. But now, having spent this evening with him, her bullshit radar was beginning to go off, and loudly too. Thirteen years was a long time, people could change a lot and she wasn't convinced he was the same sweet person as the child she had known.

She saw no merit in extending this evening any further. She'd had a long day, was knackered and really just wanted to curl up under her duvet with Netflix and then a book before going to sleep. Walking with a man she wasn't sure she trusted and raising her mother's ever-present romantic hopes was not what she wanted to be doing. She wondered if sobbing and banging her head on the dinner table could possibly be deemed acceptable once one had passed the age of three? Her own little bed in her own little flat wasn't so much emitting a soft siren call as screeching 'Come home now!' with the volume of an all-night rave.

'Of course, we think of you as family, don't we, Jim? Chosen family. After all, we have been doing things together since before you and Pips were even little twinkles. Tatters will be overjoyed to have a walk. The lead is just on the peg. Pippa knows where it is, don't you Pippa? Hurry up now, James is waiting.'

Pippa tried her death glare that had been so ineffective upon James on her mother, to much the same result. But then, to be fair, surviving three children's adolescence meant that Darth Vader could wander in the house and Jan wouldn't bat an eye, but just mention that moody boys didn't get any treats.

She tried to ignore Pete, who was shooting her looks of amusement as he cleared the table, and Polly, who was also sending looks but of envy rather than anything else, and quickly tried to formulate an excuse that would get her out of the walk. Could she have suddenly developed a leg injury? No, that would not be worth it, because it would involve her mother nipping around every day to take photos to check for improvements or for any signs of worsening symptoms. Um, could she pretend she had a pressing engagement after dinner? No, her parents would know that wasn't true and she'd never hear the end of it. Could she...?

The jangle of the chain that made up the dog's lead snapped her out of her frantically racing thoughts as Pete dropped it next to her on the table.

'There you go, sis.' He was grinning from ear to ear, clearly over the moon at his own evil as he beamed from her to James. 'Best get a wriggle on.'

Chapter Six

Pippa had taken great care with her appearance as she headed into school. It was still the holidays but Rosy had pencilled in today as a planning meeting for the Class One staff, to discuss the summer term. Pippa liked these days: she got a buzz out of helping plan what the children would be doing, and seeing how lesson built upon lesson to help develop their skills. Summer term was her absolute favourite; it was all so much fun and they spent a lot of it dashing around Penmenna doing awesome sunshiny things.

However, it wasn't professional diligence that had resulted on her trying on six different outfits this morning before deciding upon her chocolate brown, early-sixties sweater dress with cute little tan stripe detailing around the cuffs, neckline and hem of the skirt. Relaxed and stylish was the vibe she was going for and as there wouldn't be actual children in the classroom today, she could risk wearing it, the chances of getting covered head to toe in paint, playdough or glitter being hopefully next to zero. Unlike every other day, when being sprayed with art supplies, yogurt and the odd bit of wee or sick was more or less guaranteed. The joys of being a teaching assistant in Class One.

Teaming the dress with her trademark scarlet lips and the cutest little chocolate and tan court heels, and flicking the ends of her hair up to suit the outfit had made her early start more than bearable. It was just a shame she had had to look a dead seagull in the eye whilst she did it.

Her flatmate, Lottie, who ran the shop below their flat, was currently obsessed with taxidermy, having decided this would be her new career choice and being determined to become the go-to taxidermist in the UK. Lottie was often dismissed by others as a little odd, but Pippa knew she had a razor-sharp mind, a fascination with stocks and shares, which meant she owned the village shop and the flat they shared, and was far smarter than she was given credit for. It was unfortunate though that when it came to taxidermy she was still very much at the practice stage, and everything she did resulted in having slightly crossed eyes or looking like infamous serial killers of the animal world, and ended up scattered liberally over the house. Hence the seagull in the bathroom, which was, according to Lottie, an-absolutely-darling-little-touch-helping-fit-with-a-nautical-theme. In Pippa's mind it was more mangy-old-bird-riddled-with-fleas and freaking her out before breakfast.

However, even Sidney the seagull (yes, Lottie had named it) couldn't dim her excitement today. She couldn't wait to see if Kam had got the job and who she'd be working alongside. She had received an email from Rosy detailing that a Mr Choudhury had got the job. This wasn't conclusive evidence as she may have interviewed more than one male candidate, but it was definitely hopeful.

Far more hopeful than her enforced walk with James the other night had been, where he had told her how he had adored her as a child and then suggested ways in which she could improve herself. He also had revealed a quite remarkable knack for pursuing his own agenda and not even pausing in any way to hear Pippa's views. In between telling her that she could be very attractive if she just ditched the vintage thing and dressed properly, he had utterly failed to answer any of her questions about his inability to contact her after their Christmas romance all those years ago, although he did take a deep interest in the local scenery whenever she tried to discuss it.

James had no sense of humour and was rather like a shallow pool: all glinting and beautiful in the moonlight, but with nowhere near enough depth to get lost in. It was unfortunate that the pure joy on her mother's face as they returned Tatters meant Pippa was somewhat boxed in. Jan's fervid dreams of imminent grandchildren were ablaze on her face as James cunningly asked Pippa if he could take her out again whilst standing in front of her mother. Such manipulative behaviour did not play well with Pippa and she would make sure to tell him so when he picked her up next time. However, she could hardly turn him down. Whilst she didn't give a jot about his feelings, saying 'not a chance' in front of her mother would be akin to shooting Bambi at point-blank range. She just couldn't do it. Plus, she still felt she owed it to the child she had known, to scratch the surface a little deeper and see if *that* James was still in there, even if he was buried very deep indeed.

Kam, on the other hand, most definitely had a sense of humour; it was written all over his face, lighting up his eyes and even expressed in the very way he walked. It might be a shockingly bad sense of humour, but that was alright with Pippa. She had one of those too. He was the complete opposite of James in every way. If Kam had been given the job, she could see herself giggling all term.

His round face and laughing eyes were right there in her head making her smile with the possibilities of the two of them spending time together as she turned into the staff car park. And ta-daa, right there in exactly the same spot as it had been before, was the car she had sent to her father's garage. Perfect!

Chapter Seven

Kam sat at the little table in the middle of the classroom. Like all foundation stage or early-years settings, it was vibrant, alive with colour and there was a really good feeling in this classroom, the aura of a happy productive school. He was so chuffed to be here. He had heard getting any kind of job in a Cornish school was next to impossible, a bit of a dead-man's-shoes game, and this temporary position was a gift that meant he could be back on track, or at least a few steps closer, to achieving his five-year plan.

Plus, it might go some way to getting his family off his back. Having said that it may still be a while before his father forgave him.

And now he was sitting here raring to go and with a huge pot of coffee in front of him. Kam was very much a coffee man, although he was guilty of lying to his mum and swearing he only ever drank decaff. It was one of her things. His poor dad never heard the end of it and was driven to desperate measures daily. He rather hoped the women he would be working with shared his coffee love. Miss Winter, he had met for his interview, and he knew he would enjoy working alongside her, but the class teaching assistant had been out when they had shown him around, something to do with the Easter celebrations.

This took his mind back to the meeting in the car park with the Easter Bunny. She had been fab. He liked her, a lot. So much so that he hoped that she wouldn't turn out to be the classroom assistant he was assigned. He wanted to make a good impression here, and having your foot in the door within a school was key. Like most jobs, word of mouth was fundamental and he wanted to do his absolute best in Penmenna so that when it came time to move on, Rosy Winter would put in a good word for him. Good words were how one got permanent positions. Permanent positions were his only way to achieve his goals and the best chance of getting his family to see that his decisions had been good ones.

And one did not get good words by mixing business with pleasure. If the Easter Bunny was the teaching assistant, then that could cause more than a few ripples in his smooth professional life. The fact that she resembled the blonde bombshells of old and laughed at his jokes meant he had developed a minor crush in the first thirty seconds of meeting her. That was not conducive to professional workplace relations.

He poured himself another cup of coffee and was somewhat self-indulgently sniffing it as he did so when he heard the classroom door open.

'Oh wow, that smells amazing.' Blonde bombshell entered the room and Kam could feel a huge grin spreading across his face in reaction to her presence. Was it possible for one's heart to sink and to race at the same time? Plus, if anything was amazing, it was she.

She walked towards him, her curves fully highlighted in some kind of jumper that was a dress and reminded him of Mad Men and all things sixties. Damn, he needed to stop grinning. Had he not just told himself this would be a bad idea? Maybe this was just coincidence. Maybe she worked in another part of the school and had just come in here for supplies or something?

She pulled out the chair and plonked a Tupperware container remarkably similar to the ones his mother carted around everywhere, on the table in front of them.

'Is one of these mugs for me? I do hope so. I'm known to kill for proper coffee and that wouldn't be great before term even started.' She pulled one of the mugs towards her, then the cafetière and poured herself some coffee, pausing to inhale it before taking her first sip.

'Oh, this is incredible. I was hoping it was you who got the job. We're going to work well together, I just have a feeling. But this, well, this' – she inhaled again – 'this confirms it. You, Mr Choudhury, have just made my morning. Mmm.'

The pleasure she was taking in the coffee was something he understood but it was not making him feel very teacherly. Those bright red lips on the curve of the cup, the way she inhaled deep and drank with such feeling was a little bit too sensual for the workplace first thing in the morning. Damn.

After she had drunk about half a cup in one go, she cradled the mug in her hands and gestured towards the container.

'Help yourself, my mother has some kind of baking addiction and these were left on my doorstep this morning. They're pretty good, oatmeal and raisin and in the shape of pencils. You'll have to excuse that; it's her thing.'

'Oh, I can excuse that if they taste as good as they look. I have a mum that does that too.'

'Makes pencil biscuits and leaves them on your doorstep?'

'Not quite, but almost. She is incapable of leaving the house without an identical container filled with all sorts of treats which she doles out to anyone who crosses her path. She even used to bring them in at parents evening. Can you imagine how embarrassing that was? "Mrs Choudhury, Kam is very charming and particularly bright but does have a tendency to get easily distracted... ooh I know, here have some barfi, it's mango... Quite Mrs Choudhury, but the thing is... yes, I know, here have some Gulab Jamun, careful though they are very sticky..." Honestly, I swear, the teachers worked out that all they had to do to get free treats was invite her in and imply I wasn't perfect.'

'That's hilarious. Are you not perfect then?'

'Well, I am now, obviously, but no one is perfect in their adolescence.'

'Isn't that the truth!'

'Everyone tells me how lucky I am to have such an amazing cook as a mother, but honestly, I swear the whole community constantly hovers in the hope she'll drag them in and feed them. You should see how busy the house gets at Diwali.'

'Oh, tell me about it. Mine feels the need to feed the whole village at every possible festivity. Halloween and Christmas are completely out of hand!'

'Hello you two, nice to see you.' Miss Winter, the headteacher, suddenly appeared at the table, reminding Kam quite forcefully that he was here to work, not merely to drink coffee and eat biscuits. Although, how Miss Winter had entered the classroom without either of them noticing seemed a bit of a mystery. 'I see you've met each other already.'

'Yup, we met on the interview day. Kam, isn't it?' Pippa smiled over the brim of her cup at him.

'Yup, Kam Choudhury. Pleasure to meet you more formally.'

'Well, seeing as we're being formal, my surname's Parkin. Pippa Parkin, so have a giggle now and get it over with. All of us, my brother and sister were given forenames beginning with P. My parents thought it was hilarious to be alliterative. Us, less so.'

'It's a very nice name.' He smiled at her, willing himself to be bold and make eye contact as he spoke. After all, this was going to be a professional relationship so he wouldn't mess it up like he did normally with any woman he was attracted too. Kam cursed his shyness usually, but he guessed here it would work in his favour and stop him blurring those professional lines.

'Right, brilliant.' Rosy interrupted them and got down to business. 'Kam will be covering Lynne's hours so will be in the classroom with you on Mondays and Fridays, but has kindly offered to come in all week for the first week of term so he can see how the week is shaped and become familiar with the children's whole routine, rather than just the days he's in. Thank you again for that, Kam. It's much appreciated.'

'It's a pleasure, Miss Winter. It makes sense to get a good overview of the children so that I can organise my teaching to work the best it can alongside yours.'

'We're very lucky to have you, although, please call me Rosy. I feel like a character straight out of Dickens otherwise. Now, let's look at the planning for this term. Oh, I might help myself to coffee first if that's okay?'

The morning whizzed by and Kam was really happy to be here. It looked like he was going to have a lot of fun teaching the summer term curriculum in Penmenna. It revolved largely around Cornish culture with a special emphasis on their community, an awful lot of the learning taking place outdoors – some at Penmenna Hall – and tying in with the science curriculum: the growing, harvesting and cooking of produce linked to the school's regular slot on local TV gardening programme *Green-Fingered and Gorgeous* in the first half of the term. The other dominant focus was the sea, the beach, the fishing industry and all things marine. The term's work culminated in a huge demonstration of the school work at the end of summer term in the village's Feast Week, which he learnt was a Cornish celebration, a week's worth of festivities rather like a regatta but slightly more down to earth. Either way, it was going to be fun. Especially working alongside Pippa Parkin.

Chapter Eight

On the first day of term Pippa raced to work. She had always loved working with Lynne and Rosy, and had been over the moon for Lynne when she announced her pregnancy and need for maternity leave. She knew how desperately Lynne wanted to start a family and the three colleagues had celebrated the pregnancy every step of the way.

However, Pippa had been a little concerned about Lynne's replacement. Teachers came in all shapes and sizes and, like any other group in society, sometimes you could get a downright difficult one. So far, she had considered herself very lucky to never have had to work with any monsters, but she had had a little niggle in the back of her mind as Lynne's maternity leave approached. Of course, knowing that the replacement was going to be Kam changed everything.

During for the planning meeting last week she had been struck again by how nice he was, smiling and joking but contributing lots. She was really looking forward to working alongside him. Although, it was easy being nice when you had an empty classroom and a full cafetière; the real test would come when he was faced with twenty plus children, Rosy in her office and a crisis looming. And crises were ten-a-penny when you were working with four and five-year-olds.

Pippa usually got in to school early. She liked the peace in the classroom at that time of day; it gave her a chance to double-check she had all the resources she needed and to take some time out to breath in the quietness and the solitude before the chaos hit. Plus, it beat eating her corn-flakes while trying to practise a bit of daily mindfulness under the steely gaze of the stuffed stoat and the very dead dormouse that Lottie currently kept on the kitchen table next to some kind of essay on Robo-advisors and the stock market which managed to make Pippa's head hurt just by glancing at it.

Today, as she reached the door and punched in the code, she realised she wasn't the first in. There was Kam, an oversized cup in hand sending out aromatic waves of delightful awakening coffee magic.

Rosy soon joined them and the children all bowled in, chattering like starlings. Lunchboxes, reading bags and coats all jostling for space in the small cloakroom. As they gathered on the carpet the day could begin.

'Hello, class. Welcome back. I hope you all had a fabulous holiday.'

'Hello, Miss Winter,' the children chorused back at her. Pippa came and sat on the carpet with Alfie and Harry, who sometimes found it a little difficult to focus, and made sure she positioned herself as close to Billy as possible too. He was one of the oldest in the class; this was his second year in Class One, which wasn't unusual with it being a mixed key stage. Billy may be the eldest but his natural enthusiasm sometimes crossed over into slightly manic.

Pippa knew you shouldn't have favourites in a class, but she did like the more outspoken ones, the ones who other teachers or teaching assistants dreaded. Rosy and Lynne were outstanding in teaching those who would have traditionally struggled in school, but that didn't mean the children suddenly became perfect clones; they still needed plenty of very gentle reminders to comply, not whack each other with the toys, lick the carpet or shove counters up their nose during maths.

'I'd like to introduce you to Mr Choudhury. He'll be your teacher on Mondays and Fridays whilst Mrs Rowe is away having her baby.'

Sophie and Ashleigh started to snigger.

'Are you alright, girls?' Rosy queried in that age-old teacher way which was code for '*I'm not asking how you feel. I'm telling you to shut up.*'

'Mrs Rowe is having a baby… hahahahahahaha!'

'Thank you, Sophie, we are all very happy about that.'

'She's been kissing.' Sophie continued, never one to shy away from facing down authority. Pippa wriggled towards the two girls and placed a calming hand on Sophie's back, a silent reminder that this was not how one behaved at carpet time.

'No doubt she has, Sophie, but as you know that is not something we are going to talk about now. Instead we're going to give a big Class One welcome to Mr Choudhury, and try and show him that he's not about to be left with a classroom full of little monsters. And you're not little monsters, are you?'

'Hello, Mr Choudhury,' chorused the majority of the class, their little legs crossed and faces upturned, beaming a welcome as they examined the new teacher and tried to decide what they thought of him.

'Some of us are,' piped up Billy, ''specially at Halloween, I was a real big monster then.'

'And me, I was a vampire,' Sam joined in. He had been a terribly quiet child when he first joined the school but, nearly a year in, he had certainly started to find his voice.

'My mum says I'm always a little monster but my dad calls me a little heller!' Alfie added. His father spoke truth.

'Well, Mr Choudhury, you can see that most of them are beautifully behaved but some of them…' Rosy left a meaningful pause as she grinned at her class, a grin that was full of love and left the children in no doubt that she was joking.

'I can indeed. But that's okay, my mum used to say I was a monster too, and then I grew up and I became a teacher so am much less *monstery* these days. Miss Winter tells me you like to start with a story, so I have brought some of my favourites with me today and I thought I'd let you choose which one we start with.' Kam grinned at the class and held up three well-loved picture books and suggested the class had a vote.

'The trouble is, Class One, it's Monday morning and my counting brain hasn't quite fired up yet, so I might need your help…' Kam immediately got stuck in, getting the children to vote and then help him tally up the votes by counting out loud with him.

'Right, I can see you're in good hands here. I'm going to my office and leaving you with Mr Choudhury. Remember to show him that Class One are the best class in the school. Miss Parkin will be here too; I will be asking her at breaktime who has been extra good this morning, and you know she always tells me what's been happening.'

'Thank you, Miss Winter, we shall see you later. We are going to have some fun, aren't we, class?'

A very well-behaved cheer went up as Rosy turned and left Pippa and Kam to it. And it was fair to say Mr Choudhury was smashing it. He managed to combine a really approachable teaching style with the children, making their morning good fun, whilst at the same time no one was under any illusion that he wasn't fully in charge.

There was about fifteen minutes of the morning left to go, and Pippa knew she would be able to tell Rosy that Kam was utterly fabulous and the perfect cover for Lynne, when the classroom door opened and in walked Marion Marksharp. Woah! Now this was likely to become a baptism of fire. The majority of the teachers here couldn't cope with this terrifying creature and her barked commands, no matter how many years teaching experience they had. Kam didn't stand a chance. Especially as she seemed to have updated her image overnight.

Marion could usually be relied upon to prowl the corridors of the school, instilling fear and sporting a variety of tight, patterned clothes that were straight out of terribly middle-class boutiques in Fowey and Padstow – ladybirds and jaguars appearing to be this year's favourite motifs – a look that her PTA devotees immediately adopted as a uniform, although none would be quite as fitted or pronounced as those worn by their Queen Bee. But today… today she had upped the ante and for some reason had decided to come to school in what Pippa, with her knowledge of all things vintage and her generous spirit, could only describe as Up-and-coming-eighties-Essex-elite-chic.

The dress, if that was what it was, had been sprayed onto Marion in an electric blue leopard print. It sat like a second skin, cut so low over her bosom that Pippa was aware she may well get a flash of tummy button. She was half tempted to grab a scarf from the dressing up corner and cover the woman up before the children developed PTSD.

Even more alarming was the look on Marion's face as she stood in the doorway, arm perched upon the door jamb and striking a very sultry pose, as she eyed up Kam.

There was nothing for it: Pippa was going to have to intervene and get Marion out before she terrified the new teacher into running, screaming, out of the building, or brought about some other kind of catastrophe. Whatever happened she really hoped Marion's acolytes didn't start copying this new look, or Penmenna School could easily be mistaken for the casting room of 'Mafia Wives'.

'I'll only be a minute, you guys. See if you can count up this group of seeds and then this group and see how many plants we'd have if we put all the seeds together. I'll be back to help shortly.' The teaching assistant leapt to her feet and made her way towards the head of the PTA. 'Mrs Marksharp, what a pleasant surprise.'

Marion arched her eyebrows as Pippa greeted her, an arch that would have had Harmony, the Class Three teacher, running for the stationary cupboard. Luckily Pippa was made of sterner stuff.

'Mrs Marksharp, is there anything you need?'

'Yes, dear, there is, and it doesn't involve you.' Wow, that was pointed, even for Marion. It clearly wasn't just her dress sense that was ramped up to scarily aggressive levels.

'Well, as you can see Mr Choudhury is busy teaching at the moment, but I believe Rosy is in her office. If I can't help you, perhaps she can.'

Marion pushed, actually pushed, Pippa to one side as she spoke, her words to the teaching assistant shot out of the corner of her mouth like a cartoon villain. 'I think I know who it is I need to see, Miss Parkin.' Then with her scary sexy crocodile grin on, she said, 'Mr Choudhury, coo-ee dear, I wanted to come and introduce myself properly.' She slinked across the room, a colossus of self-confidence and determined intent.

Kam looked up, startled as her voice boomed around the room and some of the class began to giggle. They were more than used to Marion Marksharp's frequent visits to the classroom.

'Hello, Mrs Marksharp.' Ellie, one of the classes most confident pupils, greeted her.

'Hello, dear, do send my love to your delicious father.' But she spoke without slowing her pace, quite a feat whilst perched atop four-inch heels on a floor scattered with stickle bricks, small plastic chairs and a plethora of young children. Kam stood up from where he was sitting on the floor to meet her.

Pippa wasn't sure what to do next. She didn't want to undermine Kam's authority by rushing over to protect him – it implied he couldn't look after himself – but then again there were very few people in Penmenna who could deal with Marion. Pippa rejoined her small group of pupils no longer counting and ordering seeds as instructed but sitting agog to see what would unfold.

Kam and Marion met midpoint in the classroom.

'Mrs Marksharp, I understand. A pleasure to meet you.'

'I'm sorry to interrupt your teaching, dear' – Pippa was amazed the woman's nose didn't grow so long it hit a display board – 'but I wanted to come and introduce myself. I'm Mrs Marksharp – do call me Marion – the head of the PTA and, in my husband's absence, the acting Head of the Governors. And I'm afraid at the moment he is very absent.' She giggled and held her hand out rather like the Queen, as if she expected Kam to kneel before her, take it and bestow a kiss of supplication.

'How are you? I believe we met briefly before, when I came in for my interview.' He took her hand, rather awkwardly, and shook it.

'Quite. We absolutely did. I remember you very well, very well indeed. In fact, I told Rosy that I thought she should offer you the job.'

'Oh well, in that case, thank you very much. I think I'm going to love it here.'

'Well, I'm a great believer in having pretty things to look at and you my dear have quite the prettiest eyes I have ever seen. Pretty eyes in a very handsome face.'

Pippa jumped to her feet. For goodness sake, clearly the #MeToo movement was not something Marion subscribed to.

'Do sit down, Miss Parkin, I'm not going to eat him alive,' Marion snapped. 'At least not just yet,' she followed up, the sharpness of her address to Pippa juxtaposed against the sultry tone her voice took on once she turned back to Kam. 'I do like to get well acquainted with all the new teaching staff who come and join our wonderful community.' That was news to Pippa. She was fairly sure

Harmony Rivers had never been welcomed in such a manner, nor the far stricter Amanda Adams 'So I thought I would just slip in and invite you to dinner. I'm child-free tonight so this evening would work very well.'

Don't say yes, don't say yes, Pippa willed Kam. If he rocked up at the Marksharp house tonight she had a fairly firm idea of what might be on the menu.

There had been a whisper that the Marksharps' marriage may be in trouble, although, if anything was ever brought up in the staffroom, Rosy shut down all gossip fairly quickly, reminding people that no one knew what went on behind closed doors and the only sure thing was that rampant whispering and the dissemination of gossip could only make it worse. She also threw in her tuppence worth about how, as far as she was aware, the Marksharps' marriage was more than strong and that Richard Marksharp was merely away with work. Pippa hoped for Kam's sake that he came home pretty soon. The thought of a single Marion permanently on the prowl would be enough to drive any sensible man into his shed for the foreseeable future. School fayres and the like would become female-only affairs pretty quickly.

'That's a very kind offer, Mrs Marksharp, and I feel very welcomed by the Penmenna community but I'm afraid I'll have to…' – *don't say rain check, do not say rain check*, Pippa willed him – '…have to pass for the time being. I'm picking up the keys to my new flat after work today in Treporth Bay.' Kam named the next village over, somewhat chi-chi with its marina and high-end seafood eateries.

Far from putting Marion off, the mere mention of Treporth Bay made her eyes brighten. There was very definitely a purring noise coming from somewhere and Pippa could virtually hear the cogs turning in her brain from where she was sat.

'Treporth, oh how lovely, and how wonderful for us that you are moving so close. Very well then, I shall let you settle today, but I expect an invite to the housewarming. In fact, if you like, I could organise one for you.'

'That's very kind and I shall certainly bear it in mind closer to the time.'

'You do that,' she purred again, the leopard print was obviously having an effect. Pippa was quite surprised she managed not to rub up against his leg. 'Now I shall leave you to get on with your teaching. I do hope Class One appreciate how very lucky they are to have such a talented new teacher. I shall be watching you with great interest, my dear.'

'Ah, well, thank you very much.'

'Oh, and one more thing: I'll be organising the rota for mums to help you with the swimming classes this term. You should have a ratio of one to two and I can promise that I will make that happen. I expect they'll all be very keen. Let me reassure you, though, that I shall be the one to go in the pool with you: I'm experienced, *very* fit and highly flexible, so I know we're going to work so well together.' Pippa wasn't at the right angle to see if Marion winked but she wouldn't have been surprised. Meantime, it was taking all of her self-control not to gag at the thought of Marion's flexibility.

'Sounds fabulous, and thank you for coming to say hello, but really I should—'

'Of course, you must, dear. We shall have such fun in the pool. Such fun. And you can come to dinner next week when you're all settled.'

Chapter Nine

The day had flown past and Kam couldn't believe the speed with which it had done so. Small children really didn't ever stop so he hadn't had time to breathe from the minute they had come flying in in the morning to when the school bell rang out at three.

He had handed the children over to their parents and carers at three o'clock, which had taken ages. Almost every parent stopped to introduce themselves and make friends, which was lovely and helped contribute to his picture of the children individually, but it did go on a bit and he was desperate for coffee.

Now finally free, he went to look over the planning for the next day before heading to get himself a cup. He had hoped to have a quick catch up with Pippa before she headed off for the day, but she seemed to have disappeared. Teaching Assistants were paid by the hour so he didn't blame her at all for fleeing the minute the bell rang.

Just as he was staring at the plans on the wall, where they were placed so anyone accessing the classroom – parents, students, observers – could see how the day or week was going to shape up, he heard the door open and shut again.

'Here, I thought you might need this.' Pippa headed in with his cafetière, which he had stored in the staffroom.

'That was a belter of a day – first day of term always is – and you smashed it. I thought Marion may overwhelm you. That outfit! But you did so well. I've seen other teachers cry over that woman.'

'They cried over her inviting them to dinner?'

'Oh, that was hilarious! Trust me when I say she doesn't usually invite them over.'

'Ah! Well, maybe they don't have pretty, pretty eyes in a very handsome face.'

'Hahaha, no I guess not. Sorry 'bout that. Anyway, coffee?'

'Yes please, I thought you had gone home.'

'Oh no, I always stay and just get everything tidied away before the cleaners come in a bit. I reckon that you should just sit, enjoy that and catch your breath, a first day survival treat. I'll be done in a swizz.'

Kam smiled up at her. He had known she would be amazing in the classroom, and had been proved right. She had such a high-energy attitude that it was impossible not to be captivated by her as she swooshed around all day, livening up the classroom, singing as she went and engaging the children in every activity they undertook. He couldn't imagine what life would be like for someone so positively chirpy all day, and was rather envious. He wasn't convinced he would have been able to maintain the level of happy that she achieved on a constant basis.

He knocked back his coffee in four big gulps and went to help her wash all the paint trays and brushes.

'Hey, you're meant to be resting.'

'This is restful.' He answered as he stood next to her and filled the second sink with all the art paraphernalia.

'Washing trays and brushes?'

'Yeah, I like washing up. I'm a bit of a water babe so am quite happy. I spent a large part of my childhood washing up for my Mum. I come from a big family, and mum is food obsessed so I swear I spent as much time with my hands in the sink as she did constantly cooking.'

'That sounds nice. Family is important.'

'It is. Although mine are a little cross with me at the moment.' Pippa turned to face him, her eyes alight with curiosity, but instead of prying into why his family may be cross she had another question on her mind.

'Did I hear you tell Marion that you're picking up your keys tonight? For a place in Treporth Bay?'

'Yup. I've been staying with a friend in Newquay for the past few months. He runs a hostel so I've been helping out and living the surf dream but it's such a trek from here and it was about time I got my own place. There wasn't anywhere available in Penmenna, but I've got this place on a short-term let and it's close enough. Walking distance if needs be.'

'True. Is it dead swish? It's not one of those flats on the marina, is it?'

'It is. Do you know them?'

'Of course, they're the ultimate des res around here at the moment. I've always fancied seeing inside one of them. You'll have to tell me all about it.'

'Or you'll have to come over one night. See for yourself.' Pippa smiled in response to this, a smile that flooded her already happy face and lit up her eyes, which then developed a cheeky glint. That was cute.

'Okay, I'm free tonight so I was considering asking if you wanted a hand. We could get you all moved in and then go for a drink later, either in Treporth or walk back over to Penmenna and I'll induct you into village life in The Smuggler's Curse. You're not a proper local until you've had a pint of Rattler in there. Oh, or a soft drink, obviously, if you don't drink. Lottie, my flatmate, she doesn't but I like one now and again.'

'No, it's okay, I definitely appreciate the odd pint. That would be great but you said "considering asking".'

'I didn't know if it was appropriate, plus you've been stuck with me all day so I figured you may want to escape.'

'Hmmm, you are quite hard work…' Kam watched as Pippa's face fell. 'Hey, where's that smile gone that's been beaming all day? I was only joking. I've really enjoyed working alongside you today; I think we're going to have fun working together. It's whether you can put up with me for any longer.'

'It has been tricky but I'm a bit of a saint so I can probably cope with a little bit more. Just a little bit.'

'In that case, Miss Parkin, if your offer is still open I would greatly appreciate your help. But I don't have much to move so why don't we just meet at The Smuggler's Curse later tonight and you can fill me in on all the local gossip. And maybe give me tips to stop that PTA woman from devouring me alive in front of the children.'

'I can't promise anything.'

'Not even a drink at eight o'clock this evening?'

Pippa drained the sink, dried her hands and walked over to put trays and brushes back in the cupboard before turning around and flashing a great big smile at him.

'That is a promise that's far more achievable. That one I can make and keep. Eight tonight in The Curse. It's a date.'

Chapter Ten

Pippa smiled as she approached The Smuggler's Curse that evening. She had deliberately come a bit early so she would be there to welcome Kam when he turned up. Living in the village all her life meant she was under no illusions about the local pub but she did love the way it was a community hub with its interesting collection of regulars propping up the bar most evenings.

There was Mickey, a music sensation of the nineties who had made enough money off the back of three very popular dance anthems that meant he could spend the rest of his life in happy obscurity, pint in hand, his hair still in his eyes and missing a fair chunk of his teeth, firm in the belief that there had never been a summer to match that of 1989, and hitting on any woman under seventy who dared enter the dark insides of The Curse.

Then there was Andrew, in theory the village's taxi driver, who could guarantee to be so inebriated by half past six on any evening that he wasn't fit to walk anyone home, let alone drive them. He was, however, a good friend of her dad's and always willing to put his hand, albeit only possessing three fingers and a thumb, in his pocket to buy Pippa a drink.

Walking in was a bit like going home. If Roger liked you, there was a strong chance your drink of choice would have been poured by the time you got to the bar, alongside a packet of dry roasted thrown in for good measure.

However, as friendly as the pub was to locals, out-of-towners were a different story. The pub would go silent when someone unknown walked in, every head turning to appraise the visitor. If conversations were resumed then it was fair to assume you had been accepted; if not, it was best to make a run for it and never return, in case the proverbial pitchforks were gathered and brandished.

Somewhere back in the mists of time and at the height of Cornwall's smuggling prowess, the regulars had run the Custom's men out of Penmenna, forks, scythes and torches in hand, and the pub still rested on that reputation. In fact, Pippa suspected they were itching to do it again.

Roger, the landlord, tall, wiry, having lost most of his hair and all of his manners several years ago, deliberately kept the outside run down so as not to attract any emmets − tourists named after ants because of the way they would scurry all over the county, bright red with sunburn, come high season. Indeed, the outside of the pub looked so ramshackle that holiday makers would walk straight past, unaware that The Curse regularly dished up the best roast in the county and had highly illegal lock-ins at every possible opportunity. However, with locals regularly filling it to bursting point and it being practically impossible to secure a table for Sunday lunch unless you were sixth generation Cornish and your family had had a table for years, it meant the brewery were reluctant to change the formula. Plus, everybody knew that Roger kept a twelve bore behind the bar and wouldn't be afraid to use it.

Pippa loved the pub because of all its idiosyncrasies, rather than in spite of them. It had a roaring fire all year long, and right now it had the additional advantage of not smelling like formaldehyde – unlike her flat. She had mentioned this to Lottie who had laughed off all Pippa's concerns about toxicity, remarking that lemon juice was hardly likely to preserve the animals quite as effectively, although if she wanted to get her some arsenic she was happy to give that a go. Pippa really hoped she became a raving success soon and rented a workshop.

She had even resorted to pointing out that the chemical stench and dead wildlife littering the flat could be the reason that none of Lottie's dates ever came back. Lottie pointed out that if her dates couldn't get past her hobby and see the joy in the dormouse scene on the mantlepiece, then they weren't girlfriend material anyway.

Pippa pushed the pub door open and saw all the regulars sitting at the bar.

'Alright, darling? See you've been raiding my nan's wardrobe again.' Andrew greeted her. Pippa swirled a full circle for them in the cute little floral tea-dress she had decided to wear for tonight's date. No, not date – professional meeting of two colleagues with the intention of one welcoming the other into the community. Anyway, it was still a super cute dress and she loved it almost as much as she did the red patent Mary-Janes she had paired it with.

'Yup, she asked me to tell you to give her underwear back. Says she's sick of asking and coral has never been your colour anyway,' Pippa winked as she teased him, whilst Mickey flicked his hair out of his eyes as he laughed at his mate's face.

'You deserved that. You look fair 'ansum, little one. Come sit here and let me buy you a drink, and then you can tell us how come we're blessed with your presence on a school night.'

'I'm actually here for work.'

'For work?!' The two men chorused. 'Does that mean that headteacher of yours will be in as well?' Mickey's eyes lit up at the thought of two young women in this evening.

'Nah, a new colleague. I said I'd let him know all about the area and suggested he meet me here.'

'*He*, is it? a man? Up at the school? Hoo hoo hooo, has anyone told Richard Marksharp?'

'Stop it, Andrew.'

'You know what she's like. She'll be prowling around like a lion after fresh meat if Richard don't get e'self back here soon. And with a male teacher in school… well, that is just easy pickings!'

'Oi! Maybe he wouldn't be interested in Marion,' Pippa sprang to Kam's defence, after she had taken a huge glug of the gin Roger had wordlessly put in front of her.

'No one is interested in Marion. She just pulls you in like a hurricane and there ain't no choice about any of it! You know that!'

'I can't argue with—' Pippa's sentence was cut in half as the door was pushed open and everyone on a barstool whooshed around to take a look.

That tumbleweed silence would have filled the whole room with its echoey lack of welcome if Pippa hadn't jumped straight up and ushered Kam forward, the grin on her face as he entered so wide that it actually hurt her ears.

'Kam, come meet the reprobates of The Smuggler's Curse. Everyone' – the word had pure steel undertones – 'say hello to Kam.'

Chapter Eleven

Kam had walked along the beach, the sun setting in such glorious orange and cerise technicolour that he could barely take his eyes away from it. The seagulls were silent, long gone to bed at the end of the bay, tucked up and away from human eyes. The crunch of dried seaweed under his Reefs mingled with the crash of the waves, the smell of salt burying itself deep into his lungs as the waves reflected the summer colours of the sky.

This was living life, this simple act of appreciating the beauty around him and being grateful for what he had. Not difficult in Cornwall, beauty was everywhere in this part of the world.

Lit by the street lights and the last few minutes of the sun, Penmenna was one of these things of beauty. The warm lights of windows dappled down the hillside, a higgledy-piggledy dotting of comfort, of hearth and home.

He reached The Smuggler's Curse, light also streaming out of these windows but not quite in such a life-affirming manner as the rest of the village. Instead, light seeped out of dirty window panes, promising that it may be warmer inside but probably not as fresh. He startled as he thought he heard a moo come from the pub garden, before deciding he must be mistaken. He could see the outline of some hanging baskets suspended by the front door, but they appeared to have not much more than three bits of twig and a beetle inside, rather than the riot of colour that could be expected at this time of year.

There was laughter coming from inside. Looking at the door he wasn't sure whether, if he pushed it open, it would crumble under his fingers. He decided he didn't care. Pippa had been such a joy from the moment he had met her, constantly perky, frequently sarcastic but always funny, a proper sunshine girl. She was well worth a splinter or two. The thought of getting to spend part of the evening with her, as well as all of the day, brought the biggest beam he had felt since the age of eight and his parents had bought him a brand-new bike. Pippa was the freshness of spring and the joy of new bikes all rolled into one. He pushed the pub door firmly.

And there she was.

As he stood still in the doorway, he remembered the words of his father as he described the way he had looked at Kam's mother when they were initially introduced, and had known. He had *known*.

Kam had always thought it was romantic nonsense his dad spouted to keep his mother happy, despite the fact that his father was not usually forthcoming when it came to expressing his emotions. Still, Kam's scientific nature didn't believe in the whole thunderclap, coup-de-foudre, love at first sight nonsense. Love was a slow burn, a spark of lust followed by getting to know someone until you found a mutual respect and understanding in tandem with the continued lust thing. That was what Kam believed turned into love.

But now, risking more and more splinters per second, he wondered if he had been wrong.

For there, in front of him, Pippa stood laughing, her whole spirit lifting the dark of the bar. The laughter he heard emanating from those surrounding her showed that all were lit by her light. And without being able to name it precisely, he knew he had just felt something huge course through him.

'Kam, come meet the reprobates of The Smuggler's Curse.' She smiled as she walked to meet him by the doorway. 'Everyone, say hello to Kam.'

–

The evening passed in a whizz and a flash. Kam had imagined he would be spending it tucked up in the snug talking to Pippa, getting to know her, sharing their stories about the events that had shaped them, the things that had brought them to where they were. To see what made this sunshine girl sparkle.

What actually happened was that once she had greeted him, she pulled up a stool at the bar and ushered him to sit down. The two men she was with nodded at him and responded to her command by muttering his name, but not in a madly welcoming way. He felt a little bit like he had stumbled into the OK Corral and was about to become part of a gun fight he knew nothing about.

Pippa, however, was oblivious. Or appeared to be. She looked adorable tonight, as if she had dressed up for a dance in a village hall at some point sixty years ago, her lips matching the cherry-red of her shoes. He felt he should have bought a posy and be wearing a waistcoat, rather than chilling in a hoody and jeans.

'What can I get you?' she asked, gesturing towards the bar.

'Oh no, I'll get them. What does everyone recommend? What is the drink to welcome me to Penmenna?'

'Korev.' The shorter squatter man sat furthest from Pippa said, as the barman failed to respond to Kam's presence.

'It depends quite how brave you are, but if Roger takes a liking to you, he has a special barrel of hooch that 'e keeps for us regulars. That'll welcome you to the village. It's this 'un that we're welcoming, right?' added a man who seemed to have been involved in some extreme dental incident.

Kam grinned; an apparent attempt to poison him the minute he sat down was actually remarkably tame compared to what he'd expected when he'd first pushed open the big wooden door.

'I'll have the Korev for now then, and I'll take you up on the hooch when I return one Friday night. If you haven't run me out of town by then, obviously.'

'Exactly, after tonight you may never return. So, you won't need to know that I'm Mike and this 'ere is Andrew.' The toothless one winked as he introduced himself and his friend to Kam. 'Here, Roger, I'll buy the new teacher his first Penmenna pint. And we'll check out the cut of his jib.'

'Did you know that was a saying from back in the day, when you were checking out which country a boat was from, so it's quite pertinent here. Seeing who is friend or foe in a nautical way.' The voice was female and came from the corner, a table near the fire where sat a woman who the word dainty was invented for. Seventy if she was a day, the lace of her blouse furling up around her neck, a glass of sherry in front of her. Next to her sat a man in a dog collar, so good-looking that Kam did a double-take. The two of them were playing cards with a stack of pennies next to them, the woman looking as if she had considerably more. 'Talking of which I'd better let some sea air in; it's time for Flynn to come in for his pint.'

'Sit yourself down, Ethel. I'll get that.' The vicar put his cards down, gave Ethel a faux-stern don't-peek look and stood up to go and pull the door open, bringing in the sound of church bells striking the eighth hour.

'Oh yeah, you're going to love Flynn.' Pippa shot Kam the biggest grin as if she had a surprise up her sleeve. He wondered if Flynn was novel simply for possessing all his teeth and digits.

'And he'll love you too. Always been partial to a handsome face, bit like myself.' Ethel took a glug of her sherry and winked at the vicar.

Kam grinned. 'Well, then, I'll look forward to meeting him,' he said as Roger gave him a proper Cornish pint. He had been drinking Rattler, a cider guaranteed to put hairs on your chest, whilst he'd been living in Newquay. It was his friend Ben's drink of choice; they sold a lot of it in the bar attached to the surf hostel that Ben ran. Kam had found he'd had a couple of thick-headed mornings afterwards, with only the surf succeeding in blasting him clean and getting his brain to work again. So, for now he was happy to see if Korev might be his drink. He took a long gulp.

'This is good. I'm looking forward to Friday night, if I can judge Roger's hooch on this in any way.'

'I wouldn't,' Pippa retorted. 'That lager is considerably more legal and less likely to turn you blind.'

'Now, you madam, that were not my hooch that did that.'

The whole pub erupted in laughter.

'I'd say the majority view is that it was,' Pippa clarified.

Kam laughed along with them, taking small draughts of his beer and enjoying being part of the community atmosphere in here. They chatted away, most of the gossip about people in Penmenna, or he up Roscombe way, or that posh bloke down Treporth, but all of it harmless and no one being made more fun of than those present. He had just been invited to join the vicar, who introduced himself as Dan and seemed pretty sound, for a kick about with some of the others in the village when the door creaked open a little further. All of a sudden Kam felt a wet nose on his leg, heading towards his groin.

'See, you thought we was odd but you want to be grateful we didn't greet you like that,' Mike laughed.

'Come on, Flynn. Leave Kam alone.' Pippa greeted the dog who had snuck in through the door, 'Up you come.' And with that Flynn hopped up onto a stool that had been kept vacant and put a paw on the bar and barked.

'I know, mate,' said Andrew. 'The service in here is dreadful.' Everyone then continued their conversation as if nothing out of the ordinary was happening, while Roger popped a large dog's bowl of water and an open packet of pork scratchings on the bar.

Kam watched spellbound, only half an ear on the conversation as the dog eagerly lapped it all up, ate his snacks, barked twice at the barman, jumped down from his stool and slid out of the door again. It was Andrew this time who got up to shut the door.

'It's cute, isn't it?' Pippa whispered to him in an aside. 'Comes in every night without fail, has done since he was a pup, just sadly without his dad now. Derek passed away about three years ago, but we managed to keep Flynn in the village so he could continue with as many of his routines as possible, and his nightly walk and drink are one of them.'

'That's pretty special. I've never heard of anything like that before.'

'Penmenna's pretty special and I am happy that you are now part of it. Now, drink up. It's your round!'

–

As Pippa curled up in her bed, smile still on her face, she heard her phone beep. Reaching to grab it and expecting it to be from Pete or Polly moaning about their mother's latest heinous crime, she saw instead it was Kam whom she had given her number to when they had arranged their pub outing.

> **Thank you for today, you helped my first day go really smoothly. And tonight was lots of fun. I have a feeling I'm going to like Penmenna.**

> **Pleasure. I really enjoyed myself. See you tomorrow!**

A smile played on her lips as she placed her head on her pillow, and it stayed there until she drifted off to sleep.

Chapter Twelve

Pippa headed into the classroom, in modern and can-afford-to-be-covered-in-paint clothes and great big eyeliner flicks, with two mugs of coffee in her hands and a smile on her face. Kam had been fun the other night. He had slotted into the pub as if he'd been born and bred there, and that was a rare thing indeed. In fact, the last recorded time that had happened was when a woman had got lost in the village and came in to ask for directions. Roger had married her.

Afterwards, Kam had walked her home. She had said it wasn't necessary but he had insisted. She had let him cross her over the road and walk a full fifty yards, and then, as they reached the village shop, she had told him, with delight, that this was her.

She had toyed with inviting him in, but was aware that there was a subtext to that question that wasn't appropriate with the man who was, until the end of July, her immediate boss. Plus, as she'd been leaving to go to the pub tonight, Lottie had received a phone call about a badger on the side of the lane the other side of Lovage Farm and had practically hopped, skipped and jumped her way down the stairs, out of the building and into her car.

She was not inviting a man she had to work with – a man in possession of the most beautiful eyes and even handsomer spirit – in to deal with dead badgers after their first evening out. She had some sense of self-protection. So, although she hadn't offered coffee then, she was happy to deliver it this morning.

Bouncing in, mugs in hand, she was rewarded as Kam looked up from flicking through something on his school tablet with a great big beam of welcome.

'Here you go. I thought you would like a coffee.' She handed him the biggest mug she had been able to find in the staffroom and then took a great slurp of her own.

'Oh fab.' Rosy poked her head above the bookcases in the reading corner and smiled at Pippa, only for her face to fall a little when she saw that Pippa hadn't been talking to her.

'Oh, shoot. Um, I'm so sorry Rosy, I didn't realise you were in class today.'

'I know, fair point. I'm not. I just wanted to grab some resources to help with some special needs assessments, so I thought I'd nip in early before everyone got in, children that is, obviously. In fact, I know you're good as gold and come in early and stay late, but isn't this really early for you?'

Rosy's face was quizzical and Pippa froze to the spot. She might have a point. She hoped to god that Kam didn't pick up on it and guess she was in deliberately early just for him. Little bit awkward.

'Ha… um… I'll be right back. I'll just go get you a coffee.' Pippa fled. She was a woman who never blushed, but there was a good chance all that could change today and cheeks may decide to match her lipstick!

–

74

Kam had taught a whole lot of maths and the children were now doing various independent activities around the classroom. Pippa was in the role-play area with some of the children, creating a huge beanstalk on the side of their two-storey play loft. Before starting, they had put rollers in her hair from the dressing up area so they could act out Jack and the Beanstalk when they had finished, and they had nominated Pippa to play the mother. Ellie had pointed out that she had the perfect shrieky voice because Jack's mum could probably be heard from every side of the playground as well. Pippa's face may have scrunched up a little because Ellie quickly added, after Sam had nudged her, that Pippa wasn't shouty in a mean way though. Rather than taking offence, Pippa tried to remind herself of the social and emotional learning goals this behaviour indicated Ellie was reaching.

'Miss Parkin.' She felt the hiss upon her ear as much as she heard it, as she stood there, green painted leaf dangling over her head, staple gun in hand and spare leaves held between her knees.

'Yes,' she hissed back, feeling like a spy down a shadowy alley in a badly lit European city and rather liking it.

'The hamster door is open and I can't see Sir Squeaks-a-lot anywhere in his cage.'

Pippa spun around, handing her remaining leaves to Ashleigh, who was on the floor carefully sticking leaves to the base of the loft, her tongue sticking out slightly as she concentrated upon her task.

'Squeaks is missing?' She whispered back. She didn't want the class hearing just yet, and four and five-year-olds have some kind of magic hearing skills which mean they block out instructions fairly effectively but could always capture a secret.

Kam nodded, his eyes big and wide. Bless him, she could see that he was too concerned to even try and hide his worry.

'Okay, this is going to be fine.' She nodded at him reassuringly. She guessed that there was no teacher in the world who wanted to be responsible for losing the class pet in their first week. 'He's probably just hiding. If you were being manhandled regularly by nearly a hundred odd primary school children you'd definitely hide now and again. And if he has escaped, he can't get far.'

'Have you seen how fast hamsters run? I have, and it's fast!' Kam hissed back as they carefully wandered back to the cage, scanning the floor as they did so.

'How do you know how fast they run with such conviction?'

'I've watched YouTube videos, hundreds of YouTube videos.'

'Seriously? I'm scared to ask why. I thought my flat-mate was weird but you may have trumped even her!'

'Large family, lots of sisters. I learnt early on it was easier just to comply.'

'I like the sound of that.' Kam's eyebrows shot through his hairline as Pippa realised that she may have crossed a line into inappropriate. If he didn't know she had a bit of a crush before, he probably did now. She decided not to double down nor apologise, but just pretend she hadn't said anything at all.

They reached the cage and with her I'm-a-proper-professional-and-would-never-say-anything-dirty-in-the-workplace face on Pippa rummaged amongst Sir

Squeaks-a-lot's bedding. And then rummaged again. Oh dear.

She turned to face Kam, mirroring his expression of concern.

'Okay, you're right. Sir Squeaks has sodded off. But look, all the doors are closed. I know he was there first thing when we fed him. He can't be far. He just can't be.'

'He could be squished. We need to make sure that the children don't stampede.' They both shot a quick panicked look across the floor to make sure there was no evidence of squish so far.

Phew, lots of blue and green paint, and someone had taken some blocks out of the construction area and had started making a village near the maths corner but definitely no hamster gore visible to the naked eye.

'You've got this. Go on.' Pippa reassured Kam.

'Okay. Can you go scout the reading corner and then I'll send the children there?' Kam asked her and as she nodded in return.

'Consider it done. There won't be a cushion left unturned.' She scampered to the reading corner on tiptoes.

Kam put both of his hands in the air and used his loudest, most authoritative voice. 'Class One, can everyone stop what they're doing and freeze?' He waited for the class to respond, which they did immediately. Impressive.

'Okay, now, Sir Squeaks-a-lot has escaped from his cage so we need to be very careful and find him. I need you all to keep still for a minute whilst Miss Parkin checks the reading corner, and then we'll move there slowly from each area. I'll tell you when it's your turn, then head to the reading corner, but keep checking very carefully where you put your feet and keep your eyes peeled in case you spot him. When we are all there, we can work out a plan to find him. Does everyone understand?'

The class nodded frantically.

'Right, the reading area is clear.' Pippa shouted from across the class.

'Okay, those of you by the water and sand please make your way to Miss Parkin. Remember to watch your feet.'

Kam funnelled all the children over to the carpet, and once they were sat there, he explained how they were going to methodically explore each area, with small groups of children examining under furniture, in draws and cupboards, while others were the designated 'spotters' in case Sir Squeaks made a dash for it.

After the whole classroom was taken apart the children gathered back to the reading corner again, waiting to hear what to do next. With no sign of the runaway hamster, Pippa wasn't entirely sure what the best thing was, and felt desperate for Kam. Some of the more sensitive children were beginning to get upset.

'He's going to die.' Ashleigh bawled as they were sat back on the carpet.

'Someone is going to stamp on him and he's going to get squished.' Alfie added helpfully, and with a little too much glee. Kam raised an eyebrow at the boy who had the grace to bow his head.

'I don't think so. When I was little I had a favourite set of books, all about a hamster called Hannibal who used to escape all the time and have great adventures. If Miss Parkin fancies going to get a couple of extra pairs of hands – if anyone is free that is, maybe some of the older children – they can have another jolly good look and we can sit here, eyes still peeled, and imagine what sort of adventures Sir Squeaks-a-lot could be having.' He drew a map of the classroom on the smartboard and got the children guessing what they would do if they were an excitable hamster having an adventure.

By the time Pippa had returned with Sylvie and four of Mrs Adams' most responsible pupils (having checked Harmony and her plans to liberate Sir Squeaks on compassionate grounds had nothing to do with it), Class One had designed jet-skis for the water tray and an assault course through the sand, but Ashleigh was still sobbing, harder now and so loud it was beginning to drown Kam out.

He had tried bringing her forward and resting his arm on her shoulders as he addressed the rest of the class, but Pippa's experience taught her that with no other adults in the room it was hard to get her to stop her wailing and manage the rest of the children. Ashleigh did like to cry. And cry loudly. She did it most days. However, as this was Kam's first week with the class he hadn't got quite as irritated as Pippa had. Instead he shot her a look of pure alarm.

Pippa set the older children to looking throughout the cloakroom, and came and joined Kam on the carpet.

'Now, Ashleigh' – she slid in next to the little girl – 'everything is going to be fine. We'll find him and he'll be very tired and happy to curl up in his little bed, don't worry.'

'He won't… he's going to die…' Ashleigh started to hyperventilate.

'Oh, just stop, you're such a cry baby.' Harry rolled his eyes and let out a huge sigh, and Pippa tried not to nod in agreement.

'He's… going… to… die… in…'

'Hang on, "die in…"? Ashleigh do you know where Squeaks is?' Kam was quicker than Pippa at picking up on the extra word.

Sophie kicked Ashleigh who stopped her crying suddenly and leant over to pinch her back.

'Ow! She pinched me, Mr Choudhury. She pinched me.'

'Nice try, Sophie…' said Pippa, far less professionally than she guessed Kam would be. 'You kicked her first. Now what exactly is going on? There's something you girls aren't telling us.'

Sophie immediately burst into tears, hers rising over Ashleigh's, which to be frank was quite a feat.

'Oh, man!' Harry bowed his head and put his fingers on his ears.

Pippa looked up, caught Kam's eyes and grinned. He looked like he was in complete accord with Harry, as was the rest of the class by now. It didn't matter how brilliant you were during teacher training, or what skills you had developed in the career you had before; nothing would ever prepare you to deal with the hysterical squawking of four-year-old girls mid-meltdown.

'Sophie?' Pippa's voice took on a warning tone.

'It's not my fault, Miss.'

'It is! It is!' Ashleigh's tears dried remarkably quickly given the opportunity to rat her friend out. 'Sir Squeaks-a-lot is in her PE bag!' She shot a triumphant look across at Sophie, no qualms about spilling her friend's secret, nor apparently about taking half an hour to do so.

'Right, Miss Parkin perhaps if you take over here?' Kam stood up and motioned to Sophie to do the same.

Pippa jumped into his spot and immediately launched into some numeracy songs in an attempt to distract the class from what may or may not be found in Sophie Edmond's PE bag. Reluctantly they joined in, although clearly every single one of them was itching to watch the drama unfold.

In truth, singing about five little ducks was boring Pippa to tears as well; she also wanted to see what was happening in the cloakroom and was trying to keep half an eye on the cloakroom whilst pretending not to and hoping she didn't look swivel-eyed to the children.

As baby duck was just swimming back after the quack quacks, Pippa heard Kam shout damn and quickly apologise. Pippa stopped singing and swung her head to see Sir Squeaks-a-lot race into the classroom (Kam was right, they really did run fast) with Kam full pelt in behind him. But six foot of newly qualified teacher was no match for a hamster who was clearly thoroughly done with today.

The hamster raced across the floor, having the advantage of being able to scoot under furniture and around corners far more agilely than Kam could. It was really quite funny. Kam seemed to turn into Basil Fawlty, arms and legs everywhere. Every time it looked like Kam had the hamster pinned down, the naughty little beast would outwit him and dash the other way at speed. A few of the children started to giggle but were hushed immediately by a look from Pippa. Somehow, she managed to channel the terrifying Amanda Adams in one glance.

It was hard though not to giggle. He did look hilarious, gangly limbs flying as he sped around corners, his tie over his shoulder as the hamster disappeared on him again.

'Right, I need to go and help Mr Choudhury. Can you all stay here so we keep Sir Squeaks safe?' The class nodded, rapt by what was occurring in front of them. 'And you can sit down with the others,' Pippa addressed Sophie. She knew there would be a good reason why Sophie felt it was necessary to steal the school hamster, but now was not the time to hear it. They had to get the hamster back into his cage and try to recover a semblance of order before the parents started to arrive just before three, and peer through windows.

Pippa wondered over to the construction area where the children developed their skills with the Lego and Mobilo and where Kam was presently on his knees trying to coax the hamster out by making encouraging squeaking noises.

'Eek, eek, eek.'

It took all of Pippa's self-control not to fetch her phone and take a photo. Kam looked up and caught her eye and started to giggle.

'National curriculum, they said, early years learning goals, safeguarding, but no one ever mentioned rogue rodents. I haven't had any training for this.'

Pippa giggled back. 'It's on the job. Right, let's not be quite as gentle. You stop your eeking for a minute, as charming as it is.'

'I couldn't let you be the only one who has a special bond with animals,' he referenced their first meeting in the car park and she couldn't help but grin. He really was too cute for words. She knew you weren't supposed to be attracted to your boss, but she defied anyone not to fall a little bit in love with this man trying his damnedest to coax out the badly behaved school pet.

'It does seem to be a theme in my life at the moment.'

Kam looked at her quizzically but she decided not to expand. It felt more than a little bit wrong even thinking the word 'taxidermy' in the current situation.

'If I stop "eeking" as you call it, then what is your plan, hmm?'

'I'll clap my hands this side and scare him out. We can move that big block there and that one there and funnel him towards you.'

'Brilliant plan. You've obviously had practice at this. What if he has a heart attack? He's already had a scary kind of day.'

'Did you just swear Mr Choudhury?' shouted Ellie from the carpet, 'My daddy says swearing is not okay, doesn't he, Sam?'

'Yup.'

'Although, my friend Angelina says that daddies talk nonsense.'

'Thank you, Ellie. I don't think Mr Choudhury did swear,' Pippa jumped in.

'My daddy also says you shouldn't fib, not even little ones.'

'Okay, Ellie, just give us a minute more so we can catch Squeaksy and then we'll be back with you. You're all being very helpful,' Kam addressed the children on the carpet, presumably aware that this may not be his finest teaching moment.

Pippa knelt down the other side of the cabinet and clapped at ground level, running her hands from one side of the cabinet to the other as she did so. Sure enough, Sir Squeaks-a-lot – clearly in fine cardiac health – nipped out the other side straight into Kam's trap and into his hands. He cupped them around the little thing and raised them into the air, holding the hamster firmly and looking very Lion King.

The whole class cheered as Kam held him aloft and Pippa ran around the side of the cupboard, so caught up in the moment, so proud of their teamwork that she forgot where they were and threw her arms around Kam, heard a whooping noise come out of her mouth and kissed him in a celebratory fashion on his cheek. The class were all whooping and hollering alongside her, and as she planted the kiss Alfie and Harry both wolf-whistled.

Pippa immediately jumped back, but not before Kam had blushed to the tips of his hair and Rosy Winter had opened the classroom door.

–

> **Oh my goodness! What a day!**

> **Don't. I haven't stopped laughing all evening. Lottie is worried that I've finally crossed the line into hysteria.**

> **Crossed? Surely that happened years ago!**

Cheeky.

Do you think I'll have a job to return to on Monday?

Nah, you'll be out on your ear now! I'm joking, you'll be fine. Anyway, it was my fault.

True.

Ooh, unless Harmony kicks off about Sir Squeaks, then we'll both be desperately begging for jobs elsewhere just to escape her.

I'll start looking tomorrow ;-)

Chapter Thirteen

Kam had been mortified when Rosy had walked in on him and Pippa in what could easily have been mistaken for a lover's embrace. The headteacher had said nothing at the time but had called him in for a chat at the start of his second week to discuss how everything had been going. This was his worst fear, that he would be cast out on his ear just as he was trying to build a career in Cornwall. His whole plan rested on getting a job here; if he messed up his professional reputation this early on – he knew how teachers talked – then he was going to have to admit defeat and start from scratch somewhere else, and *that* he really didn't want to do. He wanted to be able to show his parents, and himself, that he had been right to take this leap, that it wasn't an ill-measured gamble.

He was sitting in Rosy's office now, trying to unclench his hands from the side of the chair and waiting for her to get to the bit where she told him off and then he would know how bad things were going to be. So far, she had spent the time discussing what he had found out in class about all of the individual children and reconfirmed the best way to deal with each one. She laughed, the affection clear on her face as she discussed some of the more challenging ones: the very loud Billy; the whiny and mischievous Ashleigh; Harry and Alfie who were still very boisterous; the over-confident Ellie.

Rosy had also laughed when she heard that Sophie had stolen Sir Squeaks-a-lot because her sister's hamster had recently died, and Sophie had felt desperately sorry for her and tried to remedy the situation as best she could. Rosy explained Sophie had a big heart but didn't always think her plans through. Kam couldn't help but agree.

Was he going to get out of this meeting unscathed? He couldn't believe his luck. He had heard that Rosy was not a woman who supported or engaged in gossip but surely she'd have something to say about the brief scene she had witnessed? It wasn't exactly gold-standard Ofsted– worthy teaching!

'So, you've been here a week now and it looks as if you've settled in brilliantly. The kids are clearly already fond of you and you've dealt well with some of the more unusual aspects of teaching.' She smiled.

He tried to relax but was still having to use all his self-control not to drum on the side of the chair with his now unclenched fingers, a nervous habit he had started as a child. He wished she'd hurry up and get on with the bollocking, get it over.

'I want to see how you're settling in, invite you to let me know if there are any aspects of Penmenna you're not so happy with, that you'd change if you could?'

Kam looked at her, his brow furrowed and the surprise was clear on his face.

'There's nothing I'd change. I think you have the most amazing school. I've absolutely loved this first week.'

'Thank you, although of course you couldn't say much else with me sitting here.' Kam laughed in agreement. It was true: no one would be fool enough to challenge their boss on the first week about things they may or may not like. As he approached the end of his thought he looked up at Rosy. Oh of course, she might look all sweet and butter not melty but she was wilier than he had given her credit for.

'I try and run Penmenna as openly as possible. We value all members of staff equally here, regardless of job title. However, there are some things that, no matter how flexible and open you wish to be, are sort of ingrained. Hierarchies are one of them. I can be as welcoming as I want, but you know that ultimately, I'm the head and you want to keep me happy. Hence you might be wary of being completely honest, you'd be more politic, weigh your words carefully or hold them in entirely.'

'Yes. I think I understand the point you're making. You are quite right.' And he did. She was making the point that no matter how friendly he was with Pippa, there was a power dynamic at play as long as he was the teacher and she was the TA in his class.

'Good. I would add that this is a very small community, and there is not much that anyone can do here that doesn't get discussed, dissected and amplified. Such is the nature of rural life and particularly in a community-minded village like Penmenna. For example, I know that on Monday you, with Pippa, became acquainted with the regulars in The Smuggler's Curse, and so does the rest of the village...'

Kam took a long breath. It was very warm in here.

'...and there's nothing wrong with that. It's actually a real bonus that you are keen to interact with and become part of our community. It's something I feel strongly about. I am friends with many of the staff here and seeing them outside of school is only something that strengthens us as a team. However, they do tend not to kiss me, and especially not in front of the pupils.'

There was nothing he could say, although he could feel the warmth of his blush. Even though he hadn't instigated – or minded – the kiss, it did indicate that he had created a less than professional environment in the classroom.

'Okay. I did want to talk to you about that time—'

'Mr Choudhury, Kam, I don't think you do. I wanted to mention power dynamics and imbalances in the friendliest way possible and remind you that for this term, you will be working alongside Miss Parkin. I think both of you have a natural energy and lively spirit that work very well together indeed and the children in the class are very lucky to have that. I know from experience how Pippa's vivacity really helps create a strong foundation in developing a love of school, which is why I have always kept her in the reception class. It would be a shame for that working relationship to become more complex than perhaps it should be at this point. We're only a week into term.'

Kam nodded silently. He knew everything she said was true and fair, and he couldn't blame her at all for feeling the need for this very awkward conversation. She would be within her rights to be concerned about full-blown fornication in the sensory garden by mid-May at this rate. There was nothing he could say here to make it better; just acknowledge that he understood and would try not to stick his tongue down Pippa's throat, or elsewhere, for the time he was working alongside her. July wasn't that far away; by which point Pippa would know him a lot better and probably wouldn't want her lips anywhere near him. All of which would be very sensible.

'And I also felt it only fair to warn you that there will be a position opening up here next academic year with Sarah Fielding, the Class Two teacher, retiring. I am currently keeping my eyes peeled for outstanding teachers who I can ask to come for an interview. I want you to know that if the rest of the term goes as well as this week then I shall be asking you to interview as well.'

'Wow. Thank you. I didn't expect that.'

'As I said, you've dealt with a couple of tricky situations, and taken a lot in your stride. It has been noted. From my point of view, and others who have been only too happy to pass judgement, you have settled in very quickly and your enthusiasm and cheerfulness is good for us all.'

'Thank you, Miss Winter.' He couldn't believe what he was hearing. This was fantastic. He was not going to do anything that could risk his chance of a permanent position here. That would be beyond perfect, and would mean he could shave a full twelve months from his five-year plan. In his heart he knew his decision to go into teaching had been the right one; he just wished everyone he loved agreed with him. A permanent teaching job would go a long way to make that happen.

'Rosy, please. And don't misunderstand me: your private life is your private life and absolutely none of my business. It really isn't. But as a potential friend as well as a colleague, I felt I should warn you that things do get talked about. Trust me. You may want to tread very carefully.'

Kam wasn't quite sure what to do with his face, his hands, his feet. In fact, his whole body shifted awkwardly in the chair. He knew this was a gentle warning rather than an out and out reprimand, a reminder that, as the teacher, it would be both unfair and unprofessional to try and take his friendship with Pippa any further. And that he was being watched. And that what he did could well impact on whether or not he was considered for the permanent position soon available.

'Now, let's talk about the assessments we need to start next week.'

Kam had never been so relieved to hear such mundane words in his life.

Chapter Fourteen

At the end of the week Pippa and Kam took the class to Penmenna Hall to see how the vegetables were growing in their absence. It was a long-term project and last term the children had sown all their seeds and were hoping to see that their shoots had grown into proper plants.

Rosy had told Kam and Pippa before they left that the rocket and the radishes should be ready to harvest now and, if they were lucky, the rhubarb in its most glorious, pinkest state could also be ready to pull. This meant that even the littlest pair of hands should be able to do some harvesting if they really tugged hard, and the whole outing would tie in beautifully with *The Enormous Turnip*, their literacy topic for the week.

Normally Pippa would stay in school during the Penmenna Hall trips to care for the children who remained, the classes being split into two. But this morning Rosy wanted her to go along with Kam so that the children had a familiar face alongside their new teacher. Plus, it would be unfair to leave him entirely at the mercy of the parent helpers, which Pippa took as code to mean Marion.

Hence this morning Pippa had dressed appropriately in a headscarf, boots and trademark slash of red lippy. Pippa reckoned she would have made a brilliant Land Girl and was more than ready to help the children pull the vegetables from the ground. Plus, her whole family had clubbed together to buy her some vintage Fendi knee-high wellies for Christmas last year and she didn't get to wear them as often as she wanted. They were so beautiful she would happily sleep in them (but even she drew the line at boots in bed).

Whilst waiting for Matt Masters to appear (the gardener who ran Penmenna Hall and was the presenter of *Green-Fingered and Gorgeous*, the gardening show that was filmed there), Kam led the rest of the children, with Pippa bringing up the rear, to the raised beds by the orangery that were set aside for the children's segment of the show. As they reached them, Ellie ran up to Kam and slipped her hand into his.

'Hello. I'm going to be your friend today.'

'Okay, that sounds good. How are your harvesting skills?'

'Oh good. I'm good at everything. In fact, my daddy says I'm too good for my own good. I don't know what that means but he smiles when he says it so I think he agrees that I'm good at nearly almost everything.'

'Is that so?'

'Yes.' The brevity of her answer indicated she believed it to be utterly true; however, she called over her shoulder to her friend to provide more evidence. 'It's true isn't it, Sam?'

'Well, you're good at lots of things, but—' He didn't get to finish his sentence.

'See, told ya.' Ellie looked up at Kam and smiled. Pippa hid her own grin as she watched the teacher look like he had fallen a little bit in love. Mind you, Ellie wasn't hard to love. She was adorable – sparky and confident and full of mischief – and when you knew her back story, it kind of made you love her even more. This child was a survivor.

'Why are you holding his hand? That's just stupid. You can't be friends with teachers,' Billy (whose position had been usurped as Ellie had broken the line) shouted at her from behind them. Billy had never really understood the concept of a gently pitched conversation and shouted absolutely everything. Pippa had been trying to teach him about an indoor voice for a while now, but as they were outside she decided not to muddy the waters.

'Of course, I can.' As they all stood around the raised bed, Ellie's little face scrunched up and Pippa took a couple of long strides to get to her. Kam hadn't seen that facial expression before, but she very definitely had. It normally resulted in injury to those Ellie considered had thwarted her.

'Mr Choudhury!' Pippa shouted across to try and warn him, but Ellie was too fast and her hand went straight into the raised bed beside her, grabbing a handful of dirt. Billy towered over her but Pippa knew that wouldn't matter a jot to Ellie.

Kam realised what was going on and moved like the wind to grab Ellie's hand just as it reached up, a millisecond before she rammed the earth into Billy's mouth.

Phew. Pippa didn't even want to imagine what would have happened if Billy had found himself with a mouthful of mud and worms.

'Ellie!' Her best friend Sam gave her a stern look. He was very practised at those.

'He d'served it. I can be friends with who I want. I'm friends with Miss Winter and Matt, they live next door to me so I can be friends with Mr Choudhury too.'

'They live next door to me.' Sam said, his furrow getting deeper.

'And your home is my home – your mum always says so – so they live next door to me too. You have your things at mine so it's fair.'

That logic seemed to satisfy Sam who nodded matter-of-factly at his friend.

'Hello, everybody. Welcome back to Penmenna. Now, I've got an action-packed afternoon ahead of us, so listen up and let's see how much we can fit in.' Matt Masters, who had popped up from behind a raised bed, addressed them all, his curly hair blowing around his head in the springtime breeze. His dog barked at his ankles, jumping up and down in excitement, presumably at having all the children back again.'

'Hello, Matt darling,' Marion who was accompanying them, along with a couple of other parent helpers, was in leopard print again. For a woman who had never really worn it before, she was fully embracing it this term. Pippa half expected her to break out a pair of fur-trimmed knickers any minute.

Matt smiled and waved before setting the children a whole heap of gardening jobs. Pippa kept Ellie close to her side for the rest of the day but couldn't stop sneaking glances at Kam as he dealt with the children outside of a formal classroom setting. He was smashing it.

Not only did he get down and on with the jobs in hand, letting the children take the lead where appropriate and encouraging the shyer ones to participate as fully as the more confident ones, he also managed to stop Alfie trying to saw a worm in half to see if it made two worms like his big brother had told him it would. He prevented Billy from eating the entire crop of radishes before they could bring them back to school and he also gently challenged gender stereotypes when Alfie refused to harvest the vivid hot-pink rhubarb in case Harry teased him for being girly.

Pippa was aware that she was in danger of having her mild crush turn into a massive one if she didn't rein herself in and concentrate on her work. The time she was spending with Kam on a day-to-day basis wasn't helping much. Secretly she half expected each day to reveal something that would paint him in a less golden light, something she didn't like. Did he eat messily or pick his nose when no one was looking and smear it on the furniture? But alas, so far there had been nothing. He just got more appealing rather than less as each day passed.

She was also beginning to notice Rosy watching her watching Kam around the school and as much as she loved the headmistress, she didn't want to be in trouble at work. How embarrassing would it be to be outed as that girl, the one harbouring the inappropriate crush? She was fairly sure Marion would be the first to dob her in to Rosy, should she make ridiculous cow eyes at Kam today. It was just that she didn't always realise she was doing it.

The class finally packed up all their bounty and clambered back onto the minibus excited about what they would do in the classroom over the next few days with the vegetables they had harvested. They planned to make a great big crumble and also a salad for snack time. It was remarkable how so many of the children wouldn't touch a vegetable when they first joined the school, but they would happily munch away with the alacrity of Peter Rabbit, after growing and harvesting them.

They pulled into the school grounds and Pippa was proud of herself for reining in her lustful glimpses at Kam all the way home (even though she had just seen him digging and looking properly manly, a little bit sweaty and great with the kids all at the same time). She wanted to try and put a little bit of distance between them with the intention of throwing Marion off the scent, but when she looked out of the minibus window, her heart sank and despair took over.

There, right outside the front of the school and parked on the great big yellow do–not–park zigzags was a shiny bright red convertible that screamed 'Look At Me!' and a couple of other things besides.

There could only be one person responsible for that.

Chapter Fifteen

Kam had had a great day, he had known there was something special about Penmenna School upon his very first visit but today was unreal. These children were so lucky to have this opportunity. And what's more, despite never having explored gardening in his entire life, he realised he might rather enjoy it. It was satisfying having your hands in the earth and eating what you pulled out. Admittedly. it had just been the one radish that Billy insisted he tried but still, there was a satisfaction to it that he hadn't expected.

And working with Pippa was so much fun. Her facial expressions were often so outlandish he couldn't fail to laugh at her. The way she crinkled her nose when someone said something she didn't like, and the way pure sunshine beamed out of her face when she was happy. He didn't think she realised quite how transparent she was. On top of which she didn't stop singing or humming little ditties all day, slightly off-key and not fazed by it at all. And he rather liked it.

Mia, his last girlfriend, had been so inscrutable he had never been sure what she had been thinking, and consequently was taken by complete surprise when she left saying she couldn't put up with his stupid jokes and hamster cheeks any longer. He had spent the next two weeks eating nothing but green vegetables to see if he could lose the weight on his face and make himself more chiselled and handsome. Then as he glanced around the table during a family dinner, he realised he was fighting a losing battle and it might just be better to accept his rounded face and find a partner a little less judgemental.

The break-up had proved to be the motivator to finding the courage to tell his parents that he was leaving the family business and using his degree to train as a teacher. They were not happy to lose him to begin with, but when he qualified and they realised he was looking for teaching posts outside of Middlesbrough they were incandescent; their disappointment seeped out of every glance, every meal cooked, every parental pore. If you looked at it in a kind of roundabout way, he supposed he had Mia to thank for him meeting Pippa.

He knew his decision was a good one; today for example he had had so much fun that he would have willingly done it for free. To be paid for it and to be part of these children's lives had to be the best job in the world.

The minibus pulled up at the school where the parents were already hovering so he jumped to his feet to get the children ready for their mums, dads, grandparents or childminders – one of which had parked their car on the no-waiting lines. There was always one!

He looked across at Pippa to exchange a really-who-parks-like-that look, but she didn't catch his eye, although was also looking at the car in despair.

He instructed the children to remove their seatbelts and then slowly counted them off the bus, ready to be lead back to class and then handed to their parents. They were a little bit later than three o'clock, but he had never been on a school trip that was back on the minute – children were far too unpredictable for that – and, in this case, Ashleigh had needed the loo so desperately that she had started to do that cross her legs and bounce on the spot thing while lining up to get on the bus and return to school. Kam was never sure how that helped, but it was definitely a favourite move of all young children. If he had tried it he was fairly sure his mother would have smacked the back of his legs with a spatula.

As the children were all standing outside the minibus, the very good-looking (in an over-privileged wealthy kind of way) man who had parked on the zigzags leaned out of his car's window and started waving frantically in their direction.

'Come on, darling, do hurry up. Time is money!'

Kam wondered who on earth he was addressing, until he saw that Pippa's face looked like thunder. No, surely not. Darling? He would never have thought Pippa would date someone like that. Someone who thought that saying the phrase 'time is money' was a good idea, let alone actually meaning it.

'Pippa, it's fine. You can go. We are a bit late.'

'No, I'll see the children into class, but thanks.' Pippa's scowl was a picture. She looked as if someone had just stolen all her favourite things and replaced them with rocks.

The man in the car beeped his horn. Three times.

Every parent in the vicinity turned their heads. Pippa was looking so cross, as if she were contemplating serious violence.

'Go on,' said Marion, 'He's obviously in a bit of a hurry. We can get the children back. I do love a romantic adventure!'

Pippa muttered something Kam couldn't quite catch, but as he nodded his agreement she handed Ellie and Alfie over to Marion to take them back to the classroom, and walked quickly towards the car. Kam, like everyone else, couldn't drag his eyes away as the man leaned over and kissed her cheek after she had yanked the passenger door open with some force.

'Childhood sweethearts, you know,' Sarah, one of the mums who had accompanied them to Penmenna Hall, stood behind him and addressed Alison, Ashleigh's mum. 'Best friends all throughout primary, inseparable. Susie was in the same year as them. And then he broke her heart when he went away to university, but look, now he's made his millions and come back for her. It's so sweet, a real Cinderella story. All those years yearning for him to return and he does, and in a Maserati too. She is one lucky girl. I wouldn't be surprised if they were married within the year. So handsome. Obviously devoted. She won't be a teaching assistant for long, that's for sure.'

Chapter Sixteen

Pippa sat at her kitchen table, goggles on and drill in hand as she made tiny holes in the bits of mermaid's glass she had been collecting for her Mum's birthday. It was a month away yet, but with such tricky work she knew it was always worth starting early.

The other advantage of doing this now was that it was helping her to calm down after this afternoon's nonsense. She knew herself well enough to know that with a drill in her hand then her irritation at James would subside as she'd have to use all her energy to focus on getting this right. That had to be better than dwelling on how cross she was about this whole situation.

'Hiya.' Lottie came into the kitchen and threw her handbag and tablet onto the table, grabbing it up again as she saw what Pippa was doing. 'Oops, sorry. That's pretty, what'cha making?'

'Present for Mum, I'm pretty chuffed, I've only split one piece so hopefully I'll still have enough to make a birthday bracelet. If not, you'll be with me scouring the beach at the weekend.'

'Okay, anything in for dinner?'

'Oh yes, I was meaning to speak to you about that.' Pippa lifted her goggles up and lay the drill down. 'It would appear that we have stoat for dinner!'

'Hahaha, you found him then.'

'Hmm, I didn't and normally I'd be furious with you because it is pretty gross, but in this instance James did. I'm hoping that will finally do the trick and put him off me. He's decided that now he has "won at life" – his phrase – he needs to come and get the girl he's always loved to "complete the package" – again, his phrase. So, I pretended the stoat was mine.'

'Harsh.'

'Well, keeping dead animals in the fridge tends to be a red flag at the start of a relationship.'

'And again, ouch. I'll forgive you but what on earth was James doing in our fridge? Oh wow! Are those some of your mum's biscuits?'

Pippa raised an eyebrow as Lottie pounced on the tub and peeled the lid back.

'Hahahahaha, she didn't!'

'She did.'

'Did he see them?' Lottie asked as she rammed a heart-shaped biscuit, iced pink and decorated with an inter-twined J and P, into her mouth. 'Tastes good though,' she mumbled through the crumbs.

'Yes, he bloody did. He insisted in coming in. It gets worse. Mum's interfering doesn't stop at baking. Appar-ently she's asked him to consider the name Janette for our first born; she reckons it's due a resurgence.'

'Hahaha, that's even better. You're going to have to talk to her.'

'I know, but you know she's not going to listen, like really not listen. She's convinced she know what's best for me. My plan is to annoy James so much that he gives up and sods off again.'

'I love your mum, but she's nuts.'

'Truth. With her encouragement, James turned up at school and made a complete tit of himself. I was so embarrassed, turning up in some brash bloody car and making sure everyone saw him.'

'Oh, I'm sorry. Cup of tea? Did Rosy see?'

'Yes, please. I don't know, but everyone else did. Even Kam.'

'Ooh. Well, that could be a good thing.'

'How? How can my utter humiliation be a good thing?' Pippa felt her face scrunch up, she didn't understand why Lottie would say that. It wasn't like her to be mean.

'Look, you've got a huge crush on this new teacher and it's not a good idea. If anything was to happen you'd be on cloud nine for a couple of weeks – you know you would – and then you'll do your Pippa special...'

'It's not a serious crush. It's just nice to have someone to think about as I drift off to sleep at night. I'm not letting it actually impact on my life. But pray tell, what exactly is a "Pippa special"? Bear in mind, I'm armed.' Pippa nodded in jest at the drill sat on the table as she handed Lottie her mug and tried not to look as if she knew she was fibbing a bit.

'You know. You know you know! You'll be all loved up and then he'll do something very human and you'll decide it will never work.'

'I don't do that!' Pippa put on her fiercest voice but she knew that her friend was right.

'You do! Look how much you were into that Shannon, then you saw the way she ate a snickers and boom, ended the relationship.'

'I can't spend my forever with someone who eats the chocolate from the side first! That's not right.'

Pippa's outrage was real. How could Lottie not understand? Forever meant forever to her and if she was going to get grossed out every time her partner ate chocolate she couldn't see that relationship lasting long.

'Uh-huh, and then Adam: you were keen on him but when you found he liked to play poker with the boys once a month you ended that too.'

'Poker is gambling, I can't be with someone who gambles. That could escalate badly.'

'He was a love, and he wasn't a gambler per se. He was just someone who liked to get together with his mates now and then, have a beer and play cards. A far more normal hobby than mine I'd say.'

'Yeah, but I don't fancy you and anyway your hobby bought the shop!'

'Rude. I meant taxidermy. My investing is not a hobby! Which reminds me I did a bit of digging on your new beau, and he seems highly thought off. Apparently, he's some kind of whizz kid; everything he touches turns to gold. You could do worse.'

'I'm not so sure. He's an entitled prick with outdated attitudes, who thinks I should fall at his feet because he wants to date me, but only once I've lost a little bit of weight apparently.'

'Ooh okay, maybe put the kibosh on him. But that's not what I was trying to say, not the important bit. I was talking about you and the hot new teacher. My point was that you love your friends to bits – you're the most loyal person I know – but the minute a relationship becomes more than friendship you get scared and drop people for the most inane reasons. You'll do it to Kam, and then you'll have to work together. It's a bad idea. I'm your best friend; I'm supposed to be able to tell you what I think, so I have.'

'*Hmmpf*.' Pippa scowled, pulled her glasses back down and picked up the drill. Best friends were definitely over-rated.

Chapter Seventeen

Kam sat on his longboard, feet in the water, staring up at the sky. This was his safe place, his quiet place. And he loved nowhere more than here. Being sat out at sea, just past the break and watching the activity on the shoreline, comparing it to the peace here. The perfect place to get his thoughts in order, create order from chaos and think about how he was going to deliver his lessons next week. This was mindfulness in action. And not just some recently discovered trend. Surfers had been doing this for years; the crazy adrenaline of riding a wave had its obvious reward, but *this bit*, this bit was important too.

He watched gulls circling overhead and how the clouds, few today, scudded across the sky like kittens with wool. Oh dear, maybe he had been spending too much time with five-year-old girls. He'd burst into a range of showtunes soon if he wasn't careful, whiskers on kittens and such like.

'Hey mate.' Ben paddled out back to join him, thankfully dragging him from his current train of thought. 'Waves are a bit mushy.'

'Yeah, but you know, this is what I needed. It's been a full-on week.'

'Yup. It's been weird getting used to not having you about the place, that's for sure. You settled in okay on the south coast?'

'Yeah, it's a whole different vibe, Penmenna. Well, I suppose Treporth is where I'm living. Both are very different to Newquay, but I like it. I really do.'

'You back to work with me though now, right?'

'Yup.' Kam agreed. 'I'm only contracted two full days a week in school at the moment so you've got me the rest of the time if you need me. Although, I've said I'll do any supply they've got coming up. That's okay isn't it?'

'Sure, of course. You need to get that foot in the door, and I imagine the day rate for teaching is better than what I can afford to pay you.'

'About double. How did you do this week without me, anyway?'

'Yeah good.'

Ooh, I recognise that smile. What have you done?'

'Nah, I haven't done anything.'

'But?'

'But I gave that new girl your hours this week and it worked out well. She's cheerful and gets the job done. The punters love her.'

'I bet they do.'

'And she's happy to pick up any casual hours that you can't do, so if you do get extra work at the school then I'm covered.'

'That's great. That works well for me and from the grin on your face that works pretty well for you too.'

'Well, she's helluva cute, and we've got this mad chemistry. I was thinking about seeing if she fancied coming out with us to Motion tonight.'

'That's a line you shouldn't be crossing just yet, not if you want her to carry on working for you. I've just been subject to the same conversation delivered by my new head, and trust me: workplace relationships are a definite no.'

'Okay, fair point. I could just see if she was planning on going there anyway, and then mention we would be. I reckon it would be alright though. A surf hostel is kinda different from a school. You are still on for tonight? Teaching hasn't put you off having fun has it?'

'Yeah, of course.'

'Excellent. And don't think you got that past me either. What's this about you being given an inappropriate relationship talk in your first week? If anyone had ever asked me if that was a conversation someone needed to have with you, I would have bet a fair hundred quid that no way. Not in this universe. You are the shyest man I know with the ladies, an absolute gentleman at all times. If anything, girls in the bar have asked how to get you slightly less gentlemanly.'

'That was one. One! Not girls plural.'

'Doesn't matter. Point is, how on earth have you suddenly become some kind of predator? Last week it was surf beats and laid-back riffs and now?! Now you're getting called into the headteacher's office for being a bit too handsy. That makes no sense, mate, no sense at all. It just doesn't fit with who you are, let alone your damn five-year thing.'

Kam trailed his fingers through the water, revelling in the feel of it against his fingers, laughing as his friend delivered his opinion, the kick of salt biting through the air.

'Ha! I was not being handsy, you're right about that. It was just a misunderstanding. You should have been there. I'm surprised I got off as lightly as I did to be honest.'

'What did you do?' Ben cocked his head as he looked at his friend, unable to believe what he was hearing.

'It wasn't me as such...' Kam started and his friend snorted with triumph, head rocking back as his faith in his friend was confirmed. 'It was just that the teaching assistant and I were looking for Sir Squeaks—'

'You what?'

'The teaching assistant and I were looking for the school hamster, which had escaped. When we found it, she was so excited that she put her arms around my neck and kissed me on the cheek.'

'Nice.'

'In front of the whole class...'

Ben shouted with laughter.

'...and as the headteacher walked in.'

'Oh mate!'

'It was unfortunate.'

'I'd say. But not really your fault?'

'No, not really. But it's a small village and...'

'Oh, you don't need to tell me. I know Cornwall. So, people are talking, but what specifically are they talking about? It was just the one incident, surely.'

'You're right. There isn't anything to talk about really, it's just that Pippa...'

'Isn't Pippa the name of the girl you met for a drink last week?'

'Um...'

'Woah, so you've taken your colleague for a drink in the village, and now she's flinging her arms around you in school?'

'Oh, that's not fair. You make it sound like she's a bit weird and has a huge crush, and she isn't, she doesn't and that's just not how it is.'

'Nah, that's not what I was doing. But I know you, so I imagine it was the two pints of Rattler...'

'Korev.'

'Good choice, so it was the two pints of *Korev* that made you send me that emoji with the heart eyes when I asked how your first evening in the new flat was going. Heart-eye emoji, Kam! You've gone and got a crush on your teaching assistant, haven't you?'

'She's not *my* teaching assistant. She's a professional in her own right.' Kam firmly made his point and knew that whether he had a crush or not there was nothing in this world that would make him endanger the security of a full-time teaching job in Cornwall.

'Hahaha, Pippa doesn't sound particularly Indian. Your mum is gonna have something to say!' Ben laughed and laughed. He wasn't far wrong.; Kam's mum had been chucking him under the chin from the age of six and bragging to everyone how they were going to get him married to a nice Hindu girl. Ben had been witnessing it since primary school and their friendship spanning over two decades gave him the right to tease.

It also gave Kam the right to tip him off his board.

Chapter Eighteen

May had always been Kam's favourite month. Spring was turning into summer and everywhere you looked there were signs that it was going to be a glorious year. Lambs were frolicking on fields; flowers were out in force and the vegetables in Penmenna Hall had been rioting. All was right with the world.

Today was the first bank holiday of May and he was walking through Treporth Bay along to Penmenna to meet up with Dan, who had invited him to come and join in with a kickabout this afternoon. He had loved football when he was growing up. He hadn't played in an age but was looking forward to it.

The smell of garlic and seafood wafted across the Marina as he approached the stretch of chi-chi restaurants that peppered Treporth Bay, a very different scent from the deep spicing of a decent dahl that floated out onto the street when he was at home. He decided he'd have to eat at one of them one night soon, when he thought he spied Pippa, her back to him, as she sat at one of the tables outside the swankiest of all the eateries.

He got closer, a chuckle burbling from his mouth as he saw that it had to be her, no one else in the world – surely – would have the courage to wear such an outfit!

The woman had tightly curled hair practically bouncing on top of her head and her body was clad, shoulder to ankle in what appeared to be canary yellow spandex. Her confidence meant she got away with it beautifully rather than looking like she had escaped from a time machine and was looking for her way back to the exercise segment on Eighties breakfast television. As he got closer he could see the man with her appeared to be the idiot who had picked Pippa up from school last Friday.

His heart dipped a little as he realised this meant she had probably spent the whole weekend with him, no doubt getting ready for her new wealthy life that would whisk her away from Penmenna. He gave himself a quick telling off and pasted a smile on his face as his path took him past the table. He couldn't be with Pippa anyhow, not without it messing his own life plans up, and he certainly wasn't going to do that now, not when success could be so close to hand. Despite what Ben may have to say he couldn't – didn't – assume she fancied him like he did her, especially when you looked at the alpha male she was dating. Getting jealous was a pointless, selfish waste of time.

'Hey, hey. Kam! Wait up!' He hadn't wanted to interrupt her date but it seemed as he walked by that Pippa had no such qualms, calling after him as he passed. He felt the smile broaden across his face as he heard her voice, turning on his heel to face her.

'Hi, how are you?'

'Good, good, thanks. Have you had a nice weekend?' She beamed back at him, the canary yellow of her clothing a good match for the sunshine that radiated around her, although it was so tight that it left little to the imagination.

'Yeah, not too bad. Caught some waves, chilled out and now I'm about to go and play football with Dan, you know, from the pub the other night.' He made sure he held eye contact.

'Of course, Dan's sound. I can see you getting along with him. If you're walking to Penmenna then and don't mind waiting a sec, I'll join you.'

'Yeah of course but are you not...'

'Oh no, we've finished lunch, haven't we, James? Didn't you say you had to go and see someone about something terribly important?' She directed this at her date, who was not looking quite as smug as he had been a minute ago.

'Well, yes, but—'

'Great. Then I'll walk home with Kam – we work together – and that saves you dropping me off. It's such a lush day, I'd like to do that. I'll just nip to the loo.' James looked blindsided as she moved her chair out from under the table and dashed into the restaurant. Kam didn't feel a pinch of sympathy. He hadn't anticipated seeing Pippa today, and he had been almost disappointed that the bank holiday fell on Mondays, meaning he would have one less day in the class with her. He liked the idea of walking back over the beach in her company. Already he felt lifted and he'd only been in her presence a minute or two.

James however didn't seem quite as pleased about his date scooting off. He stared at him coldly for a minute or two as Kam stood there feeling a bit awkward, and then stood up and came right up to him, invading Kam's personal space without a qualm, narrowing his eyes as he opened his mouth.

'I don't know who you are but I see the way you look at her, so consider this a gentle warning: she's mine – always has been – and no one else is getting her. I let her get away from me years ago and I'm not making that mistake again. So, if I see you sniffing around her again I'll be making sure you never walk, talk or stalk again. I suggest you suddenly find yourself busy. Got it?'

'Woah, I've only just met you. I'm not trying to sleep with your girlfriend.' That was true. It didn't mean he didn't want to, but he certainly wasn't actively trying. If anything he was actively *not* trying. Kam pulled himself up tall as he spoke, 'I work with Pippa. Her personal life has nothing to do with me, and no, I'm not suddenly busy.'

'Seriously, you're going take me on, are you? I know people, mate and—'

'Hey! What's going on.' Pippa came back out of the restaurant. 'Everything all right?'

'Yep, fine. Just chatting.'

'Hmmm.' Pippa fixed James with a hard stare. 'Okay, I'm going to talk to Mum and tell her what we discussed and then hopefully everything will be sorted. I'll let you know how it goes. Right, beachwards.' She slipped her canary clad arm through Kam's and smiled up at him, James' eyes lasering into his back as they wandered away from the restaurant.

'I don't want to cause trouble.'

'Oh, it's fine. You know what families are like. Relationships are always complicated. Plus, the cheeky bugger called me Big Bird and said I was an embarrassment.' She used her hands to indicate her outfit from hair to foot and grinned mischievously as she did so, looking a little bit like that had been her intention. Kam couldn't hide his laughter; with her hair in those tight curls and that outfit she did look a little bit Sesame Street. 'Anyway, let's not talk about him. Instead you can tell me all about you. What do you normally do on a bank holiday?'

'What, at home?'

'Yeah.'

'Well, I'd usually do what I've done this weekend: go for a surf, chill out. The only difference is I'd probably nip in to see my family. Bank holidays are nice; my dad is always in a good mood because he can charge double time if there are any call-outs; my mum moans that we never spend them with her any more like when we were kids, but has a smile on her face as she does it. But we do try to get there, unless we've got to work. Hema works in a cafe and makes it over for the evenings, and if Anuja doesn't have a performance she heads over. It's nice. Mum cooks and my sisters and I bicker. Usual family stuff. I miss them but I do love it down here.' It was true, he loved Cornwall. He could see why people made such a fuss about it. He would be happy to stay here forever.

'I'm such a homebody I can't imagine ever moving far away. I had a girlfriend once who wanted me to go and travel for six months. I was excited, but when it came to it, I was so homesick I came home again after three weeks and that was the end of that.' Pippa shrugged her shoulders as if her early return home had been inevitable.

'Huh, I spent two years touring the surf circuit, trying to carve out a career for myself, but in the end I came home too.'

'Ah, that's interesting. Why leave? Is that why you decided to teach down here?'

'Yeah, mainly. I left the circuit because my love of surfing was dwindling as it started becoming something I *had* to do rather than something I chose to do. So I went back to Middlesbrough, not because I was homesick like you, but because I realised that surfing professionally wasn't for me and my nan was poorly. I wanted to be near her, so I came home, did my degree (admittedly a couple of years later than most) and decided to stay in the UK and be near my family.'

'And your nan? Is she better?'

'No, she passed away after I finished my degree but I did get those three years with her, and then I guess I didn't want to leave my mum right away – they had been close – so I stayed in Middlesbrough for her, slid into working with my dad in the family business and before I knew it, years had passed.'

'That happens. What's the family business?'

'Plumbing. It wasn't really for me.'

They had reached the end of the marina and come to the beach. Kam lifted his hand to Pippa to help her down the steep steps that led to the beach. As she reached the sand she took her sandals off and dangled them from her wrist.

'I like the feel of the sand under my feet. I don't think I'll ever grow out of that. I know I'm being nosy, and you can tell me to stop at any time, but how did you make the leap from plumber to teacher?'

'I don't mind your questions. I'll say if I do.' He smiled down at her and she linked her arm through his again. This was nice, but he needed to be careful not to get caught up. 'I had a break-up and it made me realise that I had become stuck in a rut and ended up doing exactly what I was afraid

I would. Mia breaking my heart kind of did me a favour by making me reassess everything.' He paused in case he was boring her. Kam didn't often share such detail with people but talking to Pippa was just so easy. She nodded her head to encourage him to carry on. 'I'd been working with kids at the surf club in Saltburn in my spare time and really enjoyed it. I bit the bullet and decided to train as a teacher. I didn't want to teach business studies, which was what my degree was in, so I thought I'd try being a primary school teacher teaching a broad spectrum of subjects, and I have loved every minute of it. Best decision of my life. What's more, I can do it anywhere, and so I moved down here. My friend Ben was already here, and now I can teach and surf. Best of both worlds.'

'Your parents must be so proud.'

'Ah, no. Not at all. Well, I don't know about my mum but my dad was cross. Proper cross. He felt let down because I'd left the business. When I picked my degree, he saw it as something that would equip me for when I took over from him and then he couldn't understand how I could walk away from what he had built up. The fact that that was the point – it was what *he* had built, not me – still doesn't seem to register to this day. I think he thinks I'm being idle and feckless. And now that I'm in Cornwall, still surfing but without a permanent job, it reinforces his opinion.'

'But you're working with us.' Pippa looked perplexed and he wanted to wrap her up and keep her close. He supposed she had probably never disappointed her mum and dad so it made no sense to her.

'Yup, but it's not permanent. I kinda have this… no, don't worry about it.'

'No, go on. Tell me. You can't start and then stop. That's not fair!'

'It's a bit dull.'

'I doubt it. You haven't got a dull bone in your body. Admittedly you haven't cracked a joke and pulled a silly face today yet but I can forgive you. I get enough of those in the week.' She winked. 'I want to know more. Tell me!'

As he looked at her, he found he wanted to talk, to see what she thought. 'Okay, I have this five-year plan. It's important to me and this job at Penmenna is an important step. I guess I feel I've wasted so much time, not getting to university until I was twenty-two and then not doing my teaching training until last year, that I want to catch up. So, I need to keep my head down and focus on my career for the next few years. Everything else comes second. This temporary position in Penmenna is great. Hopefully Rosy will give me a good reference, which will help me get a position here in Cornwall. Then once I've got a full-time permanent post, while still being able to surf at weekends, I'll be living my dream. I'm giving myself five years to get established in this life, and by then hopefully I won't need to go back to the plumbing business with my tail between my legs. Once that's done, I can worry about all the other things in life – kids, mortgages and stuff – and make my parents see that my decision to leave the business wasn't a mistake, but a good move, and definitely the right one for me.'

He looked a little shamefaced, 'Does it make me sound like a kid, still looking for approval from Mum and Dad?'

'It all sounds very reasonable to me, although I'd say going to Uni at twenty-two doesn't exactly make you a late starter, but I know what you mean. I really do.

You need to do what's right for you and you feel you need to prove that to your mum and dad. Planning is the best way to guarantee it happens. I think most of us want our parents' approval throughout our lives. It doesn't stop because we've left home and having a knowledge of that doesn't make us childish. Quite the opposite. It makes us self-aware and respectful of the people who have dedicated decades of their lives to us. So no, not a kid, but a decent, switched-on human being. How's the quest for a permanent position going?'

Kam grinned. Of course she understood. He should have known she wouldn't judge him harshly; it wasn't in her make-up to be mean. 'Pretty well actually. I asked Rosy if I could put her down as a reference and she agreed. I've applied for five, no, six jobs now, across Cornwall, although one is in Devon, but I could live with that and it's just a matter of hearing whether I'm called to interview. It's early days yet.' He glanced around. Somehow, they had already reached the entrance to Penmenna beach and were pretty close to her flat. Time had whizzed by!

'And don't forget: you might get Sarah's job and then you could stay at Penmenna and everything would be perfect.'

'Everything *would* be perfect.' He smiled, knowing how much he would like that.

'Right, I'd better leave you now. I promised Lottie I'd help her with the stock inventory. Lucky, lucky me. Enjoy football!'

'I will.'

'And Kam, don't stress it. Your parents will come around. I think you're practically perfect. Any school would be lucky to have you. I just hope it's ours that gets to keep you.' And as she turned to head back to her flat she gave him a great big grin and he knew he really hoped it too.

—

Hey, was nice to see you today. How did football go?

Yeah, good. I had a great time actually. Really like Dan, he's pretty cool for a vicar.

He's def an improvement on the last one. I like him too. I know Sylvie said he was great when her mum died.

Don't doubt it.

I wanted to say thank you. I appreciate you opening up to me today. It's not always easy talking about the non-surface stuff. I felt honoured that you confided in me.

I was happy to. You're a good friend, Miss P.

And that was the way he was going to keep it! Even if you took the boyfriend out of the equation, and his own career plan, he really liked Pippa, he wasn't going to mess with this friendship.

You are too. See you Friday.

Looking forward to it. Night!

Night.

Chapter Nineteen

'Oh my god, you're about to get Marion at her worst. I don't know what's happened to her, and I never thought she could get any more intense or evil but she's extra snappy at the moment. She's timetabled a meeting in for all of us staff at lunchtime and has allocated Sylvie and Amanda on playground duty and given them two members of her committee each to help, so we can't even cry lunch duty to get out of it. Which is a bit of a bummer because that's how I've escaped every year so far. I know they're saying she has trouble in her marriage, but dear god, that woman needs to get laid. Coffee?' Pippa held out a mug to Kam, who looked a little shell shocked. 'Are you alright?'

'Yep, that was just a lot to process thirty seconds through the door. Good morning though.'

'Ha! Good morning. Sorry about that, but trust me, you need to be on full form, *now*. I'm helping you, consider this on-the-job training. I know you laugh at me but honestly, she is insane this week. And we've got swimming with her first thing, so drink up, and I really hope you've got padlocks for your teacher trunks, I'm scared for you.'

'I thought it was my job to stand on the side and oversee the pool. I didn't realise I'd have to get in the water.'

'Yeah, I'm only teasing, but still, it's worth considering. She'll try and persuade you to get changed and come in. If you want I can get Sylvie in before register to teach you some basic avoidance moves. She used to teach self-defence before the ballet school took off.'

'Sylvie is a wonder, isn't she? Best teaching assistant in the school. How are you today, Mr Choudhury? You still haven't got back to me about dinner, or a housewarming, you naughty, naughty boy!'

Marion swung into the classroom, gave Pippa her usual dismissive look and beamed at Kam, who still had his coffee in his hand and a slightly dazed early morning look on. Pippa couldn't help but think how cute he looked. She could picture him waking up in the morning, hair all jagged and mussed. with a sleepy morning smile on.

'Ah, Mrs Marksharp, how nice to see you. We've got swimming I see this morning, and Miss Parkin has just been informing me about the special meeting at lunchtime.'

'Oh, you don't want to listen to her, dear.'

'There isn't a meeting at lunchtime?'

'No, there is. I just meant generally. She's supposed to be terribly good with the children and all, but she can't count much past twenty, which is why I suspect Rosy keeps her in reception.'

'I am here, Marion. And I'll have you know I run a very successful business when I'm not in school.' The woman was intolerable. What if Kam believed her and thought she was only here as a charity case.

'Hmm, second hand clothing. Not really Google is it, dear?'

'It's a vintage clothing business that actually does quite well. And I'm an HLTA. They didn't give me that because I look cute.'

'No, well, that's true. But, from one woman to another, all this desperation, dear, it's not a good look for you. Now, why don't you pop along and put some blocks out or whatever it is you do this early in the morning before the children come in, apart from flirting with poor Mr Choudhury here.'

'Mrs Marksharp! I hardly think—'

'It's fine, Kam, I don't need you to spring to my defence. I'm used to her. I'll go and make sure everything is ready for when we get back from swimming. I should probably get this afternoon all prepped too, seeing as we won't get a chance at lunchtime.' Pippa shot daggers at Marion to reinforce her point.

'Okay, I'll come and give you a hand.' Kam responded, looking like he was trying to hide his amusement.

'Oh, don't be silly, dear. That's what she's paid for. Now I do have some things I'd like to discuss with you before we all get on the coach.'

-

By the time it was lunchtime, Pippa realised her hope that Marion may have worn herself out by being an absolute nightmare at the pool was never going to come to fruition. If anything, she was now in overdrive, pacing around the table in the staffroom as everyone filed reluctantly in, and then standing at the head of the table as a general preparing for battle.

'Right, is everybody here? Quickly, quickly, if you'd all like to find a seat… I meant the teaching staff, Alison, not you. Right, this year's May Fayre is going to be the best ever. I know I say that every year but every year we do so brilliantly and I know we can again this year. First thing is the cause. As you all know we always split proceeds between the PTA and a charity of our choosing. As I say to my boys, we are very lucky to live as we do and it's only right that we give to the less fortunate. I only discovered the other day that darling Rafe has been playing cards and giving most of his pocket money to the old dears in the Whispering Brook Care Home. Such a generous soul. *So* kind to spend time with the elderly. Anyway, I thought we could see who we wished to award the money to this year. I vote that we donate to Alex McKenzie's Foundation, thus the children will get to see the good their money does as the school is tied so closely to the Healing Hearts Orphanage. Does everyone agree?'

Marion was referring to the foundation set up by the father of Ellie in Class One. As a foreign correspondent in Central Africa, Alex had witnessed first-hand the trauma caused by the civil war in South Sudan, and since coming to Penmenna he had devoted his time to fundraising to help the displaced children of conflict. The community had done all they could to help Alex, and Penmenna school had forged close ties with the orphanages that Alex was helping to fund.

'I have compiled a list here of very worthy causes,' Harmony Rivers piped up. 'I think it's about time we diverted some money to help animals. After all they don't have a voice and, as human beings, we are their number one predator so we must take responsibility. I've been doing sterling work in advocating on behalf of guinea pigs, and whilst we're on the subject…' – Harmony shot a look at the rest of the teaching staff knowing she would have no success with Marion – 'we should also discuss the keeping of Sir Squeaks-a-lot. Not only is that name an indignity but I understand he escaped the other day and who could blame him? Who are we to have the right to incarcerate any living or breathing creature? I think we should set him free, maybe somewhere where he could—'

'Get eaten by the local cats? Any *sensible* suggestions? No? Fabulous. Alex's foundation it is then.' Marion didn't have the patience to let the hapless teacher finish.

'Really! This isn't a dictator…' Harmony's indignation trailed off as Marion fixed her with a look and Marion's minions either echoed the look or shushed her ferociously.

'This is ridiculous. We should let Harmony speak. What was it you wanted to say, Harmony?' Pippa spoke up, even though the Class Three teacher irritated the bejesus out of her. Only yesterday she had pinned her down by the photocopier and ranted at length about the lack of legislation protecting animal's sexual choices. Pippa had considered banging her own head repeatedly on top of the photocopier to see if the change in vibrations would have an effect on Harmony's monologue but decided she'd rather go without having to handwrite the twenty pencil control sheets she was copying. Plus, she was still harbouring her crush on Kam, made even worse by his openness at the weekend, and wasn't sure a gaping head wound was the most attractive look. But even Harmony at her most annoying didn't needle Pippa as much as obvious injustice. And Marion was the queen of injustice.

Harmony looked at Marion and back at Pippa while playing with the sleeves of her rainbow cardigan, sleeves that were already more than a little frayed, but before she could speak Rosy bustled into the staffroom, her tablet under her arm.

'Sorry I'm late, everyone. How are we doing?' She stopped by the fridge and pulled out a whole batch of caramel shortbread. 'I hope everyone's had lunch, but I thought we could do with some sugar to tide us over. Harmony, I made you some separately with carob and stevia. Nothing you dislike got anywhere near it.

'I wouldn't be too sure of that,' Pippa whispered to Kam whilst nodding at Marion.

'Did you have something to say, Pippa?' Rosy pulled the age-old teacher trick, gentle concern on her face and iron steel hidden behind the phrase designed to bring errant pupils to heel.

'Just that we should make it fair, have a vote on who we want to donate the money to and not let Marion steamroller us into doing what she wants. We might all end up agreeing with Marion but we should allow Harmony a voice too.'

'Oh, for goodness sake. Fine!' Marion snapped. 'Let no one say this PTA is not run on democratic lines. Right, hands up if you want to share the proceeds with Harmony's sexually-confused Guinea pigs, right no one. Fab, then that's it.'

'*I* put my hand up.' Harmony was obviously emboldened by Pippa's intervention.

Marion carried on, ignoring her completely, 'Hands up for those who would like to channel the money into a charity that we are all familiar with and that links to the schools PSHE programme? The Alex McKenzie foundation. Right, that seems unanimous to me.' She gave Harmony a glare that would induce nightmares, and then swung it around at Pippa too. Pippa bowed her head to stop herself from giggling, examining the table in depth and knowing that if she made eye contact with Kam she would be lost completely. Marion marched on. 'Next thing on the agenda is the stalls. Now, we are very good at this but we do have a few changes in personnel this year. After all, I lost my very best ladies last year and the current PTA members are still very much… um… in training. Aren't you, dears?'

Sarah and Jenny, two stalwarts under Marion's rule, looked a bit cross at this whereas the newer mums nodded supportively. They had obviously spent most of the preceding academic year being told how unworthy they were and now believed it. It was like those cults or training grounds where they beat you down and left you with nothing and then built you up again to fit the image they wished you to be. Pippa reckoned that Marion's new ladies – Alison in particular – must be about to complete the knock-all-the-joy-out-of-you stage fairly soon.

'So, let's go through the stalls list and assign any unknown spaces. Firstly, cakes. Now, Pippa your mother normally does this. Is it safe to assume she will this year?'

'Yes, she's looking forward to it, although Polly, my sister, will be cramming for her exams and can't lend a hand so without her or Mum's friend, Joanna, who can't make it this year, Mum will need a spare.'

'Oh, my mum is coming down for half-term. She will be here for the fayre and has asked if she could help. Perhaps she could do cakes with Pippa's mother?' Kam jumped in. Pippa sent him a sideways smile. That was cute. He hadn't mentioned that the other day, and she would love to meet Kam's mum. Although she had slight anxiety about her own mother being let loose anywhere near her.

'Excellent, I'll pencil that in then and you two can ensure they're okay on that stall.'

Pippa flashed Marion her fakest smile. 'Will do, also I was wondering if you'd like me to run a vintage clothes stall. I could donate half the proceeds and I have some lovely pieces at the moment. I have an original Alexander McQueen bustier for a st—'

'No, thank you. It's a May Fayre, not a jumble sale, or a chance for shameless self-promotion. Do try to think of the community.' Pippa's mouth dropped open and she saw Rosy shoot Marion her scariest warning look. Marion tittered before carrying on. 'Now, Sylvie, I understand you are happy to stage a maypole dance with all your little ballerinas, such a wonderful opportunity, and such a shame my own dear boys haven't got a place in your classes yet.'

'Yes, I'm sorry about that, Marion,' Sylvie didn't look particularly sorry. Pippa smiled across at her. Her colleague was oh-so-dainty and used it to get away with murder. Pippa often vowed to tone down things herself and take a leaf from Sylvie's book, but she never seemed to last more than thirty seconds before her natural, more ebullient self kicked right back in again and opened its mouth!

Marion carried on running through her list: Rosy and Matt were to man the plant stall and offer a gardening advice spot; Alice and Amanda from Class Four were tasked with the running of the toy stall under the caveat that this year it was not allowed to become a dumping ground for everyone else's tat; cream teas were to be staffed by Sarah, and Alison was trusted to take charge of the Pimm's stall; Davinia, from the local stables, would be bringing in some pliable ponies for pony rides around the edge of the field, and Harmony was told she should be able to manage the hook-a-duck because, as far as Marion was aware, plastic toys didn't have feelings; Sarah Fielding and her TA were put on the book stall with the same caveat as the toy stall. Other parents had signed up for a bran tub, penalty shootouts and the tombola. Marion was very clear about the type of donations she expected for tombola and had already briefed Sheila, the school secretary, about putting out a newsletter with her minimum requirements. It would seem that a bottle of brown sauce or a tin of beans were no longer welcome.

'I think we should be grateful for anything we receive, Marion. Not every mother has a cupboard full of Clarins going spare. I shall talk to Sheila and take that bit out. Penmenna prides itself on being an inclusive school and I pride myself on seeing that maintained.' Rosy was quite firm and Marion respected her enough not to mutter about a socialist state, but everyone sat around that table, and most of those forced to stand, could see her thinking it.

'Of course, you are the head. I'm merely in charge of the PTA and acting chair of governors. And after all I'm a firm believer in a level playing field...' Pippa snorted on her caramel shortbread so hard that Kam had to pat her back. She wondered if she could try faux choking if she got him on his own? He was great fun in the classroom, but she wasn't making much progress on moving them on from friendship. She reminded herself sternly that she was only meant to be daydreaming, not trying to turn the fantasy into reality. Plus, imagining the Heimlich manoeuvre in a romantic way was not normal and probably all sorts of wrong. She should concentrate instead on what Kam had told her about sorting out his career before he could think about romance, and try to stop having such thoughts in the first place.

'...when you've finished Miss Parkin. My own dear boys have achieved so much this year. I was thinking they could be in charge of a stall. They're very responsible with money. Rafe never seems to run out, despite his generosity. And did you know they are all nearly fluent in French, fluent. And dearest Rufus is beginning to speak a little Russian. Why, did I tell you—'

'Yes.' The whole school staff chorused unanimously and Pippa thought she saw a flicker of amusement in some of the PTA mums' eyes, a flicker of amusement was the first step to revolt, or at least so Pippa hoped. Surely this meeting couldn't go on for much longer? She wondered if she could get away with zoning out until it was time to return to class.

It would appear she could, only to be awakened from her daydream by Kam using her name.

'Miss Parkin and I can do that. I love those things. Can I put us both down for that?'

Miss Parkin cocked her head on one side to assess Marion's reaction to whatever she was being volunteered for. Surely she wasn't going to let Kam and Pippa spend time together, not when she was so keen on getting her own fuchsia-painted talons into the new teacher whilst her husband was away?

It would seem that Pippa was wrong.

'Thank you, Kam. That's very kind. We often have trouble getting people to volunteer for that. The children can get a little excitable and it is all the way across on the far side of the field. But with your natural authority – she looked him up and down in a fairly salacious manner – I'm sure you're going to be just fine.'

Was Rosy not going to say anything? That look was virtually sexual harassment in action. But it would appear the esteemed Miss Winter was too busy giving Kam a look of her own which Pippa couldn't quite decode.

Surely the meeting had to be over by now?

'Right, well done, everybody. I think that brings us to the end, unless anyone has any questions or further suggestions.' Marion's face clearly stated she didn't expect any. Fancy saying her beautiful bustier, in fact all of her clothes, were only fit for jumble. She really was a cow. Pippa raised her hand tentatively.

'Just before we go, I was asked to pass on a message from a highly esteemed local artisan who, at this time, would like to remain anonymous, but would like to donate a one-off, truly unique piece of... ahem... art. Perhaps you could put it down for the raffle?'

–

We're on space hoppers!

I know, right. So excited for this.

We're going to make a cracking team.

We are already a cracking team.

Mind you, we're up at the end with Davinia's horses. It could all go horribly wrong. Do you know much about horses?

Nope. But I know that if we've survived Marion today, we can easily survive that.

Bet I can go fastest.

Pshaw. You don't stand a chance.

What art were you offering?

Ah, that might have been a bit naughty. You'll have to wait and see.

Are you up to mischief?

Well, I'm not exactly sleeping. My phone keeps beeping.

Point taken. I'll leave you to sleep.

No! You don't understand. Lynne's waters have broken. She's having her baby! Oh my! Hang on a minute.

Oh goody, let's hope she falls so desperately in love with motherhood that she never comes back.

Yep, Dave just texted and said that she's seven centimetres dilated. Does that mean it's nearly here?

My sisters made me watch animal videos but they didn't teach me about childbirth! Can I guess and say probably?

I think it does. This is soooo exciting. And oi, don't think I'm letting that slide. I like working with Lynne!

But you like working with me more.

Chapter Twenty

The news that Lynne was in the hospital and had given birth meant that the school was practically buzzing with excitement. Pippa could picture the whole community of Penmenna lining up outside the maternity unit in Roscarrock, piled high with balloons, teddies, flowers and nappy stacks.

Rosy let everyone know that all was well and the baby was a boy, and then suggested that everyone give Lynne a little bit of space, with all well-wishers waiting until she was safely home before the congratulations, gifts and offers of support trooped over.

She then pulled Pippa aside and added a little more detail – eight pounds five, ten fingers and toes and Lynne suspected she no longer had a vagina left – and added that she was the only one, other than Rosy herself, allowed to visit the hospital. In fact, Lynne was demanding she got over there as soon as school was finished.

Pippa didn't need telling twice. The minute the bell rang she jumped into her car, threw aside some chocolate wrappers and empty drinks bottles, promised herself she would get around to sorting it out soon and dashed to the maternity unit.

Having been buzzed in and taken through the squeaky-clean corridors, Pippa was led into a side room where

Lynne was sitting in bed leafing and oohing and ahhing through a sheaf of celebrity magazines. Lynne had an addiction to celebrity news that it seemed even childbirth couldn't dim.

When Lynne had learnt that Angelina, a national celebrity famous for ornate hair and temper tantrums, was moving to the area Lynne had floated on cloud nine for days at the thought of bumping into her in the Londis. She still broke out into a hot sweat when she spent time with Rosy's partner, Matt. Not only was he now a national treasure in his own right but he was also Angelina's brother, the double whammy of celebrity meaning she could be relied on to hyperventilate for a short period before saying hello.

Although the biggest star of her world was currently lying in a little see-through plastic crib next to her and he was the sweetest-looking baby Pippa had ever seen.

'Oh my goodness, he is so gorgeous.'

Lynne looked up from her flicking and squealed. 'Oh, do come in. I've just sent Dave away because he was beginning to drive me potty. But isn't he?' She looked across at the crib and her face was alight with love and joy. Pippa suddenly felt emotional as she saw how deeply and utterly in love her friend was. 'I know everyone tells you that you never feel anything like it, but, Pippa, I just can't tell you what the love feels like. I thought I loved Dave, and was quite good at mildly tolerating him, but this love, this is something else instead. I feel like the fiercest wolf in the pack, and the proudest. I spent most of last night just watching him breathe; for some reason I was scared he might stop and I simply couldn't bear it.'

'I'm not surprised, and I think that's perfectly normal, although that's coming from a woman who's never given birth. but that grin on your face and light in your eyes is enough to convince anyone. I'm half tempted to rush out right now to try and make babies.' Pippa winced as she realised what she had said: Lynne had had such problems conceiving that she should have watched her words a little more carefully. 'Oh, sorry, that was a bit flippant.'

'Don't be so daft, you've got nothing to apologise for. I know I'm going to repeat myself but it really is the most amazing feeling. Never ever could I have imagined it. I mean look at his dear little fingers, and the way he's making that little sucky face in his sleep. I could watch him all day and I suspect that's how I'm about to spend the rest of my life.'

'I expect so, although please don't turn into my mother. Honestly, I love her but if she could sit by my bed and watch me sleep she'd probably still do it. What's cute at six months gets a bit creepy when you're over thirty. Anyway, tell me about the birth.'

'Do you know what? I'm going to save that for another day. I don't want to terrify you and if I give you the gory details you will never have sex again. And as a woman who is definitely never having sex again I want to hear all about your adventures and live vicariously through you instead. The village grapevine tells me you are a very popular young lady at the moment.'

'Does it? With whom?' Pippa was surprised, not surprised that the jungle drums of village gossip were in full swing – that was par for the course – but that she was supposedly very popular. 'Oh god, you don't mean James, do you? That's nothing.'

'Chuck those things off that chair and sit down, your hovering is unnerving me. You look like you might kidnap the baby and run.'

'I promise I won't do that, but okay.' Pippa sat down.

'So, spill. I want to hear all about this James fellow, and I also hear you have a massive crush on my replacement, four and half weeks in the classroom and you're smitten.'

Lynne rubbed her hands together in anticipation whilst casting glances at her sweetly sleeping bundle of treasure. Pippa felt herself blush with embarrassment. She never usually blushed. How on earth did Lynne know about her feelings for Kam. She hadn't even been in school!

'James is an irritant. He won't leave me alone. He's turned up in the village after years away and Lottie reckons he's some finance superstar, higher profits than anyone else in the game, but from what I can work out he's just an arsehole. Completely self-obsessed, no moral compass. Unfortunately, he's also decided that I'm the girl he must have to fulfil some weird childhood dream, but it's got nothing whatsoever to do with me; it's all about his ego and the fact that I'm not interested. We had lunch the other day, I made it quite clear nothing would happen and he seemed to get it. I feel so embarrassed because I did actually sleep with him once before, when I was eighteen, and now it makes me feel just urghh. Not the most romantic story in the world.'

'Oh, bless you, love. Our eighteen-year-old selves don't always make the most sensible decisions. Am I right in thinking he has delivered a floral basket or gift of some kind every day for the last week and a bit?'

Pippa sighed, 'How do you know that?'

'If you will live in the middle of a village…'

'Fair point. Yes, he does. To be honest I've never eaten so much fruit in my life. And the flowers are at least masking the smell of Lottie's formaldehyde. I still wish he'd sod off. Like I say, we had a semi-reasonable chat at lunch, I thought he had got the message, and he went back to London. But then he started sending gift baskets, so he obviously hadn't been listening. Mum thinks it's all wonderful.'

'He'll get bored eventually, but you could always get Lottie to dig a bit deeper. If he's as vile as you think she might be able to find something that will shut your mum up. I heard about her new hobby by the way, the animals.' Lynne made a face. 'I'm sure it will be a passing fad but if not, if you get her investigating you may get a bit of a break.'

'Hmm, I do hope so.'

'So this James is no good, now tell me about new Mr McDishy.'

'Mr McDishy?' Pippa's laugh flew out of her mouth making the baby startle. Both women froze, but the best-behaved baby in the world ever merely sighed and carried on sleeping.

'Yep, don't be coy. I hear everything, you know.'

'Oh, I know.'

'So, go on then. Spill.'

'Well, I don't know what you want to hear. We work really well together.'

'Are but are you playing too? Oh, my goodness, look at you going all quiet. I've known you do and say many things that most people wouldn't dare to, and now here you are, all shy, fiddling with your buttons – nice dress by the way – and not making eye contact. You've got it bad.'

Pippa brought her hands back to her side and then shoved them under her bottom on the seat so they didn't give her away any further. Lynne giggled even more.

'Oh, there's nothing I like in life as much as a little bit of romance. This is great. But I can see that now new shy Pippa Parkin's in the room I'm going to have to ask questions if I want any decent answers. Was that a groan? Wow!'

'I don't know. What do you want me to say?'

'Okay, I've seen him. He wasn't what I had pegged for your usual type, but he did have the most beautiful eyes. Even a happily married woman could get lost in those.'

'Oh my god, yes. They're gorgeous, all brown but flecked with amber, warm, you know? And his eyelashes, I've never seen anything like it. It's like he has three sets there are so many. It's just not fair. And when he laughs, I can't help but smile every time I hear it. I don't even have to be in the same room; it still makes me grin like a lunatic just knowing he's happy and on the other side of the wall. You should see him with the kids. He's so sweet. I was a bit worried that having a male teacher would mean he was a bit less forgiving, and I was worried about how it would pan out, especially with the babies in our class, but I was so wrong. He is patient and kind; he doesn't make judgements plus he designs the most amazing things with them in the construction corner. You should see the marble run he made with Billy, Harry and Alfie out of cardboard tubes and Sellotape. It took over most of the classroom. I have never seen those boys so engaged. They sent cars down it as opposed to marbles. It was awesome. And for the May Fayre we've been put in charge of the space hopper races and I know we're going to have such fun and I can't wait—'

Pippa stopped as she saw Lynne's face, eyes big and mouth open.

'What?'

'You're besotted. Absolutely besotted. I never thought I'd see the day that commitment-phobe Pippa Parkin opened her heart.'

'No, I'm not! And I haven't opened my heart. You do say ridiculous stuff. And I'm not a commitment-phobe. What is it with you and Lottie? You know that I just want to be *sure*. I want to get it right and that takes a lot. I can't see that happening with Kam. We're too different.' She cast an anxious look at the crib, aware that she her agitation had made her a bit loud. 'Oh, shhh sorry. Your baby is really good at sleeping.'

'He's really good at everything. He'll be speaking Russian by the time he's two.'

'Ha! Like Marion Marksharp's boys.'

'No, nothing like Marion's boys. Say that again and I'll ban you.'

'Okay, nothing like them at all. Nothing at all.'

'Anyway, don't try and divert me with talk of the cutest, most handsome and cleverest baby in the world. You should see how sweet he is when he feeds; he took to it like a natural. His little hands all bunched up and… no, no, stop me now or I'll turn into one of those mums that can't talk about anything without bringing it back to how perfect their offspring are.'

'Well, he is pretty perfect.'

'True. As it seems is Mr Choudhury. I don't buy this "we're so different" malarkey. Has anything happened yet?'

'No!' Pippa's face showed her outrage. 'We're colleagues. We've got to work together. I'm not looking to start a relationship with him. I can admire his good qualities and maybe… um… daydream now and again but I can hardly jump him over the water tray, and I'm not going to.'

'True. Do you see each other out of school? Oh, look you're doing that thing again with your hands and looking up to the right. That's supposed to be a sign that you're lying, or about to. Don't even try it, madam. I've not worked with small children for fifteen years without being able to spot someone being a bit shifty. Don't even think about fibbing. Do you see him out of school?'

'No.'

'No?'

'The first night we went to the pub, but we haven't been back since. And I've bumped him to him when I was out and we walked back to the village together. But that's it. Promise.'

'Promise?'

'Arggh. Yes. Although…' Pippa paused for a bit and decided honesty was the best policy. 'We do text each other in the evening.'

'Okay. So, you and I text in the evening. Like that?'

'Not exactly. We've never said anything unprofessional but… um… well… I don't really get butterflies when my phone pings and it's you.'

'But you do with him?'

Pippa bit her bottom lip and nodded.

'Okay and what about when that James fellow messages?'

'Urgh. I ignore him a lot of the time but definitely no butterflies. Shed loads of irritation though.'

'So, with the evidence presented, it's fair to say that you don't in fact have just a little crush, but rather a fairly massive infatuation?'

'Oh no, I wouldn't say that. And anyway, I'm not *doing* anything with him. You're not listening!'

'I am listening and you don't need to say it. I have. I'd be really happy for you. You deserve to be with someone good and all I've heard about this Kam chap indicates he's one of those. But you don't need me to tell you that sleeping with colleagues is a really bad idea. Really bad, especially in such a small community. So hang on to your crazy I'm-never-going-to-find-the-perfect-relationship beliefs for the time being.'

'My beliefs aren't crazy; they're how I feel. I'm not ready to settle down with anyone yet. And I'm *not* going to sleep with Kam!'

'Oh, hush with the faux indignation. All of us in this room, even nameless genius baby, know that you want to have sex with the supply teacher. And you'd be wise to carry on not doing so for now, *but* don't close yourself off to it in the future, when you're not working alongside him any more. As to this not ready for forever stuff, we never think we're fully ready for things in life. They creep up on us and then we discover we are.'

'Hmpf! Why haven't you named your baby yet?'

'Nice distraction but I'll go with it this time. Dave wants to call him something ridiculous. You know what he's like with the medieval stuff. Athelstan, Silas and

Boswell have all be mentioned and then last night when he held him for the first time he tried to call him Galore and see if I minded. I minded. I don't give a monkey's about its meaning; I'm not having my son called Galore. I'm hoping that it's just part of a convoluted plan to trick me into being madly grateful when he agrees to a far more acceptable historic name, like Tom or Richard or something, but I'm not hundred percent sure. I think there's a strong chance my husband really is that daft. Galore! For goodness sake.'

'I think he recognises his name.' Pippa giggled as the little baby began to make snuffling waking noises.

'Right, yup. He's awake. Now you're welcome to stay but this feeding is more complicated than I've made out. If you stay there's a good chance you'll get sprayed in the face by my milk.'

'Look, I'm a game gal, but there has to be some limits.'

'Limits? That's not the Pippa Parkin I know,' Dave boomed as he came through the door, loaded with food and even more magazines. 'Glad to see you've met Galore Egbert Rowe.' Pippa chuckled at the outrage on Lynne's face as he turned and tried to defuse the situation. 'I brought you pâté and blue cheese. Don't know if you can have it with the feeding and all, but I know how much you've missed it so figured it could do no harm to wave it under your nose, just in case it took your fancy.'

'Hello, Dave, congratulations, he's gorgeous but I'd better get back. It's Thursday so it's—'

'Family dinner,' Lynne finished the sentence for her. 'I'm going to start that tradition too. I like it.'

'That's because you're the mother,' said Pippa, tongue in cheek. 'Shout if you need anything and I'll nip by in a couple of days although you might be home by then.'

'Should be. Thanks for popping in.' Lynne partially raised herself, babe in arms, to give Pippa a kiss on her cheek. And as she headed to the door couldn't resist adding, 'Don't sleep with him, not until I'm back in the classroom!'

Chapter Twenty-one

'Hello darling, boys are in the shed,' called Jan as Pippa let herself into her parents' house. 'Been to see Lynne and the new baby?'

This village was ridiculous, although it wasn't outside the realms of probability that her mum had had a tracker fitted to her car.

'Yup. The baby's super cute, very well behaved. Here, my hands are full, can you hold the bin open for me? Tatters, lovely to see you but get down a minute.' She smiled at the lurcher, all gangly limbs and gazelle-like jumping the minute his favourite family member came through the door. He had very good taste.

'Why?' Jen headed into the kitchen. 'Oh my goodness, don't drop any of that on my carpet. You are a filthy little toad. Shoo, Tatters.' She flapped a tea towel at the dog to try and prevent him from unbalancing her daughter.

'I am not. I'm just a little messy. But I read a couple of articles that all said it means I'm terribly bright and have a tendency to be creative.'

'Huh! That's just the sort of nonsense that people who can't clean up their cars properly say. I'm still traumatised by your childhood bedroom. It's a miracle you didn't have rats nibbling your toes on a nightly basis.'

'Aw, that's cos I had a mum who is super good at cleaning.' Pippa leant, with her trash from the car still piled perilously high in her arms and pecked her mum's cheek.

'*Hmpf!* You might be bright and creative but that doesn't mean you can't whisk around with an anti-bacterial wipe now and again. Quickly, get that stuff in the bin before you drop any of it. Honestly Tatters, get in your basket.'

'Ta, mum. Hello, baby.' Pippa did as she was told and then bent down and made a fuss of the dog, notably not in his bed, before she turned back and addressed her mum. 'Shall we have a cup of tea before the boys come in? I wanted to talk to you anyway.'

'I need to talk to you about something I heard as well. Don't go without reminding me! But what you've just said sounds ominous, so you best go first. Oh, or is it good news?' Jan suddenly stopped looking worried and started to clap her hands excitedly. A bit like a seal, but with considerably less natural ability.

'Oh no! Don't you dare. Stop clapping!'

'I knew it, I knew it. I'm going to get to buy a hat, aren't I? Oh Pips, I can't tell you how happy this has made me. Karen and I used to daydream about you two giving us grandbabies together. This is awesome. Let me call your dad!'

'Oh my goodness. Mum! Stop!' Pippa felt like she was about thirteen again and knew her bottom lip was sticking out with teenage petulance. 'Will you *listen*? I am not getting married to James, and as to grandchildren, they are not on their way anytime soon. But it is James I need to talk to you about.'

'Well, if he hasn't proposed yet, he will do soon. I just know he will. You were spotted out on Bank Holiday Monday, you know. I can't tell you how excited I am.'

'You don't need to. You already have. It's clear with every breath. And the heart biscuits you keep leaving in my house. But I need you to sit down and let me speak. I want to be honest with you. But you need to be willing to listen, okay? Let's have a nice cup of tea. You can tell me your thing first but then you *must* listen to me.' Pippa took charge, made a pot of tea in the see-through teapot that Jan had got for Christmas and, putting it on the little table in the kitchen, encouraged her mum to sit down with her.

'Now, here you go. I never tire of watching the tea swirl out as it diffuses.'

'It's beautiful, isn't it? I know it's a silly thing but I love it so much. It's a bit like a fire, or cloud watching, it can be quite hypnotic. Okay, I'll tell you mine very quickly. You know how much I loathe that Marion woman. She fainted in the Londis today and I happened to be there. I'll never forgive the rude things she said about the WI. Hot blooming yoga indeed, most of us are battling menopause, the last thing we need is more heat. But I am worried about her. I've never seen her like that before. Luckily, Lottie was working and gave her some tea and I sat her down for a chat. Now we all know there have been rumours about her marriage floating about but she was actively gaunt, she really didn't look well. I don't think she's eating properly, and the most concerning thing of all was that instead of snapping my head off, she cried. Real tears. Like a proper human. She seemed really vulnerable and it scared me. She kept mumbling about how she had lost him – I assume she meant Richard – how he had missed the last two family holidays, and she sobbed, great big sobs that shook her body, Pips. It broke my heart. So, you see her in school most days, will you keep an eye on her? Be aware she may need a friend or two, a real one, not those fake ones who follow her around. Will you?'

'You have the biggest heart, mum. I do love you. I guess I'll have to. She's an evil old cow but yeah, everyone has their stuff, don't they? I'm not promising to be her best friend, but I'll keep an eye on her, okay?'

'Thank you. Now what did you want to talk to me about? Those boys will be back in a minute.'

'I think you know.' Pippa fixed her mother with a stern look. If she was promising to keep an eye out for Marion then her Mum could at least play ball with this.

'Is it James? I think you're being difficult about this when you don't need to be. I just don't think you're thinking any of it through, my love.'

'Thinking what through, Mum? I think I'm old enough to decide who I want to spend the rest of my life with.'

'Well, yes of course you are. But it's like you have this wall up, a wall that's stopping you taking those first steps, and I'm worried you're going to end up lonely.'

'I'm not lonely, I'm surrounded by people all day and I share a flat with Lottie and her gruesome menagerie. Plus, I've got you guys. It's cute that you're worried, but honestly there's no need. And I don't have a wall up; I've had relationships, but they didn't work out. That's quite normal. I know what I want and I'm just going to wait for it. I think that's sensible. I also think everyone should stop having a go.' Pippa meant it, she was getting a bit fed up of this now, what with Lynne yesterday and her mum now. It would seem James coming back to the village had triggered some kind of let's-attack-Pippa barrage.

'I'm not trying to have a go, love. You know I love you to the moon and back, but I'm worried you're jeopardising a chance to be happy. Companionship can bring great joy. I mean look at me and your dad. We've been together forever and he's my rock, my talisman, my inspiration.' Jan was interrupted by her inspiration coming through the kitchen door from the shed with their son, no doubt a rock-in the-making, following behind. 'Oh, for goodness sake, I'm trying to have a mother and daughter chat here. Could you sod off back outside until I call you in? Really. Always under my feet.'

Pippa could feel the grin on her face displace her irritation as she said, 'You were saying? Look, I want what you and dad have, *really* I do. I would love that Happily Ever After but it's not with James and right now I haven't met anyone who I could live with forever, male or female. Let's face it I haven't met anyone I could tolerate for even six months. And when I make a commitment and consider having children, both things I would like in my future, I want it to be with the right person. Not someone I'll regret a couple of years down the line. When they come along you'll know. *Everyone* will know. But for now, I'm happy as I am and I'm not settling. And certainly not for James.'

'All I'm saying is that you haven't experienced the joys of being in a stable relationship yet. You seem to throw the towel in before you've even tried. I am scared you are missing out by waiting for a perfection that may not be achievable. No one is perfect. It doesn't exist. James is a good bet. You've known him all your life and we know the family. For goodness sake, his family *is* our chosen family. He works hard and makes money to provide a home. And Pippa, he's very good-looking. I might be getting on a bit, but I can tell handsome when I see it and he is a very handsome young man. That makes for good babies. You tell me one thing wrong with him and I'll back off.'

'I think he could be a sociopath.'

'No, I meant one real thing.'

'I think that is pretty real, mum.'

'Only this week me and Karen went and had a good look around Debenhams for mother of the bride and groom dresses. I found the loveliest floral dress, I'll show you on the website after dinner, if you like. And Karen found a nice navy number, very flattering. I mean, Karen and I are already very organised. James is obviously keen; we just need you to hurry up, stop being so afraid of commitment and play ball.'

'Do you know what sociopath means, mum?'

'Stop saying that silly word, as if James is the sort of person who chops women into little bits.'

'No, I think you mean psychopath or serial killer, and that's not what I'm saying. He seems to lack any kind of empathy and certainly doesn't ever think he does anything wrong. It's not right. What I'm trying to say, Mum, is that I really don't like him. I don't ever want to touch him, and I certainly don't want his children, which means we can't have a relationship. His desire for me is all about ego. He only wants me because I don't want him. If I were attracted to him and I agreed to all this, he would go off me so quickly it would make our heads spin. His crush has nothing to do with me; it really is all about him. I don't want to see—'

'You're talking nonsense. Love, true love, is often a grower. I've lost count of the amount of happily married women I know who hated their husband on sight the first time they met him, honest to goodness, hated on sight. And yet they're all very happily married now, so I think you might be wrong about this. You've just got into the habit of being defensive, love. And besides think about the grandbabies, your children. You'd have such beautifully blue-eyed blonde children. You could set them up to model and all sorts, what with his good looks and your style.'

Polly bounded into the room, never short of an opinion and currently sporting jet-black hair.

'Pippa's bottle. She's not a real blonde, so she's not likely to have blonde children. You should know the colour of your own children's hair, Mum. When's dinner? I'm starving.'

'Exactly, Pippa *really* likes blonde. So she'd want blonde children. Honestly Polly, I'm trying to have a very important talk here to help your sister on the path to eternal happiness, and she's being *very* resistant. I'll call you when I'm ready to serve up.'

'Is she still trying to get you to marry James? Ha!' Polly laughed, laughed hard at her sister's facial expression as Pippa rolled her eyes and slumped her head onto her folded arms, resting on the table. She was never going to win this battle. Why was she fool enough to think she could have an adult conversation with her mother and make her see that she was no longer going out with James just to please her? Why had she ever gone along with it in the first place?

'It's not funny,' Pippa muttered, muffled by sleeves and adolescent-like hopelessness.

'It is. It's hilarious. Mum, why are Dad and Pete waiting outside? And Pips, don't marry him until he's sorted me some VIP tickets for Glastonbury. No point having him in the family if he can't pull his weight.'

> Oh, my mum's been a nightmare today.

> Only today? Lucky you! I thought you were going to see Lynne?

> I did, baby's super cute.

> Cool. What did your mum do now? Did she bake you more biscuits?

> Don't take the mick!

Pippa started to answer fully but realised Kam was the last person she wanted to discuss the Nightmare-That-Was-James with. Kam was a James-free zone at the moment and the only one it seemed not to be weighing in on her life choices. She was going to keep it that way. She decided to distract.

> **And anyway it impacts you too.**

> **Your mum?**

> **Yep. She says Marion is vulnerable at the moment and I'm in charge of keeping an eye on her at school.**

> **I didn't know they were friends. And how does that impact me?**

> **They're not. We are. Therefore, if I have to do it, you have to do it. And I've got to make Marion my New Best Friend.**

> **You can't have a new best friend. I'm your newest.**

> **Not any more.**

But I've barely unpacked. Surely that shoots me to the top of the new list.

It shoots you to the top of the most disorganised list.

Ouch. Little bit harsh.

A little harsh and a big fib. You are the most organised person I know. I bet you have unpacked really.

Of course, I have. Still want to be your newest friend though.

Uh-huh and I want a pony and a swimming pool. Life's tough like that. See you in the morning!

Hmmmm.

Chapter Twenty-two

'Kam, Kam, Kam!' A week after Pippa had been moaning about her mum and now his own mother's unrelenting squawk was piercing his head. Someone needed to record it and turn it into an app. No one was staying in bed after hearing that. Including him. He knew it was May Fayre day and he was getting up early to get to work; he just felt five thirty was pushing it a bit.

'Mum,' he answered, experience had taught him that the quicker the answer the less likely the din was to continue, even in a conversation with a door between them.

'I don't know what to wear and it's a very important day.'

'Mum, I appreciate you coming down to help but the May Fayre isn't until this afternoon. It starts at five.'

'And you said I could come in to school with you and help the PTA set it up. Well, I have to look my best for that, don't I? Now come and help me choose my outfit and I'll make you a nice cup of peppermint tea.'

'Can't the girls help?'

'Oh, you know those girls, they'll sleep until lunch if I let them.'

'Don't let them then.' By this point he had got himself out of bed and was smoothing his hair down in front of the mirror. It didn't matter what he did with it; it always seemed to stick up like it did when he was eight years old. He wondered if it would at eighty. He supposed that would presume he still had hair at eighty, at which point he'd be grateful for its sticky-up-ness. There was a sharp knocking at his bedroom door.

'Kam, Kam, Kam, Kam.' It was how he imagined machine gun fire: loud, staccato and piercing.

He pulled the door open quickly.

'Why have you not got any clothes on? Hmmm? You know better than this.'

'Mum, it's not even dawn. It's still dark and even the birds aren't up yet. Trust me: when the seagulls are still asleep, then so should you be.' He may have always loved the sea but living right next to it was teaching him that Cornish seagulls seemed particularly ferocious first thing in the morning, as if they hatched plans to make it as noisy as possible. Sometimes he swore they were playing the drums on bin lids right outside his window. Other times they emitted a noise so piercing that it chilled the soul. Either way, they were nearly as efficient as his mother when it came to working as an alarm.

'Don't you want to go back to bed for an hour, maybe two?' There was no harm in being optimistic and he smiled at his mother in what he hoped was a winning fashion. He knew he would be very keen.

'You know mornings are when I'm at my most productive.' She rammed a hot mug into his hand with a pale green liquid steaming inside. It looked nice but it wasn't coffee.

'I know, Mum. But it's going to be a really long day. A marathon. You want to be your best at the fayre tonight, so maybe just rest up and take it easy.'

'Things don't get done if you're always resting. Your father didn't rest when he was building up his business.'

'I bet he is now though,' Kam muttered, knowing his father would be having a blissful lie-in, until six thirty at least whilst his wife was away.

'Now, hurry up.' She clapped her hands together before breaking into a big wide smile and standing on her tiptoes planted a big kiss on her son's cheek. He accepted in that moment that he was up for the day and may as well make the most of it. 'Breakfast is all ready for you. Come on now.'

–

'Hiya. Good morning. Oh hello,' Pippa grinned a greeting, as a bleary Kam showed his mother into the classroom.

'Hello, darling, who are you?'

'This is Miss Parkin. She's the teaching assistant in Class One,' Kam formally introduced Pippa to his mum, not unaware of how bloody gorgeous she was looking today. A sweet little dress with flowers on made her look both demure, which his mother would like, and also skimmed her shape rather nicely, which he couldn't help but be a fan of.

'Hello, *Miss* Parkin, hmmm?'

'It certainly is. It's a pleasure to meet you Mrs Choudhury.'

'Is that *two* cups of coffee? You do know coffee is not good for your body? Caffeine is addictive. It can lead to dependence, headaches, anxiety, all sorts of things. It interferes with that natural calm that we all need. We don't want to do that, do we, darling? I'm surprised Kam hasn't told you that coffee is best avoided, and two cups at a time… It looks like the addiction has taken a full hold. He's a good boy, he listens. His father on the other hand… hmmm… he thinks I don't know he keeps a secret jar in his van and drinks it at work all day. And then he wonders why he has so much trouble sleeping and can't get up in the mornings. What can I do? I tell him and I tell him.' She shrugged as Pippa glanced at Kam and he wondered if she could see that headaches and mild anxiety may indeed be taking hold. None of which were to do with not having his morning coffee.

'I know, it's a dreadful habit, two coffees in the morning before the children come in. I shall have a good think about what you've said.' Pippa flashed her most pleasing smile and Kam's heart melted a little. He had known she wouldn't rat him out.

'You do that, darling. So, if you're the teaching assistant, does that mean my Kam is your boss, hmmm?'

'No! Mum! It means we work alongside each other. As a team!'

'It kinda means he's my boss.'

Kam's mum nodded happily. 'And is he a good one? Kind?'

'He is. I'm very happy working alongside him.' Pippa gave her a firm smile and Kam stood watching her as her personality shone from her eyes. His sunshine girl. Then he realised if his mother caught him watching Pippa and grinning, he was going to be in for nine zillion questions later. And Kam was not a fan of being questioned by his mother. It had taken up the majority of his childhood.

He remembered the boy who used to stand in front of the cooker, hands in his pockets, shifting from foot to foot, as she fired a million and one questions at him: Why are you late home from school? Why aren't you prioritising your studies? So, I hear Ben got an A in maths this week. What is wrong with you?

Questions about Pippa he was not prepared to answer. He really didn't need his mother piling the pressure on with a million suggestions as to how he ran his personal life. It was time to get his mother out of the classroom for a minute, He recognised that beady look in her eye.

'Right well, let me show you the staffroom and introduce you to the other members of staff.'

'That's very kind, darling, but I think I'll stay here.'

'Don't you want to meet everyone?'

'Yes, but I think I'd like to get to know Miss Parkin first.'

'Pippa, please. Miss Parkin sounds far too formal, and I hope we're going to become friends.'

Mrs Choudhury's face lit up as Kam heard himself let out an involuntary sigh. Quite a loud one.

'Perhaps Pippa could take me if you're determined to have me out of your classroom.'

'I'm not trying to get you out of my—'

'It's fine. I did most of the prep yesterday, I knew today would be manic. Come on, Mrs Choudhury, let me give you the whistle-stop tour. Today is going to be fun. I love the May Fayre, one of my favourite times of the year, so I'm so glad you're here to see it. I hope you're a fan of bunting. And I understand that you're helping out on the cake stall this afternoon…' Kam watched Pippa lead his mum out of the classroom, chatting nineteen to the dozen and weaving her magic. He really hoped this didn't go horribly wrong.

He seemed to wait with his breath held until both women reappeared in the classroom, Pippa offering Kam a mug of peppermint tea. 'Here you go, your mum says this was what you like to drink.' She managed not to give away anything in her face as she said it. What a trooper. 'She's been telling me all about your family. I can't wait to meet your sisters later. They sound hilarious. And she told me that your friend Ben in Newquay has been your best friend since you were four. That's really cute. She says he's very good at maths.' She couldn't help a little smirk then, and he watched her scarlet lip curve up with mischief. 'You never told me you had known him since you were babies. Why didn't you mention that?'

Before he had a chance to answer his mother, never short of words, jumped in. 'He never tells anyone anything. Plays all his cards close to his chest, don't you, Kam darling?'

'Not really.'

'Oh, he does, I've lost count of the times he just kisses me on the head, right here,' – she tapped the top of her head, bang in the centre – 'and then walks away, never answering my questions. Like *why* is he still single after all these years? Hmmm? Hmmm?'

'I can't answer that, Mrs Choudhury.' Pippa shot Kam the most mischievous look. She was clearly enjoying this far too much.

'Oh, if only there *were* answers. I ask nearly every week, I say, "Kam darling why can't you just find—"'

'Mum.'

'Let me talk. I say, "why can't you just find a nice—"'

'Mum!' Kam shouted so loud that the heads of parents who were waiting in the playground to drop their children off, spun around.

Pippa was fighting the laughter and beautifully too. She was managing to maintain her most professional face. He did not doubt for a minute that her interest was sincere, but he knew Pippa well enough now to know the crinkle between her eyes was not due to age or stress but to laughter fighting to break out. He was mortified.

He loved his mum and knew that, despite her disappointment that he had walked away from the family business, she – unlike his father – was secretly proud that he had finally used his degree and become a teacher. He knew that she was proud of what he was now doing for a living; she just wished he'd do it in Middlesbrough, get married and pop out several grandchildren for her. If he could let his mum and dad chose his bride for him at the same time, well, that would just make all her dreams come true.

He knew she had been eying up potentials for at least a decade, if not longer. One of the advantages in living in Cornwall was that he was no longer subjected to surprise dinners as he had been when living at home. He'd return home after working all hours with his dad, hands in loos or manky-smelling standing water, only to find his mother cooking up a storm having invited some girl she fancied having as a daughter-in-law over to eat. Just before he had left to move down south, she had been steadily working through his sisters' friends as potential candidates. He supposed he should be grateful she hadn't made a minibus of possible wives drive down the motorway. Although there was always time.

'Mum, I need to let the kids in. Please, can you leave any of your personal comments on my life until the classroom is empty at the end of the day? None of the children need to know what a bitter disappointment Mr Choudhury is in the marital stakes.'

Pippa sputtered into her now cold coffee. She was clearly determined to finish both cups.

'Oh, before you let them in, Kam. Remember we need to look after Marion today. You still up for it?'

'Of course.' Kam smiled back at her, trying to block out his mother who was watching their interaction keenly. Because becoming best friends with Marion Marksharp today was exactly what he needed.

Chapter Twenty-three

Pippa had had a great morning. She had really enjoyed spending the day with Kam's mum, who wasn't shy of sharing stories about her son and his mischiefs. Pippa's favourite was that as a boy he was so dedicated to his swimming that he used to spray that skin replacement stuff, the spray plaster, in between his fingers to see if he could make them webbed like the sea birds that dotted the shores. How cute was that?

She also found out that he had taken the title in the Saltburn surf competitions almost every year since he was old enough to enter. His dream of surfing professionally hadn't been an empty ambition. She had spent bits of today daydreaming about the two of them as a couple, touring around in a little VW as he surfed and she cooked sausages and hand-sewed. It was such a shame that he didn't feel the same. Perhaps if her mum knew that she had a mild crush then she'd stop spouting her nonsense about walls. No, that was a bad idea. The meddling would kill Pippa's romantic imaginings stone dead, and she was enjoying keeping this crush exactly where it belonged: in her head.

'Hello, love!' Jan wandered into the hall where Pippa was doing this daydreaming, whilst dragging tables into place for the fayre.

'Hi, mum. Thanks for helping with this.'

'No worries, sweetie. I'm sorry if you thought I was having a go the other day, you're a good girl. I know I was a little harsh, but you do need to consider some of the things I said. How's Marion been today?'

'Well, whilst I shouldn't speak ill of the queen in her very own domain, she's seemed pretty normal: patrolling the corridors and shouting at people.'

'Well, I suppose that's a good thing. Let's get this cake stall up and running. I've brought some biscuits and made a nice pineapple upsidedown cake as well. I just saw Rosy, and she's donated a chocolate cake, a coffee and walnut one and a lemon drizzle. She's a good woman that. See, baking isn't just for us oldies.'

'I never said it was. I just don't need to make cakes because I've got your biscuits!'

'That you have. Now, who am I on with this year? Joanna said she'd never be coming back after the way Marion spoke to her last year. I said that we all had to put up with that if we wanted to help the Penmenna community. She said she'd rather donate fifty quid and never run the risk of having to speak to her again. I don't think you're going to find anyone as good as Joanna.'

'Well, I think you might be in for a treat. You know the new teacher I'm working alongside?'

'The temporary one?'

'Yes. His mum's down for a few days for half term and she loves to bake as well. It would appear I have found your northern equivalent. She's already left three Tupperware containers full of sweet treats in the staffroom.' She was half tempted to tell her about Kam's mother's commitment to getting him married off – something she knew her mother could relate to – but self-preservation kicked in.

'Oh, I shall go and have a little look. When is she going to get here? Is she going to help—'

'Ah Pippa darling, there you are. Let me introduce you to my daughters, Nisha, Hema and Anuja.' Pippa and her mother turned to see Mrs Choudhury bustling over with three young women behind her.

'Hello, how lovely to meet you.' Pippa grinned a welcome to them. She had been excited all day about meeting the three sisters that Kam claimed terrorised him, and now they stood before her, all three with the same exquisite eyes as their brother – with the same identical flash of playfulness. Apart from that, though, they were wildly different from each other.

'Hello, we've heard all about you.' The youngest one, Anuja (Pippa imagined her to be a similar age as Polly) grinned mischievously. She was long-haired and long-limbed, and wearing a scarlet and gold dress that Pippa instantly fell in love with. She was glossy from top to toe, and had an assurance that radiated out of her.

'And I have heard that you force your big brother to watch animal videos online. That must take some doing.' She knew that Anuja was the dramatic one, currently working as an actress for a regional theatre company up in Middlesbrough. Looking at her Pippa had no doubt that she would become fabulously successful. The other two were a little shorter, and she guessed that Nisha, who was a history geek but worked for an insurance company, was the one in jeans and a hoodie, and Hema, who Kam had said inherited their mother's culinary skills and helped run a café, was the one with the cropped hair and huge earrings.

'Oh, he's a dreadful fibber. Can't believe a word he says,' the younger one giggled. 'He loves them, and does it voluntarily. Loves them. Makes *us* watch them with him, not the other way around. He's strange like that.'

'Don't believe Anuja. She's terribly naughty.' Mrs Choudhury gave her youngest daughter a look of such reproach it would put Jan to shame. Yet Anuja giggled rather than withered into obedience. 'She adores Kam. We all do and he is very normal, very kind, and clearly has endless patience for his sisters, especially Anuja.'

'To be fair all those years with her have meant he can easily deal with a classroom of five-years-olds,' the sister with the spiky hair spoke, her tone free of malice as she offered Pippa her hand. 'Hi, I'm Nisha.' Pippa took her hand and grinned her hello. So much for making assumptions.

'I haven't met Mr Choudhury yet,' Jan jumped into the conversation with a very pointed tone. *No*, thought Pippa, *and with good reason too. I've been keeping him safe, and you've had your hands full plotting my wedding, four christenings and my retirement with James.*

'Ah well, we shall remedy that then. Kam, Kam, Kam, Kam, come here.'

Pippa couldn't see him in the hall but his mother's call was disturbing, sounding exactly like a car alarm. Suddenly the move down to Cornwall made a little more sense.

'So, are you down in Penmenna long?' Jan had started to pump the girls and Kam's mother for information. They weren't aware that she had serious skills at this. Had she been born but a few centuries earlier Pippa was under no illusion that she would have led the Spanish Inquisition and probably had it wrapped up by teatime.

As Jan fired rapid questions at them, Pippa felt her hairs on her neck tingle and, without seeing him, knew that Kam had made his way into the school hall. She didn't know how her body knew he was close before her brain did, but it did. The first time she had been aware of it she had been in that restaurant with James and she had felt a tingle course up from the base of her spine to her neck. Not trusting her instinct, she had looked up to check the cause and there he had been, walking quietly past. She wondered if it were some sort of special phenomenon, and if it was, what did it mean?

On one level – her crazy romantic dreams level – she wondered if it meant that they were meant to be together. On a more rational, and more fearful, level she doubted they could have a Happy Ever After. Were they not too different? He was organised; she was… um, slightly more free-flowing. He was sporty; she *definitely* wasn't. That daydream earlier of her sewing whilst he surfed was lovely, but was it even a teeny bit realistic? Indulging her crush would lead to too many complications. Pure and simple. Regardless of all of that, her tingling had proved to be correct, his presence confirmed seconds later as his mother barked out her rat-a-tat-tat call again, waving at him to come over.

'Hello everyone, nice to see you've all met. Welcome to Penmenna.' He gave his sisters a kiss on the cheek. 'You must be Mrs Parkin. Pippa only says good things. It's a pleasure to meet you at last.' He held out his hand and Jan took it and shook it whilst looking at him appraisingly.

'You're the man who came into the garage and said you knew Pips. I saw you on the CCTV.'

'Well, in that case, it probably was me. I certainly came in and met your husband and, I believe, your son soon after I had first met Pippa. Your husband was kind enough to help me with my car.'

'You didn't tell me you had car problems. Why didn't you call and tell me you had problems with the car?'

'Honestly. Mum, it was nothing.'

'Oh, they never tell us anything. Pippa, why did you not tell me about young Mr Choudhury being the new teacher, huh? All these weeks and you haven't said a word!' Jan joined in with Mrs Choudhury's complaint.

Because you would have piled bags of unnecessary pressure on me and I rather like keeping my crush as it is at the moment without you smothering it to death with over-enthusiasm and frigging heart biscuits, thought Pippa.

'Mmm, didn't I?' is what she said.

'He's very handsome,' Jan said.

'Yes, I think so,' Kam's mum agreed, nodding at Jan in approval. 'And your daughter is very beautiful. She has a classic style, an elegance.' It looked like a friendship was being forged whilst Kam's sisters just shook their head at their mum whilst nudging, pinching and making silly faces at Kam who, with a quick wink at his three siblings, changed the conversation quickly.

'Let's get these tables set up then, shall we? How many do you need for the cake stall, Mrs Parkin, is two enough?'

'Oh, I normally have three. Penmenna prides itself on its cakes.'

'It's important, isn't it? Binds a family in love, a little bit of baking,' Kam's mum nodded her agreement as she spoke.

'And tooth decay.'

'Abuja!'

'Here you are then, three...' Kam dragged one table after another and another. Jan's eyes developed a gleam: she did like a man who was happy to do physical work. '...tables just for cakes and I was thinking... oh, do we need to check with Marion? Should we put my sisters next to the cake stall, and then, Mum, you can keep an eye on them and stop them damaging whatever professional reputation I have?'

'Yes, yes, that sounds like a very sensible idea. Put them next to us, so I can keep an eye on Anuja and make sure she doesn't embarrass you.'

'Embarrass him? That's a bit harsh, isn't it?' Kam's younger sister objected.

'I'm a woman who likes to prepare for every eventuality, and Anuja, with you that is very wise. Now help your brother with that table over there and you can set up next to us. That's okay isn't it, Mrs Parkin?'

'Jan. And of course it is, Mrs Choudhury.'

'Excellent, we're going to be great friends, so you must call me Geeta. Where are you going to be, Kam?'

'Ah, Miss Parkin and I...' Pippa watched as Kam didn't quite make eye contact with any member of his family. '...Miss Parkin and I are out on the field, up the back with the horses.'

'Up the back with the horses? What does that mean?'

'Is that some kind of euphemism?' his youngest sister asked.

'Anuja!' Both Kam and his mum were in unison on that one. Pippa heard the laugh burst from her lips; she liked Anuja.

'It is not. Can I remind you this is my workplace?'

'Uhuh and Miss Parkin is your colleague,' Hema noted, faux sincerity at the fore, making it quite clear that, along with her sister, she suspected there was more.

'Yes, she is and you're never coming back again if you can't behave.'

'I haven't done anything. Mum, what have *I* done? Tell him!'

'Space hoppers, what do we need to do with them?' Pippa jumped in before World War Three broke out between Kam and his sisters in the school hall. She was aware that he wanted Sarah Fielding's job next term and she wanted him to have it as well – which was not going to happen if he and his sisters had a throwdown fight in the middle of the May Fayre, surrounded by the PTA and other Penmenna school well-wishers.

'Blow them up, sit on them and bounce to the finish line?' Kam responded, at which point Hema burst out laughing until her mother leant over and pinched her just under the arm.

'I've got that bit. That's the easy bit,' Pippa said, deliberately not making eye contact with any of the sisters. 'But shouldn't we go set them up? We need to pick a good space or else our racetrack could become an obstacle course with the odd gift from Davinia's ponies in each lane.'

'Yeah, good point. Right, Mum, are you okay if I leave you here with Mrs Parkin to sort out the cakes?'

'Jan,' Pippa's mother simpered.

'Jan.' Kam bestowed on of his smiles on her, the one that lit up his deep brown eyes and radiated charm out like a heat-seeking missile. Although of course that was only an opinion, and quite possibly no one's but hers.

'Of course. You must go and do what you need to do.'

'Brilliant, and if you could keep these three in check for me, Mum, I'd appreciate it. I really like it here.'

'Yes, of course. Now girls, your brother is a teacher and we are in his place of work. You must respect your brother and his position or you will pay the price.' Geeta looked terrifyingly stern as she delivered these words, and Pippa realised even she was gulping and deciding to behave.

'Brilliant, although if you could tone down the whole flay-you-alive discipline, that would probably be helpful,' said Kam. 'Right, what do we need, Pippa?'

'Just you and me, I think, at the moment. Everything else should be there.'

'Just you and me? Sounds pretty perfect, let's go.' And Kam and Pippa headed out of the big old wooden door, knowing that five pairs of keen female eyes were watching them go and drawing all sorts of conclusions.

Chapter Twenty-four

The two hours of the May Fayre whizzed by, although Kam had forgotten how draining the extra-curricular school events could be, especially after a full day teaching. However, in this instance he didn't mind. He hadn't had as much fun in ages.

He and Pippa had giggled non-stop on the space hoppers, guiding the children and shouting '*bounce, bounce, bounce*' in an encouraging way, both adopting kids to support and then racing them against each other. People had fallen off, and others had bounced their way to victory but everyone had giggled. After a while even the der-der-der-der-der-der of the fairground music blaring out across the field faded into familiarity, and Kam swore Pippa's laugh when they took their turns on the space hoppers – she beat him four to two – was even louder. He had had to wipe the odd tear away as he raced her, the children all shouting to spur them on. So much fun. Although he was quite pleased his mother was far away in the hall, he knew she would have very firm views on the appropriate behaviour of teachers and he was fairly sure laughing riotously whilst racing on inflatable rubber balls with silly faces was not one of them.

When he had mentioned the fairground music to Pippa, she had confided that the PTA invested in the fairground organ because it could be operated without too much human intervention and still create a carnival atmosphere. It turned out that Penmenna used to have a DJ at their fayres, but a couple of years ago he had done nothing but repeatedly play 'Nothing Compares 2 U' and sob into the microphone, exhorting the children to never love and never entrust their heart to anyone. There had been a stand-off with Marion cutting the power and hauling him out, and ever since then only allowed a carefully curated soundtrack, as compiled by Marion, was allowed to play in the school hall, and the sounds of a Wurlitzer in the school field to create some party spirit.

True to school fayre form, there was still a fair amount of troubleshooting amongst the hilarity. The ponies had accidents all over the field, and Kam, unused to the country and its blasé attitudes to poo, spent a fair amount of time picking it up and binning it so no small children could fall into it. Davinia didn't seem at all fussed, just barking phrases like 'Only natural, eh?' as she ignored the heaps piling up around her, and Pippa sat on a space hopper giggling at his face as he wrinkled his nose. She had the cheek to suggest it was a good thing he was a teacher because she didn't think he'd be much good as a vet or a farmer.

There had been fisticuffs over the hook the duck where Pippa had weighed in and saved Harmony from a parent convinced they should have won a huge purple teddy and who wondered why they didn't get a goldfish in a bag any more. Pippa had positively sprinted to the stall as she heard that, to try and stop a full-on raging debate between Harmony and the family, who had now gathered to see why she wasn't unhooking the purple bear.

Then there was a fallout over a penalty shoot-out, which one of the fathers was managing in a slightly aggressive fashion, but none of these things could spoil the fun of the evening. Kam and Pippa had taken it in turns to go and get Pimm's from the cocktail tent and, as the evening progressed, both got a little swooshy. Kam was not sure that he should be drinking whilst at work but Pippa pointed out that what he shouldn't be doing was breaking with Penmenna tradition: everyone was expected to be half cut by six. Besides, it was only Pimm's, not absinthe or Special Brew. How wrong could it go?

The second half of the evening had been far less frenetic. The stalls began to wind down a little, everyone's money had been spent and people were milling about, chatting. The children, realising they had no chance of getting more pennies out of their beleaguered parents, had given up and were playing on the playground equipment or kicking a ball about on the other side of the field.

Pippa and Kam had taken the chance to sink to the ground, where they both lay down, feeling the softness of the grass and clover on their backs, and staring up at the light evening sky. Pippa started picking daisies to make herself a daisy chain as they recalled the events of the night. The alcohol had made them relaxed and Pippa gave him the biggest grin as she rolled over onto her front, her calves swinging in the air as she spoke.

'I think our mums might get on alright, you know.' She gave him a hazy half-lidded look that summed up the languor of a summer night, and he wanted so much to roll himself over as well, capture her lips with his and see where this evening took them. He knew he couldn't, not on the school field, and he knew he wouldn't because until he had completed his five-year plan he was in no position to start any kind of relationship and the way he felt about Pippa indicated it could get very serious very quickly.

'I think so too. But then they would, wouldn't they?' Kam replied, smiling but holding his body back, not allowing the distance between them to be closed in the way he would have liked.

'Do you think? Apart from their obsessive baking I'm not sure they have much in common.'

'You're bonkers. We have everything in common so why wouldn't they? Our world views are pretty similar, don't you think?' Kam's eyebrows raised. Did she really not think so?

'I hadn't thought about that. I guess they are. Family is really important to me, and community, but then so is my freedom to be who I want to be and have fun. That's still high on my list and now I'm thinking it I'm realising that um… yes… maybe we are a bit?' Pippa's tone was one of gradual realisation and he could not believe that it was only in this moment she was joining the dots to something he had found so obvious from fairly early on.

'I am. I'm with you on all the solid things, the building blocks that make up for a good life. And we both love the sea…'

'We do.'

'And music, and dancing.'

'True, but we haven't done that yet. We will though. Soon.' Her certainty cheered him.

'Only difference is that your mother isn't trying to ferociously marry you off,' Kam sighed.

'Are you joking?'

'Eh?'

'My mum is an absolute nightmare. She's doing exactly that. It seems to be her favourite thing at the moment.'

'Really?'

'Oh yes,' Pippa nodded ferociously. 'Relentless.'

'So we have that in common too: we're both really busy trying to keep our mums from marrying us off.' Kam was flustered, he hadn't meant it like that. 'Um… not to each other obviously, that's not what I meant. It sounds like we both have a lot of pressure from our mums to settle down, even though we've reached an age when they should have backed off by now! Mine just doesn't listen. It drives me mad but I'm not prepared to be forced onto a path I don't want to go down. I have to balance the love and the respect I have for my mum with my need to do my own thing in my own time.'

'Okay, I admit it. I admit defeat.' Pippa rolled over again, onto her side this time. She had a string of daisies in her hand, and was looking him fully in the eye. 'We're twins.'

'Hahaha, maybe.'

'You know, joking aside, I do understand. My mum did exactly what you're describing, last week. I was trying to talk to her about why I don't want a serious relationship right now and that, when I find the person I want to settle down with, I have to know for sure because I want what her and dad have, that in-it-for-life thing. I know she loves me, accepts me but it doesn't feel like she listens to me.'

'Truth. Tell me about it. What was she saying?'

'She was saying, in her coded way, that I need to stop looking for Mr or Ms Right and settle for Mr Right Now.'

'Really?' Kam was shocked. Surely that wasn't advice anyone should give? He wondered if her mother was referring to the blonde guy he has seen her out with, but decided against asking. He didn't want to spoil the intimacy of the moment, plus he figured that if Pippa wanted to give more detail than she would.

'I think her point was that I'm looking for perfection and I suppose, in a way, I am. I've never been prescriptive when it comes to who I'm looking for, I think I'm a relatively open-minded person and if I'm attracted to someone then I'm attracted to *them*. Gender, background, that's not important to me. The way someone thinks, the way they behave, that's what makes me like them. Mum is fine with that but she wants me to hurry up with it all, preferably with someone she chooses. She seems to agree with my friends that I have some kind of commitment issue, which I don't by the way. And it's not so much that I'm looking for perfection, but I *am* looking for someone I can throw all my eggs into one basket with. Someone I can settle down with, and yes, have kids with, but that someone has to be of my own choosing and in my own time, and that's not right now. I don't really understand why the timeframe seems more important to her than getting it right.'

'This could be – it is – a conversation that I have my mother all the bloody time. I know it's not about control, it is about love, but wow! They do want you to do what they want you to do. I sometimes think maybe parents can't accept we're adults, and mine will still be treating me like I'm twelve when I'm fifty.'

'So why don't you want to do what your mother says?' Pippa laid her daisy chain onto the grass, more caught up in the conversation they were having. A conversation he was enjoying; it felt like they were talking honest truths about their lives, rather than the surface giggling they did every day in the classroom.

'I think it's as simple as her not trusting me to choose my own partner. She thinks me being single is because I don't know what I want. But I do. I want a woman who gets me, who shares my views and with whom I can carve out a life. Before that can happen, I want to be settled, secure in myself, in a steady job, doing what I love and knowing that I have something to offer.'

'Oh Kam, you have so much to offer!'

He felt a warmth flush up his neck and across his face as he tried to answer that in any way that didn't make him look insecure or arrogant. Nothing came to him so he turned the spotlight back on her.

'So basically, you won't settle. You have a smorgasbord of humanity to choose from and you're scared of making the wrong choice. I would have never thought of you as scared of anything.'

'You are focusing on me to detract from you! That's my trick so you won't get it past me. But yup, that's about right. And you're saying you need a job, security and status before you're prepared to fall in love.'

'Ha, yep. Sounds like we're both being a bit daft.'

'True and yet we're both utterly right, and should be allowed to find the right partner in the right time.'

'True again. You are a positive fount of wisdom today, Miss Parkin.'

Pippa lent over and his heart sped up. She picked up the daisy chain and closed its final link, placing her handiwork on his head. He felt his breathing slow down as her face came so close to his he was sure she could feel his breath on her. Thoughts of job security and self-knowledge went straight from his head. Thoughts of him and Pippa being together flooded his mind and he found himself holding his breath. She relaxed back onto the grass and his breathing returned to normal. He felt relieved that he had been too shy to pull her towards him; she had *just* told him she didn't want a relationship yet.

Thank goodness he hadn't made a complete fool of himself, surrounded by all the pupils and parents. Their friendship had changed here tonight, had become deeper, more open, more honest. They smiled at each other, and he really hoped she felt the shift too, rather than thinking that either or both of them had overshared.

'Well, you two look very comfortable. Could I have the takings please?' Jenny, Marion's number two and monster-in-training appeared, hovering over them, a smug, judge-mental look all over her features. Marion had trained her well.

'Here you go.' Kam sat up and handed her the box they had used to collect the money they had taken.

'Excellent. Marion is getting ready to wind things up and asked that everyone gather in the Hall. Thank you. Chop chop!'

Chapter Twenty-five

Jenny was right; the fayre was drawing to a close with cakes and plants sold out early on and everyone packing up ready to come together for the raffle draw that took place in the school hall at the very end of the evening. With the space hoppers let down and the ponies securely tied up, Kam and Pippa walked to the hall to see how their mothers had got on.

Kam stood by his remark about his mum and Jan having an awful lot in common. It would be nice if she had made a friend down here as it would make future visits much easier. He just worried a bit that they could team up and take their meddling to even higher levels.

It had been great to see so many of the children wandering around the school with intricate henna tattoos on their arms; his sisters had obviously done a roaring trade and, as Pippa had pointed out, it was a whole brand-new thing for the Penmenna School Fayre. The parents would be over the moon to offer something to their offspring that didn't involve scrubbing green or red face paint off for the next three days.

Kam and Pippa made it through the packed school hall just in time to hear Marion tap the microphone as she stood on the small stage built out of wooden blocks kept specially for the purpose in the resources' cupboard.

'Hello, everybody, thank you once again for coming and making Penmenna's May Fayre extra special. Every year we seem to pull it out of the bag and make it spectacular, and what can I say? Penmenna, you've done it again.' She held her hands high and to the side and clapped them, waiting for the others to follow in obedient applause. Which obviously they all did.

Pippa stood at the back of the hall, next to Kam, in some kind of mother sandwich. Both women stood either side of their offspring and had bonded far too well for Kam's taste. He was having trouble enough reining in his crush on Pippa this evening, and now he was pressed up against her in this crowd. The last thing he needed was his mother deciding that she wanted to be friends with the Parkin family and making everything else even more complicated.

She had pulled him away from the school Year Six camp when he was eleven because she didn't think the facilities were clean enough; when she had discovered from Ben – three samosas and he was her number one source – that Kam was taking a girl to the cinema she had turned up and sat behind them the whole time, giving advice: 'Kam, you need to offer her a drink. Kam, she has run out of popcorn. Kam, check she is alright. This is a very scary film. You should have chosen a nice romantic drama, Kam!' He dreaded to think what she could do when she discovered Jan was equally desperate to get Pippa settled.

Perhaps if he told her about Pippa's relationship with James, whatever that was, it might put her off or stop her hatching plans. But still, for now, it was nice being surrounded by his family in the place he had decided to call home.

He looked at Marion, up there in her element, but something seemed to be off. He wondered if he was just thinking that because Pippa had flagged that she may need their support. But as he examined her face he could see it was more drawn than usual. There was a darkness around her eyes and a greyish tinge to her face that no amount of Estée Lauder (thanks to Anuja's YouTube addiction he knew all the tricks) was going to cover up. She was dressed in the electric blue leopard print again – it clearly having become a firm favourite – and had scarlet lips and nails with a flash of blue on her eyelid. He had to hand it to her: whatever was going on under the surface, she was doing a grand job up there. She was smiling down at the assembled cast of parents, staff and interested locals and bestowing her best and most regal facial expressions.

'We haven't been able to tot anything up yet, but it looks like we may have smashed last year's target and raised well over three thousand pounds…' – she paused again for applause and recognition of her genius – '…that we can split between the school here and the Healing Hearts Foundation as run by our very own celebrity, Alex Mackenzie. Talking of celebrities, I'd like to give a big thanks not just to Alex but to Matt Masters too for his stellar work on the plant stall – although I did say very clearly only *tasteful* plants. I shall be watching that extra carefully next year – and his generosity in agreeing to be a raffle prize.' She tittered as Matt waved his hand in the air and smiled at everyone. 'Although, of course, whoever wins him can't keep him longer than a couple of hours or our very own headmistress will have something to say. A big thank you also to Sylvie Rowe, whose little darlings from the ballet school made me quite emotional with their exceptional beauty and grace. So talented at such a young age, all of you.' She paused again whilst people clapped the ballet class made up of boys and girls dressed in green leotards and tights with ivy woven crowns, who had performed around the maypole erected in the field to celebrate the season.

'Now before I go ahead and draw the raffle, an extra big thank you to all the parents without whom—'

'You!' A female voice, loud and accusatory in tone rang out. Marion paused and the whole room took a deep breath and turned to see who had interrupted Marion's flow. Alison, Ashleigh's mum, who had been running the Pimm's stall wove her way to the front of the crowd, swaying and pointing at Marion, whilst repeating the word '*you*' a few more times. Each time loudly and badly articulated. Alison lent in and grabbed the ivy crown from Ashleigh's head and plopped it skewwhiff upon her own head before attempting to stand up a little straighter. She drew herself up with what she hoped was dignity, in that way very drunk people do when they've sank more than a battleship would need to keep afloat.

'You, you are a… a beashtly beasterly woman. I have come here to tell you that never never again…'

Marion was still rooted to the spot, stricken as the scene began to unfold. Kam looked around and started to gently push his way to the front, approaching Alison calmly with the intention of guiding her away before Jenny, Marion's number two, could get to her; Jenny was approaching in a much more aggressive fashion than Kam, with a face that would have worked well in Stalin's Russia. He also spotted

Rosy discreetly moving forward to the front of the stage, but figured he should press on anyway. This wasn't a too many cooks spoil the broth situation. Marion was still, uncharacteristically, frozen as Alison continued.

'…only a few months, and you have pat… pat… patronised me, snapped at me, told me I was stu… stupid… you've been…'

Just as Rosy and Kam reached Alison, another voice rang out across the hall.

'I suggest, madam, that you take a seat. My wife works exceptionally hard for this school and it is not a place where we tolerate rudeness or unpleasantness in any form. If you have something to say then there will be an appropriate time to do so. Tonight is not that time.' Mr Marksharp's voice rang out from the big wooden hall door through which he had just entered.

The whole hall remained silent, bar Rufus who shouted 'Daddy, Daddy' the minute he saw his father launching himself at Richard Marksharp's leg and clinging to it, his father stopping to ruffle his hair and plonk a kiss on top of his head before continuing, 'It looks like another splendid evening. You've clearly outdone yourself again, darling. Now, were you about to draw the raffle? I can see we have some outstanding prizes here on the table. Which lucky person…' There was a momentary pause as his eyes lit upon a stoat standing on its back legs. Kam, who had been watching Pippa beaming as Richard defended his wife, now saw her most mischievous grin flash across her face before hiding her smile. He never had got to the bottom of why she had donated a stuffed stoat in a tutu and holding a cane.

Mr Marksharp pulled himself together '... um... wonderful prizes, exotic and quite unique some of them.' He climbed upon the stage and in front of the whole hall wrapped his wife up in a great big cuddle, whilst Kam led Alison into the library where he settled her on a chair shaped like a dinosaur. Angling himself so he could still see the stage, he sat with Alison and waited as Alice bustled in with a cup of coffee.

Meanwhile on the stage, Mrs Marksharp leaned into the hug, relief across her face and, for a flash, the whole hall saw a different side of Marion, a human side. The hall was no longer silent; murmurs were beginning break out and opinion seemed divided on whether Marion deserved such an outburst or not.

Kam watched Rosy mount the stage as Marion still clung to her husband, electric blue leopard print leaning against a traditional charcoal pinstripe.

'Your attention, everybody, let's have a big round of applause for Marion, a fantastic evening and we appreciate everything you and all the parents do.' Rosy led a loud ferocious clap in an attempt to gather support for the head of the PTA, and Kam watched as the school community curled around the woman and kept her warm.

Chapter Twenty-six

Oh my goodness, that was some evening. Did you get home okay?

Yeah, I walked back along the beach. Thought it was best to leave the car in Penmenna. I didn't realise how strong those Pimm's were!

Let's face it, you're not the only one...

Right. I've never seen anything like that. I hope that Ashleigh's mum is okay, I can't help but sympathise with her. I've not been at Penmenna long but Marion's behaviour is pretty awful.

I know. But in this instance so was Alison's. I wouldn't want to be her tomorrow morning.

We had fun though, didn't we?

Oh my goodness, yes. Best. Fayre. Ever. I can't wait for you to come to Feast Week now. That's the next big thing.

When's that then?

End of summer. Remember it's in the second half terms plans. We all concentrate on Cornwall and its marine heritage. And then ta-da we celebrate it all once term ends and Penmenna has its feast week. Which is kinda like a regatta but with a bit more drink.

And everyone celebrates the village's history?

I don't know about that but everyone gets utterly, utterly sloshed. Roger tries to force his home brew on all of us and at least six people in the village will end up sleeping on the beach.

So, Cornwall in the summer is just party after party?

There's a reason people love it. It might look all quaint cottages and overpriced restaurants but we have a proud heritage to follow.

And that includes drinking until you pass out on the beach?!

We're fishermen, smugglers or miners, so um… yup, pretty much. But at least we've cut it down to once or twice a year instead of every payday.

You forget I've been inside The Smuggler's Curse.

Okay, fair point. Some still do it every payday. But even better, you haven't been to The Rats Arse yet.

There is not a pub called that! I thought Smuggler's Curse was bad.

Haha that's nothing, you know Davinia we met this evening?

Oh, I don't think I'm going to forget that in a hurry.

Well, only a couple of years ago she rocked up to the Rats Arse fete. They're having a fallow year this year so you won't see it... I'm using the dots to drag out the brilliance of this story.

What, like Glastonbury? Isn't that a bit over the top for a village pub?

Normally I'd say yes, but if you get Sarah's job then you'll see why. Anyway, Davinia rocked up one year astride her horse, long wig on and naked, bar some electrical tape in a cross over her nipples and some edible panties. She said she was the modern-day Lady Godiva. Fathers suddenly started enrolling their children in pony club quicker than anything.

What was she protesting?

Eh?

Lady Godiva was making a protest. What was Davinia's?

From what I can gather, that she was usually expected to dress in clothes when she goes out. That was it. She had been talking about setting up a naturist commune at the stables. I think this was her first foray.

> Aha, hence the rising admissions.

> Yep, fathers far and wide were suddenly very happy to take Juliana, Persephone and Abigail riding on a Saturday morning.

> We don't have a Persephone at Penmenna do we?

> No, but you can guarantee that Davinia will have. And I reckon Sylvie will have a couple soon as well. Look, I'm bored of this texting now. Do you mind if we stop?

Kam looked at the phone in his hand as he lay in bed. He kind of did mind. He wasn't sure how it had evolved but he liked his daily catch up with Pippa; it was intimate, a way of further sharing and without half the school watching and gossiping. But if she was bored, then there wasn't much he could do. He started to type back '*of course not, night night*' when his ringtone blared out.

'Brilliant, hello! I thought my fingers were going to fall off if I carried on texting at that rate. So, where were we? Oh yeah, Davinia's clothing. I think she's accepted that the neighbourhood would really prefer her fully clothed, although she does apparently still wander about her house and garden with not much on. I've always wondered about the electrical tape. Do you reckon that would hurt like hell when she had to pull it off? I remember coming back from a festival once…'

And as Pippa carried on talking ten to the dozen, Kam laid back in his bed and smiled. This was perfect.

Chapter Twenty-seven

The Saturday morning dawn streamed bright through Kam's window. Normally he would have a bit of a lie-in, maybe read whilst working his way through a pint of coffee, alternatively he would have risen half an hour ago and headed to the beach. Sitting on your board, watching the sun break over the dunes was one of his favourite ways to spend time. However, today none of these was an option. Today, he was giving his mum and his sisters a whistle-stop tour of the county. Ordinarily he would been groaning about this; he loved his mother and each of his siblings, would lay his life down for any of them without a second thought but collectively – oh my word. They were so loud!

Today though he would not be dealing with them on his own. Last night, as he and Pippa had chatted into the wee hours, she had become ever so excited and offered herself up as tour guide. She had said she had to spend the Sunday with her family and deal with the James situation – although she still hadn't been hundred percent clear what that was precisely – and on Monday she had a vintage clothes thing on in a local hotel, but would love, love, love to show him and his family around tomorrow. Relaxing and doing nothing didn't appear to ever feature on her schedule.

Kam stretched as he considered Pippa a little more. He was used to having crushes and occasionally they would be reciprocated, he would conquer his shyness and all would proceed well. But he was increasingly aware that the way he felt about Pippa was way past crush, hurtling beyond infatuation and nudging into obsession. He just could not stop thinking about her. She was constantly on his mind. The way her hair was just the right length to curve into her neck, the way she found joy in everything, the way it was impossible to predict whether she would turn up as prom queen, athlete or flapper. Then there was the way she always made time for others, and made them smile whilst she was at it, the way her curves curved into curves and into more curves.

He heard himself sigh.

He was also aware that whilst Rosy's warning about relationships in the workplace had been gentle, it had still happened. The last thing he wanted to do was put Pippa in an awkward position and he definitely couldn't afford to mess up his chances for a permanent job at Penmenna. He had had a couple of offers of interviews in other schools, which were scheduled for after the half term break, but he loved working in Penmenna so much. If he just handled his crush in as professional a way as possible, kept the boundaries firm and made no attempt whatsoever to treat Pippa as anything other than a respected colleague then he should be fine. After all he was hardly going to grab her into an embrace and declare unquenchable love for her today. Especially not in front of his sisters. Today should be fine. He'd make sure it was.

Now that he knew that she was also being pushed by her mother into finding someone and settling down, he was sure that the last thing she needed was for her life to be made messier by him throwing his feelings into the pot. Besides nothing had changed on a rational level: he still stood true to his belief that, at this point in his life, he needed to prioritise his career. He just needed to box his emotions and carry on with his life plan.

He realised that, for whatever reason, his mother hadn't been barking at him at roughly the same time as the seagulls awoke, so he took advantage of the quiet and jumped into the shower, glad to get in before the girls took over with their hour-long stints in the bathroom, a whirl of powders and pastes being splodged all over the place along with wet towels, abandoned pyjamas and shrieking.

As he stood under the torrent of water he accepted that he was fooling himself. Talking all night over the phone with your teaching assistant, giggling, sharing memories and future dreams was not keeping boundaries firm. The right thing to do would be to ring her as soon as he was dry and dressed, and thank her for her kind offer to show his family around but explain that it wasn't necessary.

As he shampooed his hair, he knew that that wasn't going to happen.

Chapter Twenty-eight

Pippa stood at Kam's front door and took a deep breath. She had a feeling today was going to be a day full of laughter, even if most of it would be at Kam's expense. She'd enjoyed meeting his sisters yesterday – they were so much fun – and watching all four of them together was fascinating: whilst they were all definite individuals there was something about the four of them that was so similar, their mannerisms, the way they laughed. It was both freaky and quite adorable. It was like one person split into four.

Just arriving at Kam's flat was making her tummy flip. She had never been there before and was fascinated to see where he lived and what it was like. She imagined she'd be walking into a man-pad, with wall to wall surfboards, wetsuits hanging over the bath and all sorts of man toys, kayaks, paddleboards and the like littering the house.

The building itself had been a great big old smokehouse and net store, part of the fishing heritage of Treporth but now repurposed as swanky apartments. She had always wanted to have a peek inside to see if they were as swish as the advertisements had suggested. She was also slightly curious as to how Kam was managing to fit his family into a two-bedroom apartment.

She felt her tummy flip again as she pushed the buzzer and waited for him to answer. She reminded herself that there was no need to be anxious; this was merely a day out with a colleague's family, not a date. However, it was a struggle to get her disobedient body to believe it: the speed of her beating heart and the nerves that were making her feel more than a little sick were convinced it was a date, and a date with the whole family at that. Which meant she had to make a good impression on everyone rather than just one person. No pressure at all.

'Hello, come on in,' Kam answered the intercom and then whispered, 'Rescue me, they're all insane.' Making her laugh before she had even walked in through the front door.

'Hello, are you ready for adventures?' She wandered into the hallway and he led her through to the living room. It was a huge room, all modern steel and glass and lots of light juxtaposed against high ceilings and old granite wall. She noted that, bar the bedding neatly folded at the end of one of the huge sofas, the room was immaculate. No smell of musty socks or damp wetsuits. Just a clean citrus smell pervading the house along with the sound of hairdryers – more than one – all of which she assumed belonged to his sisters.

Kam was dressed down in a T-shirt and jeans today, with the jet black of his hair shiny from the shower. His house told her that he was no boy but all man, his physique and smell backing that up. And those arms peeking out of the T-shirt were screaming man with every muscle, every dark hair on show. *Oh, be calm*, she told herself, whilst her mind immediately went to places that would put *Fifty Shades* to shame. His mother was in the next room and she had enough good sense not to race over there and peel that T-shirt off his body.

'Hello, I can't thank you enough for this.' Kam seemed oblivious to the filth racing through her head.

'Honestly, I'm really happy to do it. I'm just a bit worried about fitting us all in my car. Did you say your friend Ben might be joining us as well?'

'Yes, mum insisted. She practically brought him up, so he's virtually a brother rather than a friend. But don't worry, my mum's got her car and that fits eight, so we're all good.'

'Okay, is your mum driving?'

'Not unless you want to take your life in your hands. She's a demon behind the wheel, look at her…' He paused as his mother walked into the room.

'Ah Pippa, how lovely to see you. Such a good girl. I hear you are to be our tour guide, hmmm?' She enveloped her into a great big hug and Pippa breathed in a deep floral scent and felt immediately comforted, as if all was well in the world. No wonder Mrs Choudhury's family were all so close; that hug had some kind of superpower pheromone blasting out making everyone feel safe.

'I am indeed. Kam told me all the things his sisters liked so I've managed to work those in but he was pretty rubbish at telling me what your favourite thing is.'

'Ah, that's so simple.' Kam's mum went and ruffled his hair. 'Why is this still wet eh? Your guest is here and you're not ready?'

'Why don't you say that to the girls? They've stolen my hairdryer despite bringing their own, and have turned my room into some kind of beauty salon and won't let me in. They're the ones who need to get a move on.'

'Hmm. Anyway, Pippa, ignore them for now but my favourite thing is actually my children. If they're happy,

I'm happy just watching them. Now don't go telling me that's creepy,' she jumped in as Kam opened his mouth. 'Although, Pippa, the truth is I prefer them when they're doing as they're told or asleep. I *really* like them when they're sleeping.'

'Was Kam terribly naughty as a child?' asked Pippa, impressed with how she was keeping her face straight.

'Him and Ben were a handful. They turned me grey overnight. I have so many stories to tell you. Absolute pickles, the pair of them. It's a good job I had girls after that or I would no doubt be in my grave now, dead from stress at an early age.'

'You talk such nonsense,' Kam laughed at his mother's exaggerated face as she recalled her parental woes.

'I shall look forward to those stories. He always pretends he was so good. Kam said Ben is joining us today. I haven't met him yet.'

'How so? He and Kam are usually joined at the hip,' Mrs Choudhury smiled at Pippa as she said this, and then turned and flashed Kam a very cross look. 'And *nonsense*, how dare you?'

'Kam and I spend time together in work, but that's it usually.'

'In that case, we shall have to change that. Kam, Kam, why have you not taken Pippa out yet? She hasn't even met Ben. How do you expect to get yourself settled down if you don't take the first step?'

Pippa laughed as a look of utter mortification flashed across Kam's face. It wasn't enough to stop Mrs Choudhury though.

'I say to him – I've been saying for years – "When are you going to get married? Why are you not trying harder?

Look at how old I am." Now, and with his father ready to retire. We need some grandchildren and I'd like them before I'm too old to enjoy them.'

'Hahaha, are you getting the why-can't-you-find-a-nice-Hindu-bride talk again, Kam? Oh Mum, that's too funny. I thought you had stopped that. You know Kam is never going to do anything whilst you nag. I'm ready now. Where are we going?' Nisha headed into the room, and she looked more than ready: she looked absolutely gorgeous. Neither her mother or Kam seemed to notice and both turned on her at the same time.

'I don't nag! How dare you say such nonsense!'

Kam and Nisha both snorted.

'Glad to see your hair is done, sis.'

'Thanks bro, always so understanding.' She patted the short style and reached on to her tippy toes and gave her brother a kiss on the cheek. 'Hi, Pippa, nice to see you. Guess you're getting to see the family as they really are. That should put you off my big brother.'

'Will you both stop it? I'm so sorry Pippa. Ignore my mother's crazy bride talk, and as for my sister, she pretends not to be as bad but she's probably worse. You two need to stop embarrassing me, and probably Pippa as well. She's a colleague and a friend and nothing more. How many times!' He turned back to Pippa with a sorry-my-family-are-so-horrendous smile. She recognised it as a look she had thrown to people fairly frequently. It seemed Kam had been right the other night when he suggested their families had a lot in common.

Kam changed the subject, probably to save himself being embarrassed every time his mother spoke. 'I've arranged for Ben to meet us at ten, just off the A30 as you suggested heading right down west. How does that sound?'

'That sounds fab, but in that case…' she flipped a quick look at her phone '…we need to get a wriggle on. How long do you reckon before your sisters are ready?' Kam rolled his eyes as both his mother and Nisha laughed.

'Okay, I'll try but if I manage to hurry them out, we all need to recognise I am practically Superman.'

'Ooh good, it's only fair that I get to see *you* in Spandex,' came straight out of Pippa's mouth before she could think, as Nisha dissolved into giggles and Mrs Choudhury developed a very smug look.

Chapter Twenty-nine

Kam managed to get his sisters out of the flat within the next ten minutes but, much to Pippa's disappointment, he didn't appear clothed in a body-hugging red and blue costume and cape.

His mum and sisters sat in the back of Geeta's people carrier, clucking and teasing and giggling at high volume. Kam had made it quite clear that Pippa was in the front with him, for navigational purposes. She tried to offer the front seat to Mrs Choudhury, being a little uncomfortable about the matriarch being in the back seat but to her alarm, Kam's mother had a Very Determined Look and shook her head, adamant in her refusal.

'That's definitely a win for the both of us. You escape my sisters and I escape my mum.'

'Sitting in the back doesn't make us deaf, you know,' quipped Hema at the same time as Mrs Choudhury swiped her adult son around the head.

'Smacking is harmful to a child's health and largely frowned upon these days. It's banned in some countries, you know,' Kam said, rubbing the back of his head, his hair all spiky where he hadn't been able to dry it properly.

'*You're* harmful to my health with your rudeness, And we're not in "some countries". And you're not a child. There are no laws against smacking an adult.'

'I think there are. It's called common assault.'

She clipped him around the ear again.

'Ow. Are you joking?'

'Stop sitting here chattering. We'll be late for Ben. Now, Ben is a good boy. He wouldn't keep his mother waiting.'

'He doesn't speak to his mother.'

'Well, she's a dreadful woman. I don't blame him at all. Come on. Hurry up.'

Pippa couldn't stop laughing as this was going on. Kam looked like he was about eight years old, scowled at his mother and started the car. The radio came on immediately, ridiculously loudly.

'She has it on this loudly in an attempt to scare the girls into submission and cover up the sound of clanking gears and screeching brakes. She's a terrible driver. Let me turn it down so your ears don't start to bleed. Although upon reflection you should suffer for laughing when I was being slapped.' He turned the music down a smidge, so it was bearable but provided them some cover from the back.

'Look, a wise woman doesn't interfere between a mother and her son.'

'Well, I beg of you, for today, please don't be wise. I need a teammate. I'm seriously outnumbered here, always have been.'

'What about Ben, won't he be on your team?'

'Are you joking? Did you see the Tupperware container my mother bustled on board with? Yup, I know you did.'

'Oh, I did. I'm so used to it with my mum. We can't go anywhere without bringing an entire snack selection.'

'Right, although in this instance, those – *all* of those – are for Ben.' His face suddenly lit up as an old Oasis track came on the radio. 'I love this track.'

'No way, so do I. Turn it up loudly so we can sing without anyone actually hearing us.'

'You're on!' The two spent the rest of the journey singing incredibly loudly and looking at each other, possibly far more than was safe whilst driving and not without the entire Choudhury clan noting.

Chapter Thirty

The journey had been a long one, through some very twisty lanes which caused an awful lot of shrieking, eye covering and murmured prayer from the back. They had reached Penzance via Marazion so the Choudhurys could admire the beauty of St Michael's Mount, its rugged castle perched atop its mount and set on an island out on the bay. Anuja thought she might buy it once she had made her fortune.

They had then headed down through Newlyn where Pippa's suggestion to explore the fish market was met with a resounding 'No!' and through to Mousehole where Hema couldn't help but point out that the streets were clearly designed only for mice as the village name suggested, no normal car could fit through such tiny streets safely and perhaps they should all turn around rather than try.

Then had come an awful lot of narrow, winding lanes, but as they drove the hedgerows were so full of life, bursting over the road in a riot of late spring colours, pale pink and blues, whites and yellows, all delighting Mrs Choudhury, who kept 'ooh'ing and 'ahh'ing as every corner brought a glimpse of sea and a smudge of flowers against the windows.

'Okay, official first stop and we're here.' Pippa lent over and turned the radio down as Kam pulled into a car park, one of sand and grass.

'Does stopping mean we don't have to listen to you two squawking like demented parrots any more?' asked Ben in response, brushing crumbs from his trousers and smiling at Mrs Choudhury.

'It means you have a break. But we'll be back to it as soon as we get in the car,' Kam smiled, used to his friend's teasing and clearly relaxed, surrounded by all those he loved.

'Well then, I vote for a long walk. Anyone?'

Nisha laughed and punched Ben on the arm.

'That's my brother you're teasing. Mum used to try and convince us that his singing was quite beautiful.'

'Pah, you've always been too smart to be fooled by that! But my point is he's *your* brother. That's why anything I say will bounce off him like a ball does a wall. He's been tortured by you for so long, I've gotta make it harsh to have any hope of an impact.'

'What are we doing here then, Pippa?' Mrs Choudhury spoke up. She had been quiet since their arrival. If she had been Jan, Pippa would have been tempted to check her pulse.

'Well, I tried to plan a day around your daughters' interests, Mrs Choudhury.'

'Geeta, please'

'Geeta. So, we're at the Minack theatre. It really is something special and I thought Anuja would be interested because of her career and because once she's so rich and famous that she's bought St Michaels Mount, this will be her local theatre.' Anuja grinned and nodded her head in acknowledgement.

'It's going to happen, you know,' she stated, just in case they didn't have faith.

'Oh, we know. You're particularly skilled at drama,' Kam winked and the others chortled a little.

'For Hema, there was the possibility of the fish market, but even though you didn't fancy that I thought we could go to Porthminster to eat. It's one of the most popular restaurants in the county and they have just brought out a new recipe book. To give us a good appetite beforehand, I thought we could stop at an ancient village for Nisha, although I have plans to liven it up a bit for the rest of us.'

'Does it have anything to do with the bag you brought?' Kam asked. He didn't miss a trick. Shades of his mother perhaps.

'Yep, always prepared, me,' Pippa grinned as she undid her seatbelt and opened the door.

'Don't I know it!' Kam answered, a faux-victim tone to his voice, as if she had been torturing him for years. The teasing made her feel like she belonged, like she was family, and she felt the warmth of contentment traverse through her.

Within seconds, the two of them found themselves at the doors at the back of the car, and without thinking both opened the doors for the others, saying in tandem, 'Out you jump then.'

'Seriously?' asked Ben

'We're not four!' Nisha protested.

'Hmm, sometimes you behave like it!' Geeta was quick to jump in.

'Sorry!' Pippa and Kam said, laughing and again both in unison.

'This is getting freaky,' Pippa giggled, and Kam's face lit up as he motioned to the others, still sat in the back of the people carrier with their eyebrows arched.

'Shall I count them out and in, or would you prefer to? Now hurry up, we've got lots to pack in,' Pippa put on her briskest voice as Kam continued to laugh, leaning against the car as he did so.

'You're incorrigible.'

'I love that word. It's not used often enough. Say it again.'

'Happily. Incorrigible. I don't know how you don't hear it daily.'

'Will you two stop flirting so we can get down in there and have a proper look? It looks amazing.'

'We're not flirting. Anyway, Pippa's got a boyfriend,' Kam answered quickly and with a particularly devilish twinkle. Pippa clocked Ben throwing a shocked look when Kam said this, and Pippa too was a little surprised by Kam's statement. She knew she hadn't exactly qualified what she was doing with James but she thought after their talk yesterday that he understood.

'No, I haven't! He just thinks he is, and that eventually I'll believe it too. But yes, let's go and have a look. It really is remarkable. It's a theatre hewn out of the rockface.' She indicated ahead of her and they all stood there for a moment, looking out to sea and watching the gulls circling in the May sky.

'So, if I understand what you just said, you don't have a boyfriend then, but someone *thinks* that you're his girlfriend?' Hema jumped in with the question that everyone wanted to ask.

'That's about it.'

'But you're not his girlfriend.'

'No.'

'Well, don't you think you should make it clear?'

Pippa looked straight across at Kam who was watching her, an inscrutable expression on his face as he waited for her answer.

'Yes, I should, I know. And I have but he's not listening. I know I have to be firmer. It's just it's not, well… there's more to consider than just me.'

'Like my brother.'

'No, not your brother! Your brother has nothing to do with it.'

'Hema, leave her alone. Come on, let's get going!' Kam marched down towards the main building, a modern structure that housed the information about the theatre below.

Pippa fell behind, reluctant to have things hanging unresolved and fell in step with Hema to try and explain herself slightly better.

'I know it sounds bizarre, and you're right, it is odd, but the thing is… it's my mum. She has her heart set on this relationship being a success. She's planning grandchildren. She's even picked out the outfit for the wedding…'

'Hahaha. This sounds familiar.'

'And I have to get her to understand it's not happening, but she's not listening. He is her best friend's son. I have to manage this carefully so our families don't get caught up in a whole heap of miscommunication and fall out.'

'It sounds like there may be a fair bit of that already.' Hema scuffed the path with her foot as they were walking, and Pippa nodded.

'You're right, there is. But not really between me and him. I'm quite clear with him. I have really laid it on the line but it's like he thinks it's one big game. Either that or his ego is so ginormous he simply can't comprehend that I am not interested at all.'

'What does my brother think of this?' Pippa was startled again. Hema obviously thought Kam was more involved in her personal life than he was. Whilst Pippa might enjoy daydreaming about him being all up close and personal, it wasn't something that was happening or that she would allow to happen, and her desires were not something she was going to confide in his little sister when she had no intention of mentioning them to Kam himself.

'I don't know. I haven't really talked to him about it. It's kinda between me and James and our families. Kam's great, but he's a colleague so probably not going to ask him to weigh in on my love life, or lack of it.'

'Hmmm.' Hema's response sounded just like many of Kam's.

'Do all your family make that noise?'

'Yeah. It drives me mad when the others do it. They make it sound so meaningful, and then other times it's like I'm literally hovering above myself hearing myself doing it as part of me is shouting, "Stop, stop right now, that's so irritating."'

'I like it. It's nice to have a family thing.'

'Do you have a family thing?'

'Yes, we like walloping each other with tea-towels, in a playful way,' Pippa clarified.

'It's okay. I know what you mean, I didn't picture you all sitting around nursing wounds. We do that too.'

'Yes, I saw you pinch your sister in the car,' Pippa giggled. She would have done the same to Pete or Polly.

'I can't help it. Put us all in that thing and it's like being seven again. If she had pigtails I would have pulled those too,' Hema giggled.

They reached the building, and Pippa gave them time to wander through and read the big information boards that outlined the history, before heading outside to the theatre itself.

Carved into the cliff it was something that couldn't help but wow you as you stood there. The stage was made entirely of stone as were the benches for the audience. The sea, vast and open and elemental, provided the most breathtaking backdrop, one that Pippa knew from experience could often distract from the play being performed below. She also knew that although the theatre was nothing short of spectacular, bringing a cushion, a blanket and a flask was vital to help keep out the nip of the wind. Romantic it may be, but there was nothing like the bite of a cold sea breeze to kill that romance dead.

Not that cold or wind were present today. Today the sea had a turquoise sheen that made it look tropical, inviting, like it was sitting there for human admiration and perfect photographs.

Pippa sat on a bench at the top, watching Anuja's face as she took it all in. Her gaze flicked to Kam who was deep in conversation with Ben, a conversation which involved more than the odd look flicked in her direction. She wished she knew what they were saying. She wondered if they were discussing her and, if they were, what they were saying. Would it be along the lines of '*that Pippa's a gem, a definite keeper*' rather than '*that Pippa is a complete freak, run my friend, run now!*'

Or maybe they weren't talking about her at all and she was just making up nonsense because part of her wanted Kam to be saying lovely things about her. Part of her wanted Kam to be thinking of her as she did about him pretty much all of the time and definitely as her head hit the pillow in the evenings. But another part... another part of her was wondering if her friends and her mum were right all along, and she was just terrified: terrified of messing things up, of starting a relationship that may not work, of upsetting her happy life by messing around with someone involved in her work, of harbouring a crush she didn't think was reciprocated. It was all too confusing, although, as long as she could keep it in her head and not let it overspill into actual life, she had a chance to manage it without upsetting the applecart.

She knew that despite her brave words about not being ready, she wanted to settle down with someone. She *was* ready but finding the right person was such a gamble. Her mum and dad had got lucky and she wasn't sure she could expect that to happen twice. The advice the world gave was so confusing, ranging from the pessimistic 'You never truly know somebody' to the more optimistic 'When you know, you know'. All she knew for sure was that, right now, she didn't really *know* anything.

As their group returned, her phone binged. Pulling it out of her pocket she saw it was from Lottie. The others stood there for a moment breathing in the beauty of this particular part of the coast, so she quickly read the message.

Oh wow! You are not going to believe what I've heard. Make sure you come find me when you get home. I can't wait to see your face. But as ever, Pippsy, you were right.

Pippa read it twice. Had Lottie found out something she could use against James in the battle with her mum? That would be awesome. What could it be?

She pulled herself back to the moment. Anuja was still looking at the stage in awe, no doubt imagining herself in a flowy gown, hurling herself dramatically from one side of the stage to the other. Whereas Nisha was staring out over the cliffs to the turquoise sea and sandy beach next door.

'It's beautiful, like, really beautiful. Can we go down there?'

'I'm not sure that was on Pippa's plan,' Kam jumped in.

'No, but plans are like rules and made to be broken.' She winked at Kam's oldest sister, 'Porthcurno is absolutely breathtaking and there's no real reason we can't go and explore the beach. If I remember rightly it's just down the coast path, bit of a steep hill but shouldn't take too long. It's fascinating actually. Not only is it mind-blowingly beautiful and looks like it should be part of a tropical paradise somewhere far away, it's also where they put the first underground cables to communicate with America in 1870-something or other. Let's go explore, if everyone wants to?'

The walk down to the beach, a narrow path dry in the good weather and sprigged with tufts of grass, curled along the line of the coast. The path itself was unsteady and made more difficult to walk by the fact that it was next to impossible to tear your eyes away from the scene laid out in front of you. The sea was bright and clear, a myriad of blues and greens making up the turquoise that was a siren call to anyone with a soul; there were children splashing, and adults lying on their backs or sculling across the cove and looking up at the cliffs made up of multicoloured strata and scattered with grass and wildflowers.

Geeta and her daughters' voices tumbled over each other as they headed down towards the beach, claiming that this could be somewhere in the Pacific Ocean rather than part of the UK mainland.

Pippa and Kam were walking close together as they headed down, as if there was some kind of elastic bond between the two of them which meant that neither could stray far from the other for very long before they were pinged back together. Pippa was giggling – her concerns from earlier firmly put to the back of her head – and leaning into Kam as she pointed out some children mischievously throwing buckets of water over each other as they stood at the edge of the waves. Suddenly she felt her ankle twist in a dip, sending her body careering off at an angle, stumbling right by the cliff edge.

Kam moved like lightening and before anyone else had realised what was happening his arm had shot out, swooped around her and brought her back in safely. She grabbed his arm as he did so, trying to right herself on the bumpy path. Her ankle was fine but her body was shocked, not just by the near fall but also by its response to Kam's touch. An electric shock had seared through her body, making the whole of her tingle from tip to toe. She had never felt anything like it and she stared up at him, frozen to the spot as the lust puddled through her, overwhelming her. Her mind was in meltdown, her heart was pounding as she tried to thank him, whilst their hands were still holding each other, as if that was exactly where their hands should always be. Breathing in deeply, she could capture not just the salty tang of the sea air, but the smell of Kam. The woody undertones of his aftershave combined with the very core scent of him.

He made no move to change position nor to stop looking at her. Her blonde hair flicked across her face in the breeze, her eyes big and blue and communicating so much as she stared up at him.

Pippa realised, in that moment that she *was* brave, and she *was* an optimist. There was no going back, job or not. What she felt for this man was something special, something different from all her other relationships, something that she was not going to walk away from until she knew, definitively, whether this man looking at her, heart and soul on display, felt the same.

Chapter Thirty-one

> What an epic day. Thank you so much. My mum and sisters had a great time.

> Thank you for letting me join in with your family. I had the best time too. You're right, it felt like being with my own family with all the teasing.

> What was your favourite bit?

Looking at you. Delete, delete.

> Um, so much. Probably the bow and arrow battle in the prehistoric village.

That was so much fun, such a good idea bringing the toy bow and arrows. Although I thought with the fuss Ben was making we'd had his eye out.

Right, when he sank to his knees like that, wailing. For nothing! Has he ever considered a career in football?

Ouch. I shan't tell him you said that.

Well, our children in class are braver. Oh, but I loved St Ives as well.

Right? That restaurant on the beach was beautiful.

So were you when you put that blanket around your mum's shoulders. And made sure everyone's drink was topped up, and insisted that you wanted pudding because you could see Hema's face as she looked at the dessert menu and panicked no one else would join her. Pippa didn't even bother typing that, just thought it. And swooned a bit. Before behaving herself and typing something innocuous instead.

One of my favourites. They say the light in St Ives is special, hence all the artists. And watching the sun go down from that terrace; that was def a high point.

My mum loved the fact she got to visit Land's End as well.

I gathered that. She made me take about a hundred photos.

She really likes you. She told me. Quite a lot.

I really like her too.

But I like her son more. And how much does she like me, exactly?

It was the best day. Exactly how summer half term should be.

It was. And they go home soon too. I was worried about this visit and you've made it fab, so thank you.

Absolute pleasure. Best. Day. Ever. Now let me sleep, I've got my own mother to deal with tomorrow.

Good luck. Anything I can help with?

Can you hide outside the window and pass me gin at pertinent moments?

I can try.

I'll let you off the hook. But thanks for being willing.

Okay, night night. See you soon.

Night night. Sweet dreams.

Night night. Sleep tight.

Only minutes later, Pippa exhausted by a full day as well as an evening full of exciting news fell asleep in her bed, phone clutched in her hand and a great big grin on her face.

Chapter Thirty-two

'Thanks for helping me organise all this, mum.'

'That's a pleasure, love. You know I never mind helping. I'm still coming tomorrow as well, aren't I?'

'Yes, if you don't mind. But I think that's the bulk of it sorted for today. It's never looked so organised. I'll be a bit reluctant to take them out of the boxes to display them tomorrow.'

'Well, it could have hardly been any messier.'

'Mean. And I was going to put the kettle on for you whilst you put your feet up.' Pippa stood in her mum's living room, surveying the great big pile of plastic boxes complete with lids and now full to bursting with all of her stock. She had a huge vintage clothing and craft fair coming up tomorrow. Held in a large local hotel it drew visitors from all over Cornwall and beyond, and she had needed a little bit of a sort out, to create a semblance of order before the day itself. At one point her mother had even taken her life in her hands by delving into the back of Pippa's car and rifling for anything that could be considered further stock. She earnt brownie points by doing it without tutting, something Pippa wouldn't have thought possible.

Now the job was done Pippa braced herself for the real task of the day: sitting her mother down and getting her to accept that there would be no wedding, or babies, on the horizon for the foreseeable future, and certainly not with James, was not going to be easy.

Lottie's delving on the other hand had unearthed more than they had bargained for. Way more than they had bargained for. It turned out that one of Lottie's old uni friends was working for the Financial Conduct Authority, the role of which she had explained to Pippa the night before with a shake of her head. She had confided that Simone, her friend, had been amazing and had told her way more than she probably should have. The main point was that James' firm was currently under investigation. Simone had a few choice words to say about James as well, none of which were much of a surprise to Pippa. She had a feeling she and Simone might get on.

And that wasn't all. Lottie had also tracked down pictures of James on Instagram, posted by his friend, that pictured them spending their fraudulently obtained wealth in a particularly insalubrious fashion.

After a perfect day spent with Kam and his family, Pippa had returned home from dinner with them to discover all of this from her very smug-looking flatmate. There had been a lot of dancing around the kitchen table as they had celebrated Lottie's genius.

Now all she had to do was tell her mum.

'Here you are, a nice cup of tea, and I've grabbed us some of your shortbread. Is anyone else about? The house is ever so quiet.'

'No, love. Polly is out in Roscarrock; she took her guitar, muttered something at us and headed out ever so early, and I think your brother is in Plymouth today for the match. Your dad's about somewhere, probably the shed, which he uses as an excuse to escape from the things I need done around the house. That cupboard door in the bathroom is still wonky. He doesn't seem in the slightest bit inclined to fix it. He just gets that glazed look if I ask him to look at it and then, poof, I don't see him for hours.'

'That's alright isn't it? It gives us time to chat anyway.'

'True. Did you want to talk about something specific, love? You seem to be building up to something.'

'Okay, I can't get much past you. I do and I want you to hear me out before you interrupt or say anything. Ready?'

'Ready. Although I do think—'

'Nah, nah, nah. No thinking, just listening, or do I have to stuff so much shortbread in your mouth that you won't be able to talk until I've finished?'

'Ready. I'll be as quiet as a church mouse.'

Pippa's friend, Alice, spent a lot of time helping out in the village church and had fairly vocal views about the church mice, but Pippa decided now was not the time to bring that up. Plus, her mum had her most innocent I'm-going-to-do-my-best face on and it made Pippa melt a little bit.

'Okay, now I know you have big plans for me, and I love that you care so much and all of that, but this relationship fantasy you have about me and James… no, no, no, do not say a word. Quickly close your mouth. You promised! Okay, thank you. James and I are never going to work, largely because he's an arsehole. I don't ever want to sleep with him and we could never build a happy ever after.'

'Well, really.'

'Oh hush, you've had three children, none of this a-relationship-is-about-more-than-sex nonsense. I know that's true, of course it is, but you still have to have a flutter and the only flutter I have when I think of James feels distinctly more gastrointestinal in nature than romantic. He is a not a nice person underneath that veneer of charm, and I am not going along with this ridiculous charade any longer.'

'But—'

'Nope, you promised you'd listen. I know you're going to tell me what a sweet child he was, and I agree he was. The past tense being the important bit here. Just because he asks the right questions, promises Polly festival tickets, and talks to Pete about cars does not make him a decent human being. In fact, in this instance it makes him a manipulative rat who is well versed in what strings to pull to get people to do what he wants, and it has worked brilliantly. I know you think I'm being unreasonable but I have evidence for you although, quite frankly, the fact that I want nothing to do with him should be enough.'

'But—'

'Nope! Now I'm going to be kind here, but I have a deep-seated feeling that your desire for this relationship has actually less to do with me and James personally and more to do with the fact that you want to be a grandparent with Karen. And I understand that, really I do. And if we lived in the seventeenth century then you probably could get away with bundling me up and marrying me off to your friend's son, but we're not, and these days I get to have a say and I am saying no. I want children and will have them, hopefully, one day, but with the partner of my choosing not yours. Have faith that the right person will come along and I will commit to them and raise a family with them. I have faith in it and beg that you do too. But

James is not that person. Not by a long stretch. Now I know that you think I'm just being difficult…'

It was as Pippa was rattling off her defence at full speed that she suddenly realised her plan wasn't going to work. Her mother was so good, so loyal, that if she heard a snippet of what Pippa was about to tell her about James' potentially illegal business practices and the fact that the FCA were on to him, then she wouldn't hesitate to pick up the phone and warn Karen. And if Pippa managed to persuade her not to, but to come down on the side of right and understand that the hundreds of people disadvantaged by his behaviour deserved to have him in custody, the mere knowing and having to keep it from her best friend would tear Jan to bits. It may make Pippa's life easier but it would stop her mother sleeping for weeks. She paused in her speech, giving her mother a chance to respond, as she worked out what the best thing to do was.

It didn't take long.

She had no choice; she couldn't risk the trust of Simone and Lottie or the upset of her mother. She would have to keep quiet, hope the Instagram screenshots were enough and pray the FCA got their man fairly bloody soon!

'No, I don't. It's not that I think you're being difficult. I just think you're misjudging this situation.'

The irony! Pippa took a deep breath, reluctantly shelved the information about his criminal dealings and tried again.

'Mum, you may have to trust me on this, but I promise I'm not imagining things when I say this man is lower than low.'

'He's so devoted to you.'

'A-ha, because that is what he wants you to believe, but he's not. He makes a good pretence of being so, and has managed to fool his own family and ours with the exception of me, and I have proof that he is not sat in London spending every second pining for me.' Pippa pulled her phone out of her pocket and waved it triumphantly in the air. 'And I'm going to show you. Ready?'

She really hoped this was going to be enough.

'Okay, what are you going to show me exactly?'

'I'm going to show you some images Lottie recently captured off social media from one of James' friend's accounts. It proves he's never been interested in me for me; he is only interested in me because I don't want anything to do with him, and it bothers his ego so much that he can't bear it.'

'You know I don't understand social media. I don't do that. But it seems to me, if it's his friend's—'

'Shh, just look, here.' And Pippa showed her mum the first image of James kissing a very young girl as he pressed her against a wall in some seedy club. 'Look, if he was desperately in love with me, would he have his tongue rammed down that poor girl's mouth?'

'Oh no, are you sure it's him? There will be a good explanation.'

'Really, that's what you have to say? Okay. I had hoped that would be enough. Ready?'

'Oh no, I'm sure you're mistak— oh, oh, that's disgusting. Oh my goodness, okay, urggh.' Pippa's mother looked quite sick as Pippa flipped through images of James in the lap dance club with another rather young, but very generously endowed, woman writhing on his lap.

The back door slammed and Pippa's mother dropped the phone, looking as guilty as if she had been caught watching porn by her children.

Pippa couldn't help but laugh at the look of relief on Jan's face as her husband walked in. Surely that will have done the trick, no mention of insider trading needed and no more talk of marriage! Result.

'Oh my goodness, Jim. Come and look at this. you won't believe what our Pippa has just shown me.'

'Oh yes, what's that then?'

Jan passed her husband the phone.

'Oh my goodness, he's got his hand in her knickers. What sort of... oh, oh. Is that James? Our James? Oh Pippa love, I'm sorry.'

'It's fine, Dad. I don't want anything to do with him anyway, never have. This was to show you and mum what he really is like when the mask slips.'

'See Jim, I always told you he was a wrong'un. Ever since he was a boy. Disgusting behaviour. Fancy you wanting him to get involved with our Pips!'

–

As Pippa lay in her bed that night, she couldn't get rid of the smile on her face, made even broader by her phone pinging. Once her mother had flipped sides and turned against James, a burden was lifted. What was more, she hadn't needed to risk ruining the investigation, or make her mother decide between loyalty to her oldest friend or the right thing to do. She felt so much lighter she couldn't believe it. It was if all the weight in the world had been lifted from her, weight she wasn't aware had been so heavy.

Hey, how did your day go?

Good thanks, had a really nice time with my mum.

Pippa started to type how she had managed to get her to see the truth of James but then deleted it. She tried again, and again. But no matter how she wrote it she heard her own voice in her head explaining to Hema that her relationship with James had nothing to do with Kam, and that even discussing it would blur the boundaries of their friendship. She knew that the underlying meaning was that she was too scared. That if she told Kam that James was out of her life and he didn't immediately respond with 'Great, let's be together forever, build a future and make babies', she would be bitterly disappointed.

And if he did, she'd be terrified.

The others were right, she was her own worst enemy. She left the sentence as it was.

That's good to hear. No need for gin then. Have you got your vintage thing tomorrow?

Yeah, I'm looking forward to it.

Do you want some help?

Nah, my mum is excited about coming with me.

Okay, fair dues. I've got to run my mum to Falmouth at some point and do dutiful-son stuff, but she is leaving on Thursday. Fancy some celebratory drinks on Friday? One last night of fun before we have to go back to being terribly responsible adults that go to work?

Yes, please!

Chapter Thirty-three

The second bank holiday in May dawned and it tipped down. Rain battered at the windows of the car as Pippa drove to Portruthan Hotel perched up on the clifftops and looking out on a very grey sea – the sort that you wouldn't be too surprised to see dotted with icebergs.

It did mean, however, that the roads weren't as jam-packed as they would usually be. People had obviously decided to make the most of the extra day off to have a lie-in rather than race to the beach, and Pippa didn't blame them.

Another advantage, though, was that the rain was so loud against the windscreen that Pippa could, without guilt, attempt to tune her mother out as she leant forward trying to see the road as clearly as she could. However, it would take a tempest to completely drown out Jan, who, after yesterday, had taken against James so vociferously that Pippa was almost – only almost – regretting showing her the screenshots.

Polly had been furious as Jan had told her very firmly over dinner that she must not accept any freebies from that pervert. Ironically, Pippa had been forced to jump in to defend the man she had been trying to turn her mother against, by pointing out that pervert was a little harsh, seeing as, with the exception of constantly turning up on Pippa's doorstep (and the financial illegalities that Jan didn't know about), nothing James had been doing was non-consensual. Jan didn't seem to care. So much for wedding outfits and Debenhams.

They pulled into the hotel and dragged box after box in through the foyer to the big old ballroom, once filled with twinkling lights and empire-line dresses and these days playing host to high-end conferences, team building days and craft fairs like the one today. Pippa was glad to see she had a corner spot; it would give her slightly more room, and make her display more inviting, less two dimensional than had she been flat against the wall. She raised her hand to greet the familiar faces also present, who were busy unpacking their wares and making things as attractive as possible.

'Hey Pippa, lovely to see you. Jan, what treats have you got today?' asked Sally displaying her beautiful hand-made children clothes on the table one along from them.

'Hello, lovely to see you. Mum, can I leave you here? I'm just going to get the mannequins from the car.'

'Of course, love. Do you want a hand?' As Pippa shook her head, her wet hair flicking droplets as she did so, Jan responded to Sally. 'Little mini scones, clotted cream and passion fruit. I thought I'd go tropical for a change.'

'Yum, anything you make is good for me. Really, you should be selling your cakes and scones at places like this. You'd make a killing.' Pippa left the hall grinning as her friends crowded around Jan, making her mother blush with the compliments that were raining down (with the same ferocity of the deluge outside) as she peeled back the Tupperware lid. People were good. People also liked cake.

It didn't take long before they were all set up, and even Pippa was proud of how things were looking. She had an Edwardian bridal dress which she thought was the most beautiful thing she had ever seen, taking pride of place on the first mannequin. Its intricate lacework and darling little pearl buttons were enough to make the most reluctant bride swoon and Pippa just loved it. In her more indulgent moments she would imagine the women who had worn this dress as they walked down the aisle for the happiest day of their lives. She had a feeling she may weep if she ever actually sold it.

Her two 'bridesmaids' were dressed – one, in a cute Seventies tennis outfit, so sassy it hurt, and, the other, in a Nineties outfit complete with dungarees and rainbow spiral cropped T-shirt and whistle. Both looked fab and provided complete contrast to the wedding dress. Everything else was set out on her rail, and she had laminated cards, that showed every conceivable outfit she had, all over the walls and on the table mixed in with various accessories.

Lunch had been and gone and the rain had eased slightly, less frenetic but still present, which meant the ballroom was rammed. It seemed as if everyone who had considered going out for the day had decided an indoor venue was definitely the best idea. Sally's children's clothes were flying out, as were Beth's printed lampshades and Carrie's silver jewellery. Pippa had managed to sell an awful lot of stock, far more than she had anticipated and it was proving her most successful craft fair yet, and her mother was more than content, having fed most of the hall and having had compliments shower down upon her all morning. She was currently sat next to two large empty

Tupperware containers, looking like the cat who had got the cream.

'Dear god, how is a man supposed to breathe in here? This is insane. Far too many people with far too much time on their hands. Pippa, where are you?' A man's voice cut through the crowd and made Pippa freeze on the spot. She had just been congratulating herself on the sale of the most beautiful smocked top complete with floral embroidery, when she heard him. What on earth was James doing here? She flashed a quick look at her mother to see if she too had heard the familiar voice, but no, it appeared not. It would only be a matter of time.

James appeared at the table, designer sunglasses perched atop his head despite the sun being very distinctly absent.

'I don't have any more time for playing games, Pippa. This is it. Now. I need you to stop playing coy, leave this and come with me. I've got a helicopter waiting on the pad on the roof, and we need to go, now. Now! Come on. You're going to love where we're going. Quick!' He looked around agitatedly and Pippa fixed him with her fiercest look. It bounced off. What was he doing here?

Did he still seriously think she was going to go with him? Even worse, this looked like he thought she would flee the blooming country with him. Wow!

James continued, oblivious to her death glare. 'Really, we need to go now. Hello, Jan.' He spotted Pippa's mum, 'Perhaps you could take over here whilst Pippa comes with me.'

James was pushed up against the table as the crowd surged a little and put his hand out onto the table to steady himself. Then wiped it on his trousers, as if he could catch old-stuff germs.

Pippa glanced at her mum, unsure, for the first time in her life, of what her mother's reaction would be. So far, she was being remarkably quiet.

James followed her look and grinned back at her smugly. He obviously thought that if his number one supporter was here then Pippa would be forced into compliance. He reached across the table to try and grab Pippa's arm but, as he did so, four men, not your usual craft and vintage sale types, appeared behind James, one forcefully laying a hand on James' shoulder.

'Mr Carpenter, if you'd like to come with us.' His deep voice resonated through the hall.

'No, I bloody wouldn't.' He shot a furious look at Pippa before dropping his body down low and twisting to try and get out of the man's hold. 'This is your fault. I should have just gone.' With the room so packed he had no way of getting through the crowds of people, now far more excited by the drama playing out in front of Pippa's stall than they were by any lampshade.

James twisted and turned further in an attempt to escape, but the whole room could see he didn't have a hope. Another man grabbed hold of him and twisted him around, catching hold of his arms and attempting to cuff him. There was a flurry of arms as James tried to fight the men off. None of them however were prepared for Jan, who had been eerily quiet so far, suddenly coming to life and flinging herself from her chair armed with a Tupperware box.

As James writhed and wriggled and the men continued to try and cuff him, Jan launched herself at him, trying to wallop him with her container.

'Ma'am, please, stop… ma'am, we'll have to restrain you.'

'Mum, you're not helping.'

James did not know what had hit him. And Pippa wasn't entirely sure either.

The crowd stepped back and made room for what was unfolding. The men managed to get one of James' hands in a cuff as another man tried to hold back Pippa's mother, retired nurse and volunteer hospice carer, queen of the cakes and one-time chair of the WI. Despite their interference, Jan was managing to take a few good hard whacks at James with her Tupperware as she punctuated her attack with the words 'pervert', 'disgrace' and 'filthy'.

One of the detectives managed to peel her away and return her to Pippa, warning her to keep her mother under control unless she wanted to be visiting the police station herself, whilst the other three managed to finally contain James and read his rights.

He wouldn't be using that helicopter now.

Pippa still stood frozen to the spot in shock at everything that had happened in such a short space of time. She stayed like that as the crowd parted to make way for the plain clothes policemen to lead James away and as her mother shot the room a triumphant glance before returning to her chair and resuming her normal demure expression.

As James was led out, hurling curse words over his shoulder and blaming Pippa for all his ills, Pippa started to giggle, the laughter coming over her in waves and feeling out of her control. She wondered if this was what shock was.

The room had just gone from silent to the beginnings of murmuring, when suddenly another voice, loud and bold, pierced the whispers.

'Woo-hoo. Hello, darling. We thought we'd nip by and take a look.' And there, standing on tiptoes, with all her adult children standing behind her, was Geeta. It was Hema who piped up next, a great big mischievous grin on her face. 'So, does this mean you're single now?'

I imagine it's been a long day but do you think we should set our mothers up as a wrestling team?

You're so bad.

But not as bad as your mother! Should I be terrified?

She was awesome, wasn't she? The police should consider asking her to join. Didn't work out so well for James though.

What did they arrest him for?

Not entirely sure, but I think it was to do with his work. Insider trading and so on. I had heard a whisper that they were after him. I didn't expect him, or them, to show up today though!

It could be seen as romantic that he risked his escape by coming to get you first.

Yeah, if romance means refusing to listen for consent and trying to bully someone into running away with you.

Okay, good point. I assume that's put an end to your mother's matrimonial dreams?

Let's hope so! On the car journey home she said that she understood I would find the right person when I was ready. Although she did add that she wished I'd hurry up! Honestly.

> **Ha! Some progress though. You must be pleased. Still on for Friday?**

> **Oh yes. I think I deserve a drink.**

You deserve the world. It was Kam's turn then to hit the backspace button and tap out '*See you then, then*' instead. But he knew both were true.

Chapter Thirty-four

Half-term week had whizzed by in that way that school holidays do: incredibly fast and filled with the awareness that this was it now for another few weeks. In Kam's case it was especially bittersweet because for him the end of the summer term would not just mark the start of six glorious (well-earned) weeks of holiday but the end of his time at Penmenna.

He knew Sarah Fielding's post had been advertised just before the end of term and that interviews would occur at the very start of July, but despite Rosy telling him about the vacancy all those weeks ago when he'd first started, she had said nothing since. Kam was usually prone to optimism, but in this case he couldn't help but fear that no news was very definitely not good news.

He supposed on the positive side of things that he would be staying in Cornwall. He had four other interviews lined up in June, he could get lucky and get one of those. All were for permanent full-time positions, which would give him the security he wanted. If all of those failed, there was always supply work or hours with Ben, and once he wasn't working alongside Pippa then he could finally nail his colours to the mast and see if she felt the way he did. He hoped she did. At times, like on the footpath at Porthcurno or as they had been falling around on space hoppers, their chemistry was so intense, sparking between them, fizzing and shivering in blue spiky jags of desire, that he had to suspect she felt as keenly as him. He was also aware that she was so full of sunshine that she was lovely to everyone, making whoever she was talking to feel like they were on top of the world, the only person in the room. It was possible that she may not be attracted to him at all and her presence just made him feel special, like it did everyone else.

In which case he'd feel like a real idiot.

His mum and sisters had headed home yesterday and had declared the visit a success, which meant they'd be back in the summer, possibly twice. Hema had spent the days after their trip to Pippa's Vintage and Craft Fair whispering plans about how to seal the deal, each one more ludicrous then the rest. Her very last suggestion being trails of vintage shoes à la Hansel and Gretel to his bedroom. Although all that would prove was that Pippa really liked shoes. He wanted to try without the trickery when the opportunity presented itself, once they were no longer working together and he had a secure position in place.

Tonight she was coming out with him and Ben and he was determined that they have a good time. He had wanted to pick her up but she insisted she'd be already in Newquay meeting friends. He was a little disappointed. He liked the idea of picking her up; it felt gentlemanly plus he wanted to see the inside of her flat, if for no other reason than checking out the freakiest stuffed animals man had ever seen. That stoat she had brought to the fayre had crossed eyes which, combined with its tutu and cane, made it one of the oddest things he'd seen.

Instead though, she'd be meeting him at the club itself, he forgot that with her being born and bred in the area she was going to more au fait with things down here than he was. He wondered if he would have simply met her out one night. Maybe, maybe they were meant to meet, job or not.

He stood nervously at the bar waiting for drinks whilst Ben tried to sweet talk a girl he had seen around town and taken a liking to. Like most of Ben's crushes Kam wasn't convinced this one was going to pan out well either, but he had to give his mate points for tenacity. Perhaps if he had his friend's courage he wouldn't be feeling quite so sick now.

'Kam!' He heard his name a split second before he felt arms around his neck giving him a kind of backwards cuddle. His sickness and nerves disappeared in that moment; he turned and couldn't help the grin that spread across his face, surely marking him out as hopelessly besotted, as he saw Pippa standing there, a lopsided smile on her face. 'Yay. We're out, finally! We should have done this ages ago. We're going to have the best night.' He looked at her and thought it was quite probably true.

'We should have, but we're doing it now. What do you want to drink?'

She ordered tequila, managing to drag the word out for its full three syllables and add a whooping noise as she said it. She then downed it with considerable skill – not a wince in sight– hinting at experience, and managed to persuade Kam into having one too. And then another.

They found themselves on the dance floor, her arms in the air and Kam getting completely lost in the music, caught up in the bliss of being out with Pippa and seeing her throw herself fully into enjoying the evening.

She seemed to know most people here and Kam noted, many of them remarking that they hadn't seen her out for ages. To which she'd grin and say she was here now, and then introduce Kam. Introductions that, as the evening progressed, became more and more elaborate. By the time midnight had struck he was the best teacher in the world ever, and apparently had adorable eyelashes! She had taken to stroking his face as she pointed out this feature, to emphasise what she called his beauty. It made little sense to him, but he did know he was having fun and didn't want this evening to end.

However, soon the club played its last track, with Pippa still jumping around like a lunatic. He wasn't sure how she did it; he was beginning to tire but then he guessed he had been up at six to catch the dawn waves. He stood back to watch her as she bounced around like Tigger, high-fiving people she knew, and not just shaking but downright rattling her head to the beats. She danced as she lived. No half measures for Pippa Parkin.

As they all piled out the club, Ben invited everyone back to his, but the truth was, even though he didn't want the evening to end, Kam knew it made more sense to head back to Treporth now rather than later, and had already made arrangements.

'Are you going back to Ben's?' Pippa bumped her hip into him to get his attention.

'No, I'm going to head home. Not as young as I used to be and I pay a price for an all-nighter now.'

'Tell me about it. In that case wanna share a cab back?' She grinned at him winningly and again he felt like the luckiest man in the world.

'Of course. Being dead grown-up and sensible I've already booked a cab for Treporth. I'm sure they won't object if we go via Penmenna.'

'Fab, let's go then.' They both did the whole round of goodbyes, Ben giving him one of those you-lucky-sod-all-your-dreams-come-true kind of looks and Kam shook his head subtly to make sure Ben knew that was not the case. He and Pippa were not going home together. He was just making sure she got back safely. It was important to him that Ben understood that this was not some kind of post-club hook-up.

He and Pippa piled into the cab, all jumbled legs and laughter and carried on giggling at all sorts of nonsense on the journey home, when Pippa's phone binged.

'Oh damn.' She checked the screen.

'What's wrong?

'Oh it's okay. It's just Lottie has been on a Tinder date and brought her back to the flat.'

'And you don't like Lottie having Tinder dates?' If Pippa had a mad crush on her flatmate then Kam may as well give up right now.

'Oh, I don't mind at all. She's always much nicer after a successful date. Sometimes when she's snappy I pull the app up for her and practically force her out the house.' Kam breathed a sigh of relief, that did not sound like crush like behaviour. 'It's just that she can get quite loud, if you know what I mean.'

'Oh, yup, I do.'

'And as much I love her, listening to her having sex all night – and she goes on for hours. We're not talking a five-minute quickie here. I swear the walls shake and even the seagull in the bathroom looks frightened – is my own personal idea of hell. I'd rather she stuffed my bed full of her disgusting creatures, than listen to that again. I wish she had said sooner. I would have stayed in Newquay. I guess I could try and get into Mum and Dad's. I suspect the key is still under the squirrel. Oops, I shouldn't have said that.'

'You can stay at mine.'

'Really?' Pippa gazed up at him. 'Are you sure?'

'Of course, I changed it all after mum left, so it's spankingly clean, screaming out for a visitor.'

Pippa giggled drunkenly. 'Spanking and screaming huh?' she said as Kam blushed. He hadn't meant it like that. He just wanted her to feel welcome. He tried to think of some witty reply that would assure her he wasn't attempting anything sleazy but was so flustered he couldn't get a word out.

Pippa didn't seem to notice and sank against him. 'You're such a nice man, such a nice man. How on earth are you still single, huh?' He didn't have an answer to that. He just let her rest against him and found himself wordlessly stroking her hair as she chattered away.

'All the mean ones, they have women coming out of their ears, but the nice ones, the ones like you, well, it just doesn't make sense.' She placed a hand on his chest and sat up, as if she were trying to right herself. 'Ooh, ooh.'

'Oi mate, your girlfriend had better not be sick, that's fifty quid extra if she don't get out my cab in time. Bloody Newquay.' The taxi driver issued his warning and then trailed off muttering about the evils of drink and the youth. Kam felt quite pleased to be called youth. Being nearly thirty he didn't think he qualified any more but the driver was right, Pippa was looking distinctly queasy.

'Are you okay? We can get the cab to stop if you want. Have a walk around for a couple of minutes, that would be alright, wouldn't it?' He addressed the latter bit of his sentence to the driver.

'Yep, better that than my upholstery getting trashed. I'll be keeping the meter running though.'

'No, no need. I'm absolutely scrum-dabbi-doozily fine,' Pippa slurred her words before lying her head back onto Kam's chest and beginning to snore.

Chapter Thirty-five

'Hmmm… ummm… yummm… hmmm.' Pippa snuggled in deeper to Kam's chest. He could have happily stayed like that for a fair bit longer, but the taxi driver was definitely not of the same cheerful disposition.

'Mate, your girlfriend snores like a warthog. I'm sure it's dead romantic that you don't seem to mind, but I don't want to be parked up all night while you look like some moony teenager and she sleeps the night away. Wake her up and get her inside. She can snore as loud as she likes in there.' He waved his hand towards Kam's apartment building.

'Yep, fair point.' Kam wanted to revel in the 'your girlfriend' bit but appreciated the cabbie would not be willing to indulge any more 'teenage' behaviour. Kam shook Pippa very gently and then, when that clearly wasn't working, a little bit harder. She made a few more nuzzling noises and then her eyes fluttered open a bit and she smiled the biggest smile that Kam had ever seen.

'That's nice to wake up to. Hello, gorgeous. Mmmm.' And then her eyes closed again.

'Hey, hey. Pippa. We're back at mine. We need to get out of the cab.'

'The what... oh... oh, of course. I must have fallen asleep. Sorry.' She smiled up sleepily at Kam and then lent herself forward to apologise to the taxi driver as well.

'That's alright, love, just get out now, eh,' the taxi driver said, considerably nicer to Pippa than he had been to Kam.

'Oh yes, yes, of course. That I can do. Ooh...' Kam opened the car door and the cold air hit them both like a slap in the face. Summer may be here but nearly three in the morning was still pretty chilly. Pippa missed her footing, as she climbed down from the cab and stumbled slightly with Kam catching her arm and helping her up. 'I think I might still be a bit drunk... yep, def a bit wobbly still. Sorry.'

'Don't be daft, you're fine. Let's get you to bed.' Kam made sure she was steady on her feet.

'Oh yes, please. I thought you'd never bloody ask. Oh shit, did I just say that out loud?'

'You did.' The grin wasn't leaving Kam's face, although he didn't dare to dream that she had meant it.

'Um, can you forget I said that? More than a little bit embarrassing.' She giggled, and the pitch he recognised as the one she used when she was even just slightly mortified.

'Of course, I'll chalk it up to that last tequila. You were a demon this evening.'

'Were? There's no past tense about it. Pete always gets cross that I'm half his size and can drink him under the table. Bit like the chin, I blame my father.' Kam wasn't entirely sure what the last bit meant but wasn't at all surprised. He reckoned based on tonight she could probably outdrink the local rugby team.

'I believe you.'

'I don't drink very often though, before you go thinking I have some kind of problem, but I haven't had a blow out in months and months and it is the holidays.' She gave him her most winning smile and swept her hand across the marina, the lights twinkling on the jetties down to the boats all moored up. 'Do I have to go to bed just yet? Look how beautiful it is. And I bet the beach is empty.'

'Probably.'

'Can we go have a wander? I can show you my favourite rock. I'm a bit lightheaded and a bit of fresh air might do me some good.' She was teetering a little.

'True.'

'And if she's sick it won't be in your flat. Look, as charming as it is sitting listening to you two lovebirds, I'd like to get back to my own wife now. That's forty quid mate and can you shut the door so I can get home.'

'Oops sorry.' Kam realised he had been so focused on getting Pippa out of the taxi safely, he had forgotten the important things like shutting the car door and paying. 'Here you go.'

The taxi driver didn't even bother saying goodbye and zoomed off at great speed. Kam and Pippa stood there watching him race down Fore Street, past the marina and up the hill out of Treporth, presumably home to his wife who was sleeping soundly and not teetering on the pavement in crazy heels and wearing a slightly lopsided grin.

The moon lit the streets and Pippa let out an involuntary shiver before she turned to address Kam. 'Come on then, let's go sit on the beach for a bit.'

'Okay, if you're sure but here, you're shivering.' Kam took his jacket off and draped it over her shoulders.

'Thank you.' Pippa looked up at him and then, word-lessly as they started to walk towards the tiny little cove to the side of the village, slipped her hand into his.

He didn't know what to think but could feel his heart beat faster.

Yes, they had had a fab night, dancing together all night long, laughing like fools and, in truth, for Kam the evening had been about the two of them, the rest of his friends and hers fading into the background while the two of them had inhabited a fun-filled, tequila-fuelled bubble. But her subtly taking his hand... what did that mean? Even with the informality of their night out, Kam was crucifyingly aware that nothing much had changed, apart from the fact that Pippa was now free of James. They still had to work together and he still had to be aware that, despite their working relationship being very much one of two equals, if he made some kind of move it could be perceived as him taking advantage, not to mention the potential awkwardness in the classroom afterwards. And, no matter how strongly he felt about her, and despite the interviews lined up he still wasn't secure in Cornwall yet, and he hadn't worked so hard to establish himself, risked so much to mess it up now.

Was her hand a signal of platonic ease or was she trying to give him another message? It was all so compli-cated trying to decode what he thought was for the best, then throwing what Pippa was saying into the mix was making it all the more confusing. He decided to just carry on holding her hand and pretend it was about sharing warmth, like brother and sister. He was determined not to read more into it.

'How you feeling?' He thought it wise to stick to a safe topic.

'Okay, tonight was fun, wasn't it? So much fun, but I think the drink is beginning to wear off a bit. I still feel very – very – whooshy, and light-headed. I'm a bit scared that when I put my head on the pillow then the whole room is going to spin, so like the taxi driver said, a short time on the beach might be sensible. Get me past that phase. Although now I feel guilty for dragging you out with me.'

'I'm quite happy.' Kam felt it would be wise to under-play how he was actually feeling, which could be covered by the words: ecstatic, besotted and joyful. He heard the pitch of his voice lower as he tried to mask quite how perfect this evening had been for him. 'I'm hardly going to be comfortable with you wandering around by yourself.'

'Treporth isn't known for violent crime.'

'And let's keep it that way, just because somewhere seems incredibly safe doesn't mean it can't turn on a sixpence, and I couldn't bear to tell all those little faces in Class One that I had let their Miss Parkin wander off in the middle of the night and get kidnapped, fall off a cliff, get washed out to sea, that sort of thing.'

'True. They'd never forgive you, but in all the months I've known y—'

'All the months,' Kam grinned as he repeated her state-ment.

'Shhh, don't interrupt, in all the months I've known you, you've never been a negative nelly so what's with the whole cliff sea death thing? What about Miss Parkin had an amazing adventure and, I don't know, ran into some pirates – that sort of thing – and set off to sail the seven seas. That would be a tale they loved. I'd send postcards.'

'Not if you didn't come back to the classroom. I think they'd rather have you than postcards.' Kam knew he would. They clambered down the steps, Pippa taking her shoes off again, making him smile as he remembered the first time they had done this, and wandered across the sand for a couple of minutes before she came to a halt.

'Shall we sit here?' Pippa waved her hands, indicating a smooth set of rocks hidden within the curve of the cliffs.

'Can do.' Kam kicked away the dry seaweed at their base and sat down on the side to give her plenty of room to sit, without them needing to touch, still very aware that he didn't want to muddle the boundaries.

'Oh for goodness sake, come in closer.' Pippa clearly had no such concerns as she sat down and dragged him across the few inches between him and her. 'I've got your jacket, but this rock is hardly toasty, so we're going to need to cuddle up to keep warm. Don't tell me you haven't sat out on the beach late at night before!'

'Of course, I have. I spent most of my time when I lived up north on the beach at Saltburn and then there was my time on the surf circuit but that was usually with a fire and a gaggle of people.'

'Well, right now it's only you and me.' She smiled up at him and then pointed to the moon, huge in the sky and hovering over the calm sea, draping its glory over the water and enchanting everything with its light. They sat in silence for a moment, just breathing in and listening to the rhythm of the waves, and Kam couldn't have been happier.

'Isn't this the best?' She grinned and lay her head on his shoulder. 'The sound of the beach at night is so calming. There is nothing better for the soul. My brother and I used to sneak out sometimes with one of Mum's Tupperware boxes and just go and sit on the beach in Penmenna. There's something about it, the dark and the sounds of the waves continuing to crash onto the beach regardless of time of day or year. It makes you feel like such a little cog in a great big machine and really secure, all at the same time. It makes my soul happy.'

'Mm… huh,' Kam answered, too blissed out to think of anything more meaningful to say. This was the perfect way to end such a busy evening; it had combined the two extremes of Cornwall, and he was so pleased to be here.

They sat like that for some time, all curled up together and keeping each other warm. Pippa turned to him again and looked him square in the eye instead of out to sea. He looked back. Had this been any other girl he would have taken this as the perfect time to move in. But this wasn't any girl – this was Pippa – so even if he overcame his shyness, he couldn't overcome his principles, Rosy's words still clear in his mind.

Pippa smiled mysteriously and leant forward and gave him a peck on the lips. She sat back with a look on her face that was partly proud of her own bravery and partly nervous in case she had overstepped boundaries. He could feel lust whooshing through him at a rate of knots but still felt frozen to the rock. How he wanted to lean in and kiss her properly, feel her mouth on his, not merely a peck but a full-bodied, fully intent kiss.

But not only was she his colleague, she was his drunk colleague. It would be wrong. He felt himself clench as he tried to hold back on everything that every particle of his body was urging him to do. To cup her face with his hands, pull her close and not let her go. To run his hands through her hair as he pulled her face to his, to feel her back arch against him.

Instead he did nothing.

Pippa tentatively smiled, held eye contact and leant forward and pecked him smack on the lips again. He loved her courage and felt such a sham of a man. But if this were to happen, it had to happen right. And whilst sitting on a moonlit beach was pretty damn perfect, it couldn't be. Not tonight.

Kam held his hand out and stroked her face, fighting the pull, his body, his heart and his soul were screaming at him to lean in and lose himself in her. But she was still very drunk. Kam had never taken advantage of a woman in his life, and a woman encouraging him, having drunk the amount of tequila that Pippa had, was not what he considered to be consent. Damn the romance of a moonlit beach, and double damn himself for having principles.

Chapter Thirty-six

Pippa couldn't believe what a fool she had made of herself on the beach. Not only had she leaned in and given Kam a peck on the lips – with the hope it would lead to considerably more – she had done it twice and been rejected each time!

In fairness he had been very gracious and moved the conversation along seamlessly, making her feel less awkward than he could have done, but still she was gutted. And majorly embarrassed. She had hoped it had all the ingredients of the perfect romantic moment: the moonlight, the sea crashing on a beach that was empty apart from the two of them. You only got one first kiss and this one was staged beautifully. It was just unfortunate that Kam didn't want to play.

It had taken a lot of courage to move in like that, but the tequila had helped. The alcohol had freed her, made her consider taking the advice so freely given to her over the last couple months, to take a gamble, to trust her instincts, to know that no one on this planet knew if things would work out but that you would never discover if you didn't try. Besides, she wasn't planning on jumping into a full-on relationship – she hadn't sorted out *that* many issues in the course of one evening – but she would be happy right now with a one-night thing, see if anything developed over time. So, lots of deep breaths, a fair few shots and the most romantic of settings had made Pippa bold. She wouldn't be doing that again! She'd heard it said that 'Faint heart never won fair lady'. Tonight, she had learnt that the only thing Pippa's boldness had won was a whole ton of mortification. So much for instinct and old sayings.

They wandered back to Kam's apartment block with him keeping up chatter as if nothing monumental, like the baring of her soul, had happened. Pippa kept her hands to herself this time. Why the hell had he held her hand as they walked to the beach, and then let her cuddle in, if he wasn't interested? She was just flipping it over in her mind and wondering if there was more to it when she stopped still in her tracks.

Damn. She couldn't have just seen that? Surely not?

She had assumed that at this time of night they could wander around without being seen by anyone they knew. She should have known better. This was the trouble with living in Cornwall: everyone knew everyone and talked and if there was no rumour to be had, one would soon get made up. But she certainly hadn't expected to bump into the Chair of Governors at gone three in the morning.

In fact, thinking about it, what the hell *was* Richard Marksharp doing sneaking out of the apartment block? She shot a look at Kam to see if he had noticed who it was that had just left through the front door and he raised his eyebrow in acknowledgment. For a man struggling to find time to come to Cornwall to spend time with his family in Penmenna, it was certainly odd that he had the time to be sneaking around Treporth Bay in the middle of the night.

Oh damn, now he had seen them as well. This was all she needed. She nodded at him as formally as she could and hoped he wouldn't say anything to Marion. If Marion got wind of the fact that Pippa was heading back to Kam's apartment in an itsy-bitsy dress and stratospheric heels at this time in the morning then the whole village would know by breakfast and if Rosy found out…

Ding!

Was that why Kam had been reluctant to kiss her on the beach? She knew about and respected his five-year plan, but was the reason he had said no to a one-night thing because he was aware that nothing stayed secret in Cornwall for long? Was it not that he found her sexually repulsive but rather that he just was trying to protect their professional relationship? That made more sense. Not in an ego driven how-could-he-resist-me kind of way – Pippa hoped she wasn't that person – but you kinda knew – had a sense, or hoped you did – when someone liked you back, and she was pretty sure that Kam did. They had been flirting now for months; she caught him looking at her all the time, and not with disgust either. There had been moments, like on the path to Porthcurno, when she had been sure he'd wanted to kiss her, his desire had been shooting out of his eyes like laser beams. Then on the dance floor tonight, the way they danced together, the music throbbing as they matched it beat for beat… how could that *not* be a precursor to having sex? She certainly had never danced with anyone else like that. In fact, for a man who was usually super shy in the real world, Kam was certainly adept on the dance floor. That boded well.

All of her thoughts were jumbling in her brain, which was beginning to bang, and bang loudly, as if an army of dwarves were mining right at the very front of it. Ouch!

She needed to stop thinking and get herself to bed.

The trouble was once she was there, after Kam had very gentlemanly shown her to the spare room, she could not get thoughts of him out of her head. He was just on the other side of the wall. Was he lying there awake thinking about her as well? What was he wearing? Ugh, she sounded like some sleazy heavy breather, but still… did he sleep in just pants, pyjama bottoms, or nothing at all? It was as if imps had taken control of her fingers and they were itching to get next door and peel that duvet back.

How had she turned into such a letch? But was he lying there wondering the same thing? Should she shout through the walls that she was naked?

No. No, she most definitely shouldn't!

Pippa lay there for some time, trying to get some order in her head amongst the thumping. If he had turned her down because he didn't want their first kiss to be public, then maybe he was waiting for her to come in and try again? Should she get up?

Or maybe he is just not interested. You're drunk, horny and with a crush that's out of control. Maybe you should let the man sleep in peace instead of prowling his house like a mini Marion Marksharp, dribbling at the thought of fresh young man flesh.

Nah, I could drink all the tequila and never be that bad, Pippa sank back into the pillows, smirking before she fell asleep.

–

Pippa woke up the next morning to a gentle tap on the bedroom door. She shook her head a little, just to test it. By rights she should have the hangover from hell but was it possible that she had got lucky and slept through it? Maybe her headache before she fell asleep was the beginning of it. That would be a result. It would appear, however, that her drunken decision to 'trust her instincts' and try and get into Kam's pants was still was still in place this morning. Although this time she had enough awareness to know she hadn't been 'brave', just lustful.

She heard another gentle knock. Oh, this was almost as good as waking up next to him. She wriggled up in bed, tried to smooth her hair down and put her most sultry smile on. Hopefully when he opened the door she would be sitting there, slightly mussed and oh so sexy. No harm in being hopeful.

'Hello, come in.' She tried for her breathiest Marylin Monroe tones, although she was aware that; having seen her squawking across playgrounds for the last half term, he may not buy it.

'Are you decent?'

Absolutely not. Very definitely indecent and very hopeful, she thought.

'Yep,' was her slightly more sensible reply.

He poked his head around the door and she was hit with the enticing aroma of fresh coffee as well as a slam to the pit of her stomach as lust washed back all over her.

He looked delicious. She was right about the way his hair stuck up slightly first thing in the morning the way she had always imagined it would. He stood there in pyjama bottoms and she wasn't sure where to look first. She had always had a thing for men with strong upper arms and shoulders, and he very definitely had both. And then there was the downy line from his chest all the way down to the top of his trouser. She remembered how in secondary school she and her friends all had giggled about that bit, calling it the pathway to paradise.

Now that damn phrase was stuck in her head, her eyes on that line of hair, and she was struggling to speak.

'Argh, um, arghhh.'

'Go back to sleep. I can bring you coffee later.'

'No!' she squeaked the word, high pitched and desperate, and as he turned back to face her she patted the duvet next to her, feeling spider-like – come into my web, little fly.

She had to make a decision. She was, she assumed, now sober and had to work out what was more important to her: saving face or finding out the truth. Luckily, she had never been particularly shy. She may never get this chance again.

'Are you sure?' Kam asked.

Oh yes.

'Mm, coffee would be great. This is so kind of you.'

'That's okay. You've been bringing me coffee every morning since we started working together. It's only fair I get to return the favour. How's your head?'

'Surprisingly good actually. I think my hangover kicked in early.'

Kam sat down on the bed next to her and she had to use all her self-control not to take the coffee from him and run her hand up his arm.

She looked up at and saw that he was looking at her in a way that made her feel brave. She *knew* she was right. She *knew* he liked her as she liked him. Was she brave enough to try again? The worst that could happen was that he would reject her again and put distance between them for the remaining half term. Was that worse than dragging this out even longer? The not knowing. She could deal with rejection but she was fed up of this limbo. As far as she could see she liked him and he liked her, and right now he was sitting at the end of her bed, well, his spare-room bed, wearing very little. She could do this. She wasn't suggesting forever. Nothing had to change. She knew he was shy; his entire family and Ben had taken great pains to tell her this at every opportunity. Shy was fine. She could take charge. But how should she pitch it? How to do it in a way that enticed him in and didn't make him run a mile? She could feel her tummy squirming with nerves and the rest of her squirming with something altogether different.

She wouldn't just lunge this time. She'd try and pitch it in a Kam-friendly way. If only she could come up with the right words.

'Are you alright. You're looking at me a bit oddly. Do you need me to get you some aspirin?'

'No, don't go anywhere,' Pippa squeaked as she quickly tried to refocus her eyes to look more normal.

'Now, you look like you're having a stroke. Have a quick sip of your coffee. See if that helps.'

'I'm not having a stroke. That's so rude.'

'I'm not trying to be rude.'

Pippa wished he bloody was.

'I'm really grateful that you let me stay the night. What are your plans for the rest of the day?' For goodness sake, this was small talk. She'd be asking about the weather next.

'Chill out really. I've left the day blank because I thought I might feel a bit rough after a night of clubbing. What about you?'

'Same. Do you want to spend it together?' That was good. Bold. Confident.

He looked straight at her and grinned, as if all his wishes had been granted. In that smile, she saw the boy who had sprayed plaster between his fingers, and nearly melted. This man.

'Yes, please. That would be great.'

'Okay. Can we clear something up from last night?'

'Go on…' Kam's tone was tentative now but he was still looking at her, and without knowing what she was doing, as if she had no control over her body, her arm jerked up and she found herself stroking his face.

Oh sugar, she thought about pulling back but he hadn't flinched. If anything he was smiling. Okay, this was good. Um… she still needed to sort out last night.

'Okay, I want to apologise for kissing you on the beach yesterday.' She did try and move her hand away now, but Kam reached up and clasped it, keeping her hand on his face.

'I'm so sorry. I didn't want to pull away. I really didn't. I spent most of last night lying awake and regretting it. But Pips, you were so drunk, and I care about you so much I didn't want a drunken fumble to spoil our friendship. You've become my friend and I was terrified we would mess that up. Not to mention the whole working together thing.'

They both dropped their hands down from his face, but their fingers remained entwined, resting on the duvet.

She knew it! He did want to kiss her. Stars and unicorns and silver sparkles were all exploding in her head.

He did want to kiss her. He was just being a bloody gentleman.

Well, there was a time to be gentlemanly and a time not to be, and this surely was the latter.

'I'm not drunk now.'

'Sure?'

'Pretty sure. Not drunk and still very keen.'

She looked at him.

He looked at her.

He was stroking her hand in little circles as it lay there. Was this going to be it if she leaned in this time?

Pippa leaned forward and said again, 'Kam, I'm not drunk but I am right here.'

Kam leant in, 'Pippa, what if we mess work – *us* – up?'

'And what if it we don't? What if we just forget all our worries, every niggle about the future and our plans and just enjoy now? Right now.' She lent even closer and he moved to meet her.

She shut her eyes, and as she did so she felt his lips touch hers, tentative at first and then deeper, more searching and a lot bolder.

Oh, Kam Choudhury, not such a gentleman after all!

Chapter Thirty-seven

Kam stood in his doorway giving Pippa a long, lingering kiss goodbye. He had one hand on the small of her back and was holding her so close that you couldn't have fitted a whisker between the two of them. He'd quite like to keep it this way forever.

The weekend had been spectacular. They had spent the whole of it inside his flat, with him only nipping out to buy bits and bobs with which to treat her, cooking for her as she wrapped herself in a sheet and watched, occasionally getting up to help him or to kiss him. They would fall into bed again giggling, eyes never off each other. Dinner took three hours from conception to completion so good was she at helping.

They had spent the rest of it entangled together, making love and talking about everything under the sun. He had felt before that they knew each other; after this weekend he was convinced he knew no one better and that no one knew him as she did. His plans for his future shelved, Pippa was what he wanted his life to revolve around now, but he knew she had talked sense when she had broached their next steps, when she had turned her blue eyes on him – the same bright blue as the sea that day in Porthcurno – and reminded him that they needed to be careful, that if they weren't, gossip would spread like wildfire. She had asked if it would affect his job prospects and he'd told her about Rosy's warning. At this, she had laughed as she imagined his embarrassment; and then she had became serious as she told him how she would love for him to stay at Penmenna, and how this weekend, if known about, could make that less likely. He knew she was right and he wanted to say he didn't care. But he did care, he wanted to stay.

She also pointed out, and it hadn't occurred to him, that the minute they became talked about, her mother would know, his mother would find out too and the pressure piled upon them would become as heavy as the Earth itself. Pippa wanted to keep what had happened just between them a secret for now, a secret they would hug to themselves throughout the next half term, reverting back to being professional, appearing to be friends, colleagues and nothing more. Then in July they could see how things lay. When they no longer had to work side by side, they could see if they felt as they did now, and have six weeks just like this weekend, to spend together with no outside distractions.

He knew she spoke sense.

Now on the doorstep, their weekend coming to a close, they paused their kissing and stared at each other all happy, and safe in the knowledge that neither would have rather spent the last twenty-four hours any other way.

'Thank you for a fabulous day. And night. And morning.' He could hear mischievousness in her tone as she spoke. 'I had the best time and I shall see you in school, Mr Choudhury'. Pippa stood up on tiptoes and whispered it in his ear, a smile on her face that summed up all that joy one feels at having a new lover, new plans, and shared secrets.

He leant in for one last kiss, determined to remember how this moment felt, to fix it in his head and make it a memory to hold on to, to get him through the next six weeks.

'Mmmm. I must go, or my mother will be having kittens. I promised to take her out for lunch for her birthday, and I should probably get home and change first, and grab the present I made. I'll see you on Monday.'

'You will. But we won't be able to do this.' He kissed her again.

'No, we won't.' She gave a little half-smile, a shrug. 'You cannot out me as the woman who sleeps with her boss.'

'I'm not your boss, Rosy is.'

'I know, if only she were interested, huh,' she winked. 'Put me down and let me go. My mother will kill me if I'm late.'

'She'll forgive you when she sees the bracelet. I reckon we can gamble on one last kiss.'

'Oh, go on then.'

As he watched her walk away, he knew his grin had taken over his face. She rounded the corner and his phone vibrated against his leg. He pulled it out of his pocket. Maybe it was her, saying she'd be back after she had taken her mum to lunch.

It wasn't.

'Where are you? I'm sitting in the car park at Fistral and you're nowhere to be seen.'

'Oh shit, Ben, sorry. My weekend panned out differently than I expected. Um, I'll grab my stuff and jump in the car now. Start without me and I'll see you in the water. Sorry, mate. Right behind you, promise.'

Chapter Thirty-eight

The two men sat on the beach, boards by their side, staring out to the sea, watching the beach live its summer life: families with small children, buckets and spades, and cooler bags full of food; old stalwarts with their beach windbreaks and a sturdy mallet; teenagers meeting, pleased to escape the presence of their parents; and of course, the surf community, out in force today. Ben had started a fire once the sun started to go down and they were both sitting there with a flask of coffee, drinking from old tin mugs and looking out across the ocean.

'Honestly, mate, I'm not sure what you're making the fuss about. You really like her.'

'I *really* like her.'

'Right, so that's great. You really like her; she liked you enough to stay over the night, sorry, to stay-over-and-have-the-best-weekend-of-your-life-like-ever. Surely that's job done and all's good.'

'No. Not at all. When we were together it made sense for us to have this weekend and then wait because...'

'Oh no, tell me you did not ruin this by telling her about your five-year bloody plan!'

'She knows about that and *she* thinks it's a good idea.' Kam grinned as Ben shook his head and placed it in his hands, as if all hope had left the world. 'But no, not that.

To wait and get this half term out of the way, see where I stand on the job front, have a chance to be together and see how things go before everyone knows.'

'And before your mum descends,' Ben laughed knowingly. 'All sounds very sensible to me. So what wrong with that?'

'I'm worried that this will turn into a one-night stand, that we will move back into the friendzone and not be able to leave it again. I want a relationship with Pippa and I want it now. The rest will all sort itself out. It seems bloody stupid to spend the next six weeks being in the classroom with her and acting like nothing's happened, when to me everything's happened. Sod my plan. This throws it all up on its head and twirls it around. I'm prepared to take the gamble. I'm in a good place. Even if I don't get the Penmenna job, I've got all these other interviews coming up. Dad might not be happy with my decision to teach, and I've always wanted to make him proud, but you know what, I'm a good man – I am – and if that's not enough for him, then why would I put my future happiness on hold for approval I may never get. Pippa's awesome. I want to give this a go and I want to give it a go now.'

'Okay. I've never seen you so fired up. I agree with pretty much all of that, but some perspective perhaps? You've spent one night with her. Maybe you're pushing too far, too fast? Maybe you should slow down, keep it professional at work, wait out the term and see how things develop, you know, slowly. Slowly, slowly.'

'Yes, I appreciate that. But it's not slowly, slowly. It could be stop, stop. It feels fraudulent. I want to speak up, know for certain what's going on in her head. I was so convinced we were on the same page, but now, in the cool light of day, what if we weren't? What if I was a quickie and she wants to get on with everything with nothing changing, and then she can let me off the hook completely when we've finished working together? She told me her friends accuse her of being a commitment-phobe and they've known her a lot longer than I have. Why would she change that now, after one weekend? Perhaps the doubt will seep in, perhaps the doubt never left?'

'Did you ask her?'

'Not outright, no. In the moment it didn't occur to me.'

'So now you're out of the moment, perhaps you should find your voice?'

'Yeah, maybe.'

'Well then, do it. Even if you're postponing things until the end of term, you *are* able to speak to her! Come on, you're a lion. Let's hear you roar!'

'Meow.'

'Yeah, thought as much. I was trying to be kind but you're your own worst enemy.' Ben laughed at his friend.

'Aren't we all?'

'That's the truth. Look, this seems to be eating you up a bit.'

'It is. I seem to veer from being completely loved-up to being full of doubt, and that was just on the drive over. I don't like it.'

'So sort it out, and if you feel too awkward saying it to her face, then write her a letter, and that way she gets time to process it, think about things and isn't forced into an immediate answer. It might just be the perfect solution.'

Kam looked at his friend in amazement. He was fond of Ben for many reasons but his friend had never been known for his great ideas, but this one was brilliant. It would totally solve all the worries circling around in Kam's head without turning him into that James, the kind of creep who followed Pippa around insisting she became his girlfriend. Kam took a slurp of coffee.

He knew he was good at lots of things and was super secure in the person he was. He was just a bit shit about talking about his emotions with anyone. He didn't know why but the words just wouldn't come out. He knew good communication was the way to help take things forward but when he tried, his mouth would dry up and nothing would come out. He'd make an idiot of himself and worsen the chances of what he wanted to achieve rather than helping them. A letter meant he could be really clear in what he wanted to say, and Ben was right: it would achieve that without putting Pippa on the spot.

'Ben, you're a genius!'

'Yeah, one would have thought you would have spotted that before now.' They both chuckled into their mugs and Kam realised his oldest friend had hit upon the perfect solution. He looked up as the sun set across the coastline, knowing he had had the perfect weekend and was surrounded by people he cared deeply for. Life was good, and he had a letter to write.

Chapter Thirty-nine

Pippa wandered into the classroom early and with coffee in her hand. She still couldn't manage to wipe the grin off her face. Her mother had loved the bracelet on Sunday and had assumed that Pippa was so happy because of the thoughtful nature of her gift. Pippa wasn't about to tell her any different.

Now it was Monday and she was still smiling. It was going to be tough acting normally around Kam. She hadn't stopped thinking about him from the moment she had skipped down the street away from his flat in Treporth Bay, and it had taken all her self-control not to text him last night. The texting was a habit – a really nice habit – they had fallen into but since sleeping together she was a bit worried about texting him straight after. She'd been super clear about this not turning into a relationship, about keeping things on the down-low because she didn't want to jeopardise him getting the full-time position. To text now might blur the clarity of that. She wondered if she had done the right thing, but the night of the school fayre, as they had lain on the grass, she had seen how important it was to him to keep his career on track. She cared too much about him to let anything jeopardise that.

But principles aside, the thought of seeing him this morning was making her dizzy with anticipation. The whole of her was fizzing as she walked through the door to the classroom.

'Hello.' She so wanted to give him a kiss hello. Argghh, this was awkward. She knew she couldn't. That would be a direct contradiction of everything they had set out. But it would be oh so easy just to reach up…

She had to make do with smiling at him instead to which she received a grin from him that lit up his whole face.

Oh goody. He was obviously feeling it too.

'Anything extraordinary for today?'

'No, all on plan. Big introduction of the new half term's topic – which has to be the easiest cross curricular ever.'

'Right? How great Cornwall is and why. How is that anything other than bliss? I could help teach that all year round.'

'I think you do, just without realising. Oh shit, I've left the resource bag in the car. Um, if I dash and grab it, are you alright here?'

'Of course. Run, they'll be in in a minute.'

'I know.'

'And they'll all be desperate to see their new favourite teacher. The one who before half term proved he was the second best in the world at space hopping!'

'Well, I'm first in the world at space hopping, so I'll take that with the amendment obviously. But favourite teacher, don't think so.'

'You're mine.' She gave him a cheeky wink and watched his eyes widen. As she held her hands up, she continued, 'My bad. Rule breaking and I've only been in a few minutes. Will abide by them all from now on, promise.'

'I think we both know you enjoy bending the rules now and again.' He stood close to her and an image of Saturday whirled into her head, the way he had placed his hands on her back, her shoulders, her tummy, her inner thigh. Whoosh, the flood of lust came flying back.

She needed to get her head back in the game. She had barely been in three minutes and she was already about to mess everything up. Boundaries had been laid down for a very good reason and she wasn't changing them now. If they wanted to make this work long term, they couldn't fall down at the first hurdle.

'No. We need to keep it how it is, and there's no way I'm letting you put the Class Two job on the line. Oh shit, there's Marion.' Pippa spotted an immaculate blonde helmet of hair heading their way through the window, stopping to speak to parents she deemed acceptable on her way to the classroom and sniff at those she felt weren't. 'Go, or you'll never get your stuff from the car. Quick. I'll field her.'

'Are you going to tell her? About Richard?'

'Argggh. I don't know, girl code says I probably should, but then we're not really best friends. I don't want to be the one passing on gossip that could turn her life upside down. The sensible option is to stay out of people's marriages. We don't know what we saw. it could be completely innocent.'

'Hmmm. At three in the morning?'

'Yes. We can't jump to assumptions. It's not as if we saw him standing in a doorway kissing someone.'

'Like we were.'

They maintained eye contact as Kam spoke and she felt all the feels zing through her body. This was crazy.

They were going to get caught before the register had been taken at this rate.

'Stop and go and get your things! You're so bad.'

Kam grinned naughtily – conspiratorially – at her as he left. She looked around the classroom, knowing it was only going to be empty for another thirty seconds, and breathed in a deep sigh of contentment. This really was her happy place: the bright colours, the effort she knew that had gone into every picture, every piece of work around the classroom, the laughter that fuelled the room, the hustle bustle of the children learning.

'Hello, Miss Parkin. Is Kam about?'

'Hello, Marion, he'll be back in a minute. Can I help you with anything?'

'No, I don't think so, dear.' Marion sniffed. She really was an arse. Pippa could not see why Rosy, Sylvie and Alice had so much time for her.

Pippa stood eyeing Marion and Marion stood doing the same right back, when Pippa decided to be the bigger person and break the spell.

'Wasn't the May Fayre a success? You must be so happy.'

'Well, there was that dreadful woman. *She* won't be allowed back. We can only have the most responsible parents on the PTA, not some half-drunk slattern who can't behave in public. Imagine if she had acted like that when we were out with the school. What if she had had an outburst at Penmenna Hall when they were filming for the show?'

Pippa, and she suspected most of the other people in the hall that afternoon, felt that Marion had had it coming for quite some time, but because of the hazy after-glow from the weekend, or the excitement of working alongside Kam today, or maybe the promise she had made her mum before the half-term holiday, Pippa felt like trying again.

'Did you have a good half term? Did the boys do anything nice?'

'The boys had very full, very productive days. Rafe had drama school all week, very exclusive, and the others did a week-long surf school. Then in the evenings we had an intensive Latin course for all three of them.'

'Latin? Rufus is only five.'

'Never too early to start a classical education.'

Pippa felt herself about to say 'Hmmm', and stopped in time as she realised that was the Choudhury family's phrase. 'It was nice to see Richard at the fayre,' Pippa said instead, as the children started to stream in.

'Yes, lovely to have him back. He was here for the whole of half term, absolutely wonderful. We got to spend a lot of time together, although he did have to go and work briefly with a colleague who lives down here, same building as Kam I think. Lovely woman, hard worker. I did think she'd be a good fit for Alex actually, before he found Sylvie. Ooh, there's Kam now. Of course, he must have opened the door to let the kids in. Walk, don't run, young man.' Marion tapped Billy on the head and turned her full headlamps beam onto Kam and stalked across the room towards the teacher, already deluged with small children clinging to him and telling him their tales of summer half term.

Pippa went to fetch her tablet so she could enter lunch numbers, and wondered if she was doing the right thing by not mentioning Richard sneaking out of that flat at daft o'clock, although from what Marion had said it was probably work related. Spotting Kam still talking with Marion, Pippa clapped her hands and lead the children to the carpet where they could all say good morning. Kam caught her eye – those eyes – and issued a silent thank you as he manoeuvred around Marion and towards the children.

'Hello, Class, lovely to see you all back and well rested and ready to do tons of hard work, yes?' He laughed as the class made faux groaning noises. Once they dispersed to their activities, Kam went over to a pile of papers and started to rifle through them. Pippa watched him (she hadn't actually taken her eyes off him since he'd come back into the class). He seemed to have lost something, going through the pile and checking three times. He ran his fingers along the inside of his collar and brought his eyes up, flitting about the class, dwelling on window ledges and worktops to see if he could see what he had misplaced.

Pippa approached him, reminding herself to keep to the agreement whilst really wanting to say, 'Oh my god, let's spend every day and every night together.' She definitely deserved a sainthood for this.

'Everything okay?'

'Um… yeah. Yes. Nothing to worry about. I had something to give you. I spent all of last night getting it right… um… but I must have carried it over to the office and left it on Sheila's desk when I was photocopying on my way back from the car.'

'Do I need it before breaktime?'

'No. No, not at all.'

'Then I'll nip over and grab it at break time, if it's nothing major.' As she spoke Kam looked like he was about to argue but suddenly his focus switched.

'Billy! What do you think you're doing?'

Pippa turned to see what Kam was staring at. Billy, who was by the art supplies ready for his activity, was wearing a whole heap of paint. It was yellow and currently pouring down his head, onto his shoulders and over his aertex shirt. His classmates surrounded him, aghast and silent all apart from Ellie who had a very bad case of the giggles.

'I'm Cornwall! I'm sand and sunshine and ice cream,' Billy shouted, as Pippa dove across the classroom grabbing some green paper towels on the way. Kam raced her to it, both of them trying not to laugh as they attempted to wrap the child in aprons and lift him out of the classroom and into the shower they had installed for children with additional needs, and this sort of thing.

—

At breaktime Pippa headed to the staffroom and stopped by Sheila's desk, which was constantly overflowing with bits of paper, paperclips, piles of post-it notes and records of achievement. It looked terrifying, a mountain of paper and blue files that could topple at any moment.

'Are you alright under there? Can I bring you a cup of tea and a biscuit?'

Sheila popped up, glasses resting wonkily on her nose.

'Lynne's baby – Piran, they've decided upon – is doing really well, you know, although the poor woman has got mastitis. I said to her, "You think that's bad? Wait until he starts getting teeth." Bless his little face.'

'Oh, um. Okay. Tea? Oh, and did Kam leave some papers here? Something for me possibly?' Pippa adored Sheila, but she did have some odd ideas about what was alright to share. However, she made a mental note to check in on Lynne later.

'That would be lovely. And yes, somewhere. Give me a sec.'

Pippa watched her move pile onto pile, off of one pile and to the side. It was like primary paperwork version of Find the Lady. Pippa thought she may get dizzy just looking at it.

'Any second now.' Sheila smiled up at her, adjusted her glasses with her finger and went back to super speed shuffling.

'I'll go put the kettle on for a minute then.'

'Okay, dear...' Pippa turned to head to the staffroom. 'Hold on, is this what you're looking for? Sheila was somehow now standing directly behind Pippa, as if she had teleportation powers, and thrust a small sheaf of papers under her nose. 'This?'

Pippa glanced down at the papers. It was Kam's new literacy plan, a project he had taken on to breathe a bit of extra life into... Well, it was all very exciting and so forth, but Pippa wasn't quite sure why Kam had been getting hot and bothered by it. Yup, there on the corner of the top sheet was her name so this must have been what he was talking about.

Smiling a thank you, she headed to get tea whilst wondering if the yellow paint under her nails would stay with her for life.

–

That was quite a day!

> **Oh yes, Billy is a monster, but how can you not love him?**

> **Relatively easily. You should have seen his mum's face at pick up.**

> **I saw her dragging him from the playground. She had a face like thunder.**

There was a long pause as Pippa watched the moving dots appear indicating Kam was typing. Then they stopped and started again. And stopped. It took about ten minutes before the next message came through.

> **Did you get to read it?**

Really? She knew Kam had put quite a lot of work into the phonics package but was he sitting there nibbling his nails whilst she read it? It seemed unlikely, but if he wanted reassurance that she had read it and paid attention, that she could do.

> **Yes, I read it when I got home.**

There was no immediate answer and she found herself nodding off as sleep began to curl its drowsy fingers around her. Just as she drifted off, her phone pinged again. She reached her hand out, her eyes bleary, to read the message.

And? What do you think?

What did she think? Right now, all she could think of was how her pillow and duvet were emitting a call to sleep. She tapped out what she hoped was a supportive reply…

Great, you obviously put loads of work into it. Well done.

…and fell fast asleep, the phone still in her hand.

Chapter Forty

The remainder of summer term had whizzed by, but Pippa had not enjoyed it as much as she normally would have. Yes, there had been lots of trips to the beach, even more to Penmenna Hall, and the glamour of corralling small children whilst being filmed. Lots of the lessons were taken outside, which was Pippa's favourite thing, with the school field and the playgrounds being commandeered as teaching spaces and the classroom itself smelled permanently of sun cream.

But despite the term being as fun packed as usual, something had happened in the classroom and she was more than a little bit broken-hearted. After that first day, Kam had withdrawn into himself. No longer did they banter back and forth, no longer did he try and catch her eye and make silly faces, or mutter appalling jokes under his breath. Instead, he had become very remote, closed off.

He hadn't put a foot out of place, he was still utterly professional, and very kind, but the spark they had once had, had disappeared.

Poof! Gone.

She alternated between furious and sad.

Heart sad.

She had thought he wasn't like other people, had been convinced that what they had between them was special, the stuff of romantic dreams, the we're-in-this-together-forever feel. She had thought that they could pause things until they no longer shared a classroom and then work on building a life together, or try to. She had put aside all her fears about her future and tried to do as others had suggested and take the leap. But no, it turned out that once he had got into her pants he was no longer interested, and everything she had wanted to avoid had come true.

She had tried every way she could think of to fix it, but he always had an excuse at the ready these days, a reason for not spending time together after school. And what was worse, no one else seemed to notice the fractured nature of their friendship. If they had, they weren't discussing it with Pippa, who had taken to ranting at Lottie every evening, the only other person who knew the truth of what had happened.

Today, however, had been a great day. She and Rosy had been helping the children put the finishing touches to the fish and boats and mermaids sculpted out of wire and paper, that they had made for the torchlight carnival that took place on the Thursday night of Feast Week. Laughter had been boinging around the class all day, finishing with Ellie insisting that the cat she had made, complete with whiskers and a boat shaped hat was in fact a sea lion and that no one in Penmenna knew what they were talking about.

But that was part of the problem: now she enjoyed her days far more when Rosy was teaching than when Kam was in charge. She dreaded the days he was in, when it seemed her poor judgement was rubbed in her face as the air no longer crackled with the excitement of unresolved sexual tension but was spattered with misunderstanding, hurt feelings and incomprehension. Or at least on her part – she had no idea what was going on in Kam's head. That was a swamp she couldn't wade through. The only explanation that made any sense was that he was a bit of a twat, and that in itself didn't – couldn't – ring true.

She put her key in the front door, relieved to be home and planning to slide early into her pyjamas and shut out the world for a bit. Half way up the stairs to the flat she stopped as she heard a scuffling noise.

What on earth could that be? Lottie was still working in the shop downstairs. She really hoped it wasn't the dormice on the mantlepiece coming back to life and tap dancing across the living room floor.

She crept up the rest of the stairs, half wishing it wasn't summer so she would at least have an umbrella to hand. Instead she'd have to rely on her natural survival skills. If it was a burglar she'd scream, go for the balls followed by the eyes and then peg it back down the stairs to the shop.

As she hit the top step she heard a woman's voice ring out. It was her mother. How had she not guessed? Of course it was. Now she knew who was upstairs, her heartbeat slowed and she relaxed, her shoulders slumping back into their natural position. She was about to push open the door to the flat when she caught specific words.

'…it's not just your boy; something *has* changed. She's so despondent these days. I haven't known her like this since she was a teenager. It did cross my mind it was regret over James…' Her mother paused and was clearly receiving short shrift for such an idea from whoever was on the other end of the phone. Pippa couldn't identify it

– she was behind the door after all – but even with such a barrier she could still make out some kind of squawking. Hopefully it was a squawker with more common sense than her mum, who was currently declaring that 'We're going to have to do something…'

Pippa had heard enough. The last thing she needed was her mother getting involved again, and roping others in. It was time to stop this right now.

'Hello, Mum! What are you're doing here?' Pippa burst into the kitchen in the same way she used to stealth-attack Pete when they were kids. It would seem that the pleasure in kapowing the door open and watching someone's mouth drop open in surprise didn't dim with age. It being her mother's mouth brought an extra special joy as, apart from anything else, it temporarily stopped her from speaking.

But only temporarily.

'Ah, Ge… I'm going to have to go. Pippa's home. Let's talk tomorrow.'

'So?' Pippa arched her eyebrow at her mother and for fun put her hand on her hip. Her mum sat at her kitchen table with phone in hand and shock all over her face, an expression that soon turned to mild martyrdom as if she had been misjudged yet again and was doing nothing wrong.

'Hello, love.' She got to her feet, gave Pippa a peck on the cheek and sat down again. 'Did you know you have a dead squirrel in your fridge? I don't really know where to begin. I thought I had taugh—'

'Yes, it's Lottie you need to subject to your talk on hygiene, disease and germs riddling your system. At the end of the day, it is her home. But nice try. Now, what

287

are you doing here? As much as I love you, I've talked to you about this before. You can't just let yourself in. What if I had someone, you know, here.' Pippa waggled her eyebrows to make her meaning clear without being inappropriately explicit.

'Well, if you had, I wouldn't have needed to make these, would I?' Jan pushed forward the inevitable plastic container, full of Raspberry Bakewell biscuits, the raspberries forming the shape of happy faces. They were her favourite biscuits, and her mother's good intent, and the fact that she had picked up on Pippa's recent downturn in mood, made her heart squidge. Her mum might be irritating, constantly bloody present and way too involved but all was born from love. Pippa knew she was so lucky to have that. Not everyone did. Poor Sylvie had lost her mum just over a year ago, and Alice's was an absolute nightmare, although thankfully lived on the other side of the world.

'Come on then, you've clearly popped the kettle on. I guess I should join you and make some inroads with those biscuits.'

Pippa drew a chair out and sat down to talk to her mum.

Jan waited until Pippa had her mouth full of biscuits before she asked the question she had clearly been dying to ask.

'So, how's work? You and Kam still getting on very well?'

Pippa may have had a mouthful of crumbs but managed to fix her mother with a look that spoke volumes.

'I'm not interfering, love. It's just a question. You seem low, and have done for a while now. Plus, your dad said when you were at the Feast Week planning meeting the two of you took great efforts not to sit together. Now, I may not be Sherlock Holmes, but I'm not completely daft, Here, have another biscuit and then tell me what is going on with you.'

'Nothing. We're not joined at the hip you know? I don't know what Dad was talking about. These are good though, Mum, maybe one more.'

'Good, take that one. It's been sprinkled with truth serum and then you can answer my question again. I know you think I'm just interfering, but that's my job.'

'Mmm, maybe when I was six...' mumbled Pippa through a mouthful of almonds and raspberries.

'And now too. So, come on, what's going on?'

'Oh my goodness, Mum, nothing! *Nothing* is happening between Kam and me.' Pippa declared stoutly. And that was the truth. Absolutely nothing. They worked together, and now the magic was lost. Every now and again, the two of them would get caught up in the moment in the classroom, and a flicker of their old friendship would return and then it kind of fizzled out with awkwardness, feeble excuses and moving apart.

Pippa had even tried to invite him out for friendly drinks, where she was hoping to get him to loosen up a bit so she could address what on earth had gone wrong between the two of them. But when she had invited him out to The Smuggler's Curse, reiterating that it was for platonic drinks, he had refused her invitation.

'Hey, you're off on a daydream. Are you really trying to tell me that you and Kam have not had a fall out and that's not what's upsetting you? Because my mother senses are tingling like mad and we both know my mumma senses are never wrong!'

'No! We're not children. We haven't fallen out at play-time and will make up before the home bell. It's a professional working relationship and that's it. Nothing has gone wrong. Can we talk about something else please?'

Pippa got up to rinse out the mug her mother had used. There was no way on earth she'd admit she had slept with him and he had then frozen her out. She could feel Jan watching her as she took out a J-cloth, sprayed the worktop and wiped it down. Hard.

She could almost hear the cogs turning in Jan's head.

'There you are. That's better.'

'Oh love.' Her mum's tone was so chock full of sympathy that Pippa was scared she might well up. She quickly decided to switch tack and divert her mother's attention, otherwise Jan would be like a terrier with a rat, sympathy or not.

'Have you heard the latest about Marion?'

'What has she done now?'

'Nothing. But you asked me to keep an eye and...'

'Oh no! What's happened?' Jan's mouth dropped open and her eyes scrunched up. She and Marion may not see eye to eye, but her mum wouldn't wish harm on anyone. 'Did that woman from the May Fayre mount a proper rebellion? Tell me it's that and not more bad news about her marriage.'

'No, it's not school stuff I'm afraid, although Alison has resigned from the PTA and is spending a lot of time talking loudly about how Ashleigh is excelling in Sylvie's ballet class. It's driving Marion mad as she couldn't get her boys in. All quite amusing, but no, not that. Nothing solid but...'

'The boys are alright, aren't they?'

'Dear me, yes. I think those three could probably survive Armageddon.'

'I suspect they may well herald it in.'

Pippa giggled at her mother's naughtiness. Subject changed successfully.

'So…?'

'It's just those whispers about her marriage seem to be gaining traction and you said yourself things weren't looking good.'

'Yes, and then Richard came swanning in and put the rumours to rest that night.'

'Yep, but not well enough apparently. He's been very absent again the last few weeks and it's all started up again. The playground is abuzz with rumour and Marion is looking far from her usual self. Mind you, now now I feel bad, like I'm gossiping without knowing anything concrete.'

'I'm your mother. You're not gossiping. You're passing on important village news, still rumours are horrid. Poor Marion.'

'And you know how they snowball in a community like this. I've tried to be kind to her, redress the balance but you know what she's like: she just looks at me as if I'm dirt and sweeps by to talk to someone – anyone – else.'

'I don't like the woman but I don't wish her ill.' Jan reached for another biscuit, 'Do you think there's any truth in it?'

'I hope not. Whatever you say about her, her dedication to her family is evident. I think it would destroy her if that tumbled apart. But you know, Kam and I did see Richard Marksharp creeping out of some woman's flat in the new apartment block in Treporth Bay, at gone three in the morn—' Pippa stopped midsentence as she realised she had relaxed far too much as her mother's eyes lit up.

'And what were you—'

'Nothing!

'At three o'clock in the morning? I'd say you were definitely doing something!'

'Eurgghh… nothing, nothing, nothing!' And Pippa and wondered if the day would ever come when she'd be able to get something past her mother.

Chapter Forty-one

Kam couldn't believe the last week of term had come around so quickly, with term ending on the Thursday, this was his final day at Penmenna. His initial feelings about the school had proven right: he had felt honoured to get the temporary position and was now waiting to see if he had been offered the permanent one after Rosy had invited him to interview. He felt the other interviews he had been to had gone well, but it was this one – despite his disappointment over Pippa's response to his letter, or lack of it – that he really wanted. Rosy had promised everyone would be informed whether they had been successful or not by today, and she was like a clam around the school. He found it impossible to call based on her behaviour towards him since the interview for the Class Two job had taken place last week.

If he got it, he could really start to build a life in Penmenna, but if not, then he would be watching his inbox with baited breath or signing up for supply come September. Either way he would no longer be in the classroom with Pippa after this week. Which, in itself, was bittersweet. He knew he had a tendency to be a closet romantic, but he really had had high hopes for the two of them.

The night they had spent together still replayed in his mind at various times. Images would pop into his head: the curve of her spine, her neck, the freckle nestled in the mid-point of her clavicle. But there was no escaping that she had very clearly brushed him off. She had, at no point, referred to the letter he had written to her. Nothing, nada. She had ignored its existence completely, which he had to accept was her way of letting him know that she was not in the slightest bit interested in taking things further, in recreating the weekend he had found so magical.

He had been so very careful with the letter, taking hours crafting it as he laid out the depth of his feelings and his hopes for their future. His heart had been in his mouth all the time while he was writing it, and the day he had brought it into school for her had left him a bag of nerves. It was a miracle he had got through the day without anyone realising how elevated his blood pressure was.

Her lack of response meant he didn't know to this day if she had ignored it because she wasn't interested in anything other than a one-night stand or because she was scared off by the clear intensity of his feelings. Either way she had never explained, and the letter, which at the time he had thought was such a good idea, had instead sounded the death knell for their friendship.

Maybe if he didn't get the job, he would ask. Putting his head over the parapet again was terrifying but he needed to know one way or another. However, he also he cared enough for her not to want to embarrass her any more than the letter obviously had. Arghh!

However, today was not the day to dwell. It was going to be their last day working together and he was going to focus on the positive. She still brought such light to the classroom, and every now and again he would think their friendship was getting back onto an even keel when all of a sudden she would get flustered and make her excuses to dive across the classroom for some imagined sand tray emergency. If nothing else, her determination to avoid him meant that she had spent a lot of time scrubbing non-existent dirt from things both before and after school. He wondered if the sudden cleaning spurt was a tool to avoid him. She seemed to be taking it to excessive and uncharacteristic levels, but he was also aware that he could just be being paranoid and she really didn't give two figs.

Kam was excited for Sports Day though. He had loved it at school and was keen today and most looking forward to the egg-and-spoon and the three-legged race.

He had bought end of term presents for all the parent volunteers and a something for Pippa, that he had managed to source through eBay. He hoped she was going to love it, and that they could then end on a high, sweeping any misunderstandings under the carpet. He didn't want to end the term with bad feelings between them but was nervous about giving it to her. He was worried she may read more into the gift than he intended. It was supposed to be a thank-you-very-much-for-being-such-a-pleasure-to-work-alongside gift, not a this-is-my-last-ditch-attempt-to-get-you-back-in-my-bed present, which it absolutely wasn't.

'Hello!' Pippa came bouncing into the classroom dressed in an old-style tracksuit and Kam couldn't help but grin as the memory of her yellow spandex popped into his head. 'Oh, look at all the flowers. Aren't they beautiful?'

'They're for the parent helpers. But here, I have something for you as well.'

Her face fell. Damn! This was supposed to be a pleasant moment. It wasn't supposed to make her worry.

'I haven't got anything for you.' Her voice was small, like a young child who had been caught scrumping apples.

'And nor should you! You were in the room when I made it quite clear I didn't want any end of term presents. Whilst the intention is kind, it gets so silly and competitive. Parents are under enough pressure simply bringing up small children, without having to conform to that nonsense. And the same rule applies to you.'

'You did say you would be happy with home-made cards.'

'I did.'

'So I made you one of those.'

'Really?'

'Yes. It's just a silly thing and I know we've been a bit rocky this term, but I'm hoping we can put that past us and just enjoy today.' She stood there looking at him, eyes big, nerves painted all over her face. He could tell how much courage that admission had taken and he could easily meet her half way. He had been building up to saying something similar himself, so he knew how daunting it was to be so honest.

'Of course, let's make today the best. Let me grab your gift.' Pippa clapped her hands like an excited child, jumping up and down on the spot. He hadn't realised how much she loved presents, although he should've guessed, and despite the tension of the last half term his heart soared at the pleasure on her face.

He really hoped she liked it. It was a bit of a gamble and he wasn't a natural present buyer. He handed her the gift, which he had tried to wrap, again wrapping not being one of his natural skills. It did look a bit rough; he just hoped the saying that it was the thought that counted stood true.

The expression on Pippa's face said it was. In fact she let out a sound, a kind of intermingled giggle squeal, as she tried to get into it.

'I wanted it to be secure,' Kam shrugged apologetically, fetching a pair of red-handled primary-school scissors to help her hack through the many layers of tape he had used.

'It's certainly secure. Ooh, hang on, I've got a corner.' And she had. She managed to peel back a corner of the layers of wrapping paper and started to rip. With the help of the scissors, her tenacity and occasionally her teeth, she finally managed to pull the remainder of the paper off to reveal a pair of vintage Dior cat's eye sunglasses, decorated with little bits of bamboo. Pippa was silent and he was desperately hoping that it was out of pleasure not disappointment. His own breath caught in his throat as he waited for a reaction.

Slowly she looked up and met his eyes, the glasses cradled in her hands as he spotted a teeny tear just brimming on her lower eyelid. He hadn't wanted to make her cry! This was supposed to be a nice thing!

'I… I… I don't know… um… what to say. Kam, they are so beautiful, I could cry. I think I am crying. I've never seen such a beautiful pair, and they're mine. They are mine, aren't they?'

'Yes, they are all yours. Definitely. Although you have to admit they would look great on me.'

'Hahaha, they would.' They laughed together and just for a moment it seemed as if they had recaptured how their friendship used to be – how it should be – and Kam wondered if this was making Pippa as happy as it was making him.

'I'm a bit embarrassed about your card now.'

'You said it was home-made?'

'Yes.' She made a sobbing noise as she agreed, and looked a little shamefaced.

'Well, then I know I'm going to love it! Go on, let me see it before the kids come in.'

'Okay. Hang on.' Pippa raced over to the window sill where she had stashed her handbag. 'Here you go.'

She looked down at her feet as she handed the card over. He ripped open the envelope and pulled out the card. And there, on the front, was Sir Squeaks-a-lot, or at the very least a very similar looking hamster on the cover, photoshopped with a bindle – a handkerchief on a stick à la Dick Whittington – and a naughty grin as he straddled a space-hopper and fled from Pippa, Kam and his family, an image that had been snapped on their day out.

Kam started to laugh, proper big laughs that came from his tummy and shook his body.

He heard Pippa breath a deep sigh. How could she have been embarrassed about this? It was the best card ever. She had obviously spent an age on Photoshop trying to get it right. And it was. It was perfect.

'This is amazing. I couldn't ask for a better card. It needs to go in a frame.'

'Oh, you can't do that!'

'I can, and I will. Pippa Parkin, you're hilarious.'

'You're not too bad either, Kam Choudhury.' Pippa grinned at him, sunglasses still in her hand as he clutched his card, wiping the tears from his eyes as he did so.

'Hello, Pippa. How's tricks?' Rosy opened the classroom door and headed in. 'Kam, could I have a quick word?'

'Of course.' He grinned one last grin at Pippa as he left the class and followed Rosy to her office. It was such a shame it had taken him until the last day of term to get back on an even keel with her. His heart would mend – it would teach him not to be so soft – but it was her friendship that he had missed so much. It hadn't taken a long time for her to become such a big part of his life, and when the distance had sprung up between them it had left a gaping hole where her friendship had been.

He followed Rosy into her office, keeping one hand behind his back and crossing his fingers. He so wasn't ready for this to be his last day in this amazing school.

Chapter Forty-two

Ten minutes later Kam floated out of Rosy's office. The headmistress had been happy to inform him that Penmenna school would like to offer him the full time, permanent position as Class Two teacher starting in September. He happily accepted and now raced to the classroom to tell Pippa, only to find her knee deep in children, parents and PE kits, as she listened to endless reminders about how Parent A was not a fan of competitive sports, and Parent B wanted to make it quite clear that they expected the races to be undertaken seriously as children needed to learn to win and to lose, none of this namby-pamby 'taking part' nonsense, and Parent C wanted to make sure Pippa knew how to administer Kayden's inhaler, despite the fact that Pippa had been doing so perfectly well for the entire academic year.

The minute he entered the classroom, he too was besieged by parents who, mindful that today would be his last day in school before the long summer holidays, wanted to wish him well and thank him for all he had done for the children. He was itching to tell them all that he would be back next term to teach some of the children who would move up into Class Two with him for the next academic year (although he would be making sure Billy was kept away from the squeezy paint bottles), but he felt he should keep the news to himself for now. Partly because he knew Rosy wanted to make a formal announcement at the end of the day as Sports Day was wrapped up, but also because he wanted Pippa to be the first to know.

The children were spending their morning putting the finishing touches to their wire and paper sculptures, which they would carry through the streets of Penmenna on the Thursday of Feast Week. A celebration of sea myths and monsters was the theme for this year, and Penmenna School was busy churning out a huge Kraken, tentacles and all, and a beautiful mermaid with flowing hair and iridescent scales, as well as lots of little versions that would contribute to make a showstopping colourful display.

Kam had been blown away by watching the sculptures come together; all the classes had worked on them, as well as various people from the village popping in and making it a truly inclusive community project. Dan had come and helped, his Hollywood good looks making several of the mothers swoon. Lottie had come to lend a hand as well, although Rosy had carefully and gently declined her kind offer to donate Sidney the Seagull to ride along with them.

The children were also making individual models to carry through the street, and there were sea serpents and dragons, sirens and giant jelly fish. Some were huge. Ellie and Sam, for example, had shelved the idea of the sea lion and were making instead a huge squid-like creature with giant googly eyes and a gazillion wavy tentacles that needed four sticks to hold it up it was so big. With Pippa beavering away with the children, her creative side coming fully to the fore, Kam didn't get the chance to tell her his news until lunchtime.

Despite their rapprochement, Kam was a little uneasy about telling Pippa his news. It had crossed his mind that the reason they were getting on so much better today was because she thought that there was a chance this was his last day ever in the school, and thus she felt relief that soon she wouldn't have to face him at work. He knew that her nature, her very being, meant that there wasn't a mean bone in her body, but then he hadn't expected her not to even fully acknowledge his letter, so he was aware that his assumptions about her were no longer reliable.

As the children were walked through to the dining hall to eat their lunch, he caught Pippa's eye and this time she met his gaze and smiled. That boded well. He edged closer to her, his heart beating fast. He felt like he was his fourteen-year-old self trying to deliver a valentine to the most popular girl in school.

'Hey.' He smiled tentatively at her.

'Hey.' She smiled back. Her sunshine smile lit up the room and Kam's heart bounced. He knew he was still smitten. He also knew smitten wasn't a professional term. 'Ellie and Sam's squid is looking great isn't it? I was worried they wouldn't finish it in time, but they've really cracked on.'

'They have. Although we both know Ellie was in charge of that,' Kam replied.

'Ha! Probably, although, you know, Sam has a quiet authority that makes me think he's secretly the one in charge. I wouldn't be surprised if, over time, Sam was to become the more dominant one. Ellie won't have anyone upset him. You should have seen her when she first joined the school. She took out anyone who was mean to him with the violent swiftness of a professional assassin!'

'I can imagine. I wouldn't want to cross her, and she's still only five. Imagine what she's going to be like at twenty or thirty.'

'Running the country probably, but what I really want to know is what Rosy had to say.' Her tone faltered as she asked, and Kam wasn't sure why. Was it because she wanted him to get the job, or was it because she was scared that he may have been given the post?

'Okay, well…' he dragged it out, a little hint of his old mischief back in his voice.

'You toad! Come on… did she offer you the job? She did, didn't she, or you wouldn't be messing about!'

'I'm sorry. I went to her office and she… um… well, I think that she wanted me to hear the news in private so I didn't… you know… make a fool of myself.' Kam managed to work his face into a suitably sad expression sneaking a peek out from under his eyelashes to see if she was falling for it. She looked a little suspicious, so he decided to ramp it up a bit. 'Rosy said there were some standout candidates and that it was a tough call, but hey, let's not get too despondent. Lynne will be back in the classroom in September, so that's great!'

'Did you really not get it? I thought you had it in the bag! I don't believe it. The new teacher had better be some award-winning superher… oh you, you! I should have known you were messing about.' She gave him a quick punch on the arm as she realised he was teasing, exactly as he used to do when it was just the two of them, her action greeted by a shocked chorus of small voices all shouting, 'Miss Parkin!'

–

303

Kam ended the day on a high, Sports Day had been fun and he hadn't been able to stop grinning all afternoon. He had been given the job of his dreams, the girl he adored was talking to him again and when Rosy had announced his appointment a huge cheer had gone up from all the assembled parents, children and staff. This had to be the best day ever in the history of his world.

He was walking back to his car, after giving Pippa a goodbye hug while managing to keep all his emotions nicely pent-up as he did so. He felt content and, although he knew he had to accept that Pippa didn't feel the way he did, the fact they were back on good terms was enough for him right now. Most of the love songs and stories in the world dealt with unrequited love. There was nothing special about him. He was just experiencing one of those things that made humans human.

His phone vibrated in his pocket. He hadn't told anyone outside of the school his news, but he wouldn't be at all surprised if his mother had some kind of minicam installed in the top pocket of his suit and was ringing to shriek at him. He stopped as he reached his car and pulled out the phone to see what she had to say.

Only it wasn't his mother texting, it was Pippa's. How had she got hold of his number?

Hello! Good news travels fast. Congratulations! I thought I'd get in touch to see if you wanted to join our family for the sea shanty singing in The Smuggler's Curse on Monday night, it will be great fun and you'd be more than welcome. We'll be there from half six on. Jan.

The phone beeped again.

That's Jan, Pippa's mum, by the way. Hope to see you Monday!

Chapter Forty-three

Feast Week had arrived which meant that Penmenna was filled with fluttering bunting and very high spirits. The bunting was a mish mash and there was so much of it that it was wound around some unusual places as well as flying high in the air, fluttering from lamppost to lamppost. A lot of it had been made by the children at school a few years ago, and in addition there had been some guerrilla knitters in action, creating seaside scenes and yarn bombing the village. Pippa's money was on Ethel and her friends. Street names (not that there were many) had been framed with knitted seashells and the outside of The Smuggler's Curse had been prettied up with woollen sea monsters and beach scenes in keeping with the carnival theme.

Yesterday had seen the raft races down on the beach where families had to construct their own rafts out of any material they pleased, launch them in Treporth Bay and then try to sail them the length of the coast to Penmenna. Everyone who stayed afloat won a medal, although you could guarantee only three or four would complete it. This year Pete and Jim had made a contraption that managed to meet all the conditions of the race and was built largely out of empty plastic bottles that Jan had collected all year long. It had been great fun as Pippa, Pete and their dad had optimistically climbed aboard it in

Treporth Bay, only to have it sink halfway around, just past the huge rock that protruded out of the sea and that teenagers liked to clamber upon. They had waded around to Penmenna beach, soaked to the skin and roaring with laughter as Jan met them on the other side with towels and a thermos of tea. This was what raft race day was about. This year the summer sun was beating down from the sky, making the capsizing a pleasurable relief rather than an unpleasant soaking. Feast Weeks were not guaranteed to be sunny, so it had been lovely to be splayed out on the beach, munching crisps and gulping water, surrounded by the majority of the village and wider community, with the sun drying them out and warming them through.

Now, though, it was Monday evening and Pippa was sat inside The Smuggler's Curse with her family and a whole host of regulars, giggling with the choir before they started their performance properly. This was one of Pippa's favourite nights of Feast Week, steeped in history, tradition and Roger's hooch. She steered clear of the latter, experience having taught her that this week was a marathon not a sprint, and as always it would culminate in an It's-a-Knockout tournament that took place on the school field followed by spectacular fireworks over the cliffs.

She sat there happily, chatting away to Ethel as her mum and dad nattered together. Ethel was telling Pippa the story of when she had driven through Paris in a white, open-topped sports car in the Sixties with two strangers she had met in a bar, when the door opened and, as per usual, everyone turned around to see who had entered. The general feel was a little friendlier today. During Feast Week strangers were almost welcome into The Smuggler's

307

Curse as long as they showed the correct deference, i.e. let anyone local get served before them without kicking up a fuss.

Pippa was slow to turn with everyone else, her mind still busy whizzing past the Eiffel tower, hair streaming, and Ethel shrieking with laughter in an Aston Martin, so it took her a second or two to process that it was Kam who had just walked through the door.

He stood, as if unsure, looking around the inside of the pub to see someone he recognised. Pippa waved, her mind immediately a-boggle as she realised that now, formally and officially, they didn't work in the same classroom any more. That changed the whole dynamic of their relationship, surely?

With him getting the job in Sarah's class, they would still be colleagues but not in such a strict sense. It also meant that his five-year plan was not only on track but going faster than he had expected, which would have boded well for her, had he stuck to the romantic plans they had made that fateful weekend. If the reason their relationship had fallen to pieces was because he was concerned about protecting their professional reputation, now it was the summer holidays and they were a lot freer than they had been this time last week. She shot a grin at him but he had already been enveloped into a giant bear hug by her dad, her mother having nipped off somewhere. Pippa decided she had better rescue him before he was subjected to the topic of how he should have replaced his car by now with something Japanese and reliable.

'Ah Pippa, now I *know* you know this young man.'

'Yes, Kam's my colleague.' There was a split-second silence where both she and Kam realised what she had said. Not friend. Colleague. Ouch. Pippa wished for all her life that she could take it back as she saw the hurt flash in Kam's eyes. Jim steamrollered on, unaware of any undercurrent.

'Not if your mother has her way.' Her father smirked at the two of them, both so embarrassed by this point that they looked at everything but each other. Kam seemed suddenly interested in the beer taps and Pippa studied her toes with the intensity of a podiatry PhD student.

'Who's taking my name in vain?' Jan rejoined them but not quickly enough to prevent Jim's initial embarrassing statement. Or to stop him compounding it.

'I was just telling Pips and Kam that you had high hopes for them romantically'. Pippa heard someone groan, loudly and with feeling and then realised it was her.

'Oh no! You're mistaken. You know that I've promised Pippa I'll no longer interfere in her love life. She's a big girl. I'm sure she can sort it out on her own.'

'But you said that you and Kam's mum had been talk—'

'Who wants a drink then?' Jan's tone was loud, and smacked of forced cheerfulness and Jim let out a yelp before leaning over to rub his foot. Pippa fixed her mum with her fiercest what-on-earth-are-you-up-to-now glare, which bounced off her like lambs in springtime.

'Ooh, and look the choir is about to start.'

At this point Kam stopped looking as if the Carlsberg and Korev pumps were the secret of all knowledge and smiled wanly at Pippa. She smiled tentatively back. If nothing else she knew Kam understood what it was like to have a mother who was sure she knew best and constantly interfered.

The singing began and the rousing sound of *Trelawney* rang through the pub. As the drums began to swell so did every Cornish heart, and most of those sitting stood to their feet. The song roused such a strength of feeling one would have been hard pressed to find a Cornishman or woman not stirred into action or emotion by this song. Pippa stood facing the choir and knew that the love she felt for her county was beaming from her face, as it was from the faces of the majority of those in the room as they all joined in with the chorus '*here's twenty thousand Cornish men shall know the reason why.*'

It was a song that they grew up with, and one that took pride of place in all Cornish choirs. It told the story of the imprisonment of a Cornish bishop. Pippa knew that the men did not actually march upon parliament as the song suggested, but she also knew no one in the pub gave a sod about historical accuracy in this case. It was all about the feeling.

The choir moved seamlessly onto *Robbers Retreat*, another Smuggler's Curse favourite, and Pippa looked over at Kam gripping one of those little pamphlets that the choir had put on the bar, with all the lyrics written down for those who may not know them but wanted to sing along with the locals.

She stood watching him for far longer than was polite as he tried as hard as he could not to spend too much time looking at the words, fixing his eyes on the choir and singing loudly, trying to gauge the tune and what was coming next.

It made Pippa sigh; he was so beautiful, inside and out.

She didn't like people who didn't sing with the full force of their being. Teachers and teaching assistants by the very nature of their job tended to sing loud and proud. Even if, as in Kam's case, they didn't really have a clue what they were singing. Her eyes caught on the line of hair running from his hairline down the back of his neck and her tummy flipped as she remembered running her hands through his thick hair as she pulled his head down towards hers with an urgency that was now trickling back and beginning to swirl around in the pit of her stomach, spreading a tingle all the way across her body. The day and night they'd spent together had been so great, everything she had dreamed it would be. Sometimes you could get on brilliantly with someone, have so much in common and yet not be sexually compatible. This had not been the case between her and Kam. They had matched each other move for move, the desire of one mirroring the other's. She could imagine, and unfortunately right now was, making love for a lifetime and never ever getting bored.

Maybe now that they had the holidays stretching in front of them, she could try and speak to him again. See if they could resolve their issues and go back to that weekend and start afresh. Tonight could be the night. Maybe any minute now.

For goodness sake, woman! Where is your dignity, huh? Have some self-respect. Her inner voice kicked in, its tone dripping disapproval and disappointment. Yes, his hair may curl oh-so-beautifully over his collar; yes; he may have been the best sex, the most meaningful sex, you have ever had and yes, it's a shame it's not going to be repeated. But it's not. This man was charm personified, your new best friend until you slept with him and then, for no reason, after a couple of days back in school, became awkward, cold and detached.

She remembered the sting of rejection so harshly that it almost put paid to the lust currently coursing through her body. Not completely though, so she determinedly dragged her eyes away from his frame – they had moved from his hairline towards his shoulders, across his chest and then down a bit, the entire time she had been telling herself off – and fixed them firmly on the choir in front of her. If she stared at Mr Gwynn long enough, who very definitely still had some of last night's supper stuck in his limp and sticky handlebar moustache, that should cool off any further sexual desire her disobedient body may feel. If it got really tricky, there was always Roger. *To put her off!* she quickly clarified in her mischievous, revolted mind.

Once she had regained control of her body, (which was a desperate relief, as she feared she had been barely a step away from grabbing her 'colleague', hurling him over the bar and straddling him there and then) she took a look around. The pub was absolutely rammed, with all available spots full, with the exception of one stool at the bar. It took her back to Kam's first night in the pub, and sure enough, as if she were psychic, Flynn the dog pushed his way through the open door and the throng of people and hopped up onto his seat. Kam stopped singing for a minute to watch Flynn jump up, and then turned to look at her with an expression that said he hadn't forgotten the fun they had had that night either.

Dignity. Self-respect. Dignity. Self-respect. If only he hadn't frozen her out, they could be starting out together now and living the romantic dream. Dignity. Self-respect.

She could not help but grin back though. It felt so good to be back on friendly terms again. Maybe it wouldn't be so bad if she tried to spend some time with him over the summer. If she could get their easy-going friendship back then that would be enough. Not perfect – true – but pretty damn good. Perhaps she could talk to him later. Or even better, text him tonight as they used to. Then she wouldn't have to deal with a possible rejection face to face, watch his face fall and the freeze set back in again. A freeze that she was worried even the July heat would be unable to melt. Yes, that was what she would do, text him later. For now, she would just sing standing next to him, loving the season, loving her county and loving the family and friends around her.

Chapter Forty-four

As the choir finished their last song and were standing at the front beaming at the rapturous applause, Kam turned and thanked Jan for her invite.

'I've had a brilliant evening. This has been fab. Thanks ever so much for inviting me to join you all. I'd love to stay but I need to get home. I'm helping my friend with breakfast tomorrow. It's crazy busy now the holidays have started and he's a bit short staffed.'

'Of course, I'm so glad you could join us. Will we see you about this week?'

'For sure. I'm part of the carnival parade along with Pippa, and I've heard that the It's-a-Knockout competition and the fireworks are not to be missed.

'That's the truth. We shall look forward to seeing you then, then,' Jim jumped in. 'Won't we, Pippa?'

'Of course we will. I'll see you on the Thursday.'

'You're on.' Kam shook Jim's hand and gave Jan a kiss on the cheek, and then turned to Pippa and bent down and repeated the gesture. Pippa couldn't control the grin that spread across her face as she felt his lips brush her cheek and wondered whether if he went to kiss the other cheek could she move her face quickly and catch his lips with hers? Then she realised that the middle of The Smuggler's Curse was not where she wanted to stage her get-her-tongue-down-Kam's-throat-again plan. Plus, that smirk on her mother's face was really annoying.

As she watched him go, she spotted Sheila bustling through the crowd and heading her way.

'Hey Sheila, how are you?'

'Aren't they fabulous? I love hearing the choir sing. Quite magical. They hit me right here.' She touched her heart and Pippa grinned in agreement. She was right; there was something that uplifted the spirit and soothed the soul, when the community got together and sang. 'Anyway, dear, that's not why I came to say hello, I was hoping to see Kam as well. I'm so pleased he has Sarah's job, such a cheerful addition to the team.'

'He is.' Pippa deliberately didn't look at her mum or dad.

'Yes, but look, here.' Sheila rifled in her bag. 'I don't know if it's important but I found this on my desk when I went in to school this weekend for my big end of term tidy up. I thought I'd best get it to you. I don't know how I didn't realise before.'

Pippa took the slimline envelope that Sheila held out to her and instantly recognised Kam's handwriting on the envelope where her name was scrawled.

'Thanks, Sheila. I have no idea what this could be.'

'Well, open it and find out, love,' her dad chipped in with his ever so wise advice.

'I will do.' Pippa smiled and ignored him, slipping the letter into the bag. It could just be a note about timetables or curriculum, but she didn't know and Kam hadn't mentioned it, so there was no way she was going to open it in front of the entire village. No. If Kam had put something in this envelope that wasn't school-related, she wanted to be alone when she opened it.

Pippa left the pub and wandered down to the beach. It was a place she went to, like most of the locals, for anything that could be vaguely emotional. There was nothing as grounding as the smell of the ocean and the rhythmic smash of the waves on the shoreline, and at night it was particularly magical, especially if there were any boats far out and lit up, bobbing on the waves.

Today she headed for the cave on the right side of the beach. As she reached it, she sat down in front of her favourite Penmenna rock (she had one for each local beach), which having been smoothed over the years by the sea provided the perfect place to rest, although right now it felt cold against her back.

She moved the crunchy dried seaweed from around her and pulled the envelope out of her bag. She was going to feel like a right tit if this was more literacy work.

She lifted the sticky envelope flap and took a deep breath. As she unfolded the paper inside she could see by the dim light of the half-moon that it was a letter, but she couldn't quite make out the words. Pulling her phone from her bag she flipped the torch on and braced herself for whatever it was she about to read.

It didn't have a date on the top but as she scanned down it became clear that he had written it shortly after their weekend together.

Dear Pippa,
    That was the most amazing weekend ever.
I decided that I was going to write you a letter, so I could stop ranting at Ben about

how I feel about you and tell the person in question instead. By doing it this way you aren't forced to give a polite-to-my-face, in-the-moment answer to my question. You can pack your bags, flee Penmenna and rue the day you agreed to stay at mine. Or just ignore the letter, behave as if it had never been written, and I will know, wordlessly, to back off.

I figure I can be honest in a letter, and by doing that we won't have the misunderstand-ings and the miscommunications that plague so many friendships and relationships.

Here goes.

This weekend was awesome. I may have said that already, but it bears repeating. I would like to have more weekends like it, lots more like it. And preferably before July. I know that pretending nothing has happened until the end of term was what we agreed, and you're right: it's very sensible. But you know what? I want to stamp on Very Sensible, ball it all up and hurl it over a cliff. I want to do Not Very Sensible, I want to shout from the rooftops about our weekend and I don't want to spend the next six weekends of term wishing you were here with me, or I was there with you.

I want to be with you properly. I want to be in a relationship with you and I would love that to start now. I don't want to miss out on any time we could spend together.

You've told me how you want your Happily-Ever-After to be forever, and I think you and I could be that. Really, I do. This letter is to ask if you do too?

This may sound like it's come out of the blue, like the ravings of a madman. The latter may be true but the former definitely isn't. From the day of my interview when I met you in the car park all big bunny paws and fluffy tummy, I was a bit smitten. That morphed into a massive crush. Why?

Because I love the way you light up every room when you enter it; the way you tackle everything life throws at you with tenacity and a never-ending cheerfulness; the way you sing all the time as you work – loudly and very very off-key – and are completely unaware you're doing it, lifting everyone's hearts as they hear you; the way you crinkle your nose when you laugh and the way every emotion you feel is displayed all over your face. I love that you are utterly true to yourself and at the same time cherish and protect those around you. And I swear there is no one on the planet who rocks spandex with the verve that you do. This list could go on forever but I don't want to freak you out more than I already am.

So, it would seem that I am a hopeless romantic and one who is hopelessly devoted to you – yes, I wrote that so you could sing it.

We both know you just did. And I am really, really hoping you feel the same about me.

So I leave you some choices: you can ignore all of this and I shall back-off, understanding that you do not feel the same and are mortified at getting this letter, or you can find any way you like (words, semaphore, face paints) to let me know that you are quite keen to spend a lot more time with me before the end of term and very definitely outside of work, and if some of that involves stripping me naked and doing bad things then know I am here and I am keen.

Pippa, you are ace.

All my love,

Kam.

Breath seemed to have left Pippa's body as she read through the letter. Once she had finished it she sat there, back still against the rock, waves still breaking on the beach, trying to catch a breath, any breath. It was as if it had all been taken from her and she was in shock. There was such a swirl of emotions whirling around her head, around her whole body, that she didn't know what to do, how to respond. She lay her phone down on her lap and on top of the letter and found she was now gulping great big breaths of air.

This was ridiculous.

Eventually she regained control of herself, slowing her breathing down, tying it to the rhythm of the waves. She tried to use some of the mindfulness techniques that she and Lottie had practised. She spent a minute or two dragging her mind back from the contents of the letter to the way her body was feeling, focusing upon the sand under her fingers, until she was calm enough to consider what the letter in front of her was saying. She felt the breath playing across her lips as she picked up the piece of paper and read it again, just to double check that she wasn't imagining this.

Wow.

Chapter Forty-five

Wow.

This was still the word on her lips as she fell asleep that night, and awoke again the next morning.

Wow.

She had seriously screwed up.

She didn't dare count the weeks that Kam had been waiting for an answer from her, waiting for her to say 'Yes please', screw her clothes into a ball and do all sorts of things that were very definitely not suitable for a school setting.

Which, thanks to Sheila, she hadn't done, hadn't known he was waiting, had just thought he was being an arsehole when he was clearly hurting like mad and assuming her silence was a cold-hearted rejection of all that he was offering. What must he think of her?

No one had ever written her a love letter before, although her brief spate of internet dating had indicated that many men thought dick pics were an acceptable declaration of interest.

Not only was this a love letter, but it was written by a man she had been prepared to take a gamble on, a man for whom she'd been prepared to overcome her fear that no one would ever give her what her parents had, a man she knew she would choose to spend her life with if a genie ever came down and granted her three wishes. The first two of course would go on things of global importance, like world peace etc., and maybe an endless wardrobe. But the third, the third she would have definitely used to get herself Kam. And now, now… ooooohh, she could scream with frustration.

The obvious thing to do was to get out of bed, stop beating herself up and peg it over to Treporth Bay, or better still to Ben's surf hostel in Newquay where he'd actually be, and screech 'Yes, yes, yes' at him. Although maybe an explanation first of why she was shouting that would be better. An explanation and an apology.

If Sheila hadn't been so damn lovely Pippa might have felt like killing her right now, stretching her innards across Penmenna, like the bunting already up and on display, and winding a bit around the knitted squids on the lampposts. Mind you, Pippa didn't think she'd actually enjoy the practicalities of that and anyway, everyone had stopped getting cross with Sheila years ago. She was reliably unreliable but meant well, it was just fact. Getting angry with her was tantamount to cruelty and would achieve nothing other than a prolonged bout of self-loathing.

Which it appeared she was engaging in anyway.

Her phone sat on the bedside table beeped and she grabbed it, praying with all her heart that it was Kam telling her he simply couldn't live without her.

Help me! Mum is driving me crazy.

Her heart sank as she realised it wasn't Kam. Of course it wasn't. They had stopped texting after she had *not* got the letter he had written. It was Polly who had been away for the weekend and clearly only just landed back at home.

> Well, of course. That's her job. Did you have a good time at the festival? Back to walking and talking yet?

> Nooooooooooo! And you're meant to be here helping with the pasty and you're not so she's trying to get me out of bed and I feel like I haven't slept for four days and my eyes are literally going to bleed out of my face if I don't get some rest soon. Rescue me. Please. Best Sister *ever*.

Pippa jumped out of bed. There was no time to get sucked into maudlin self-pity for cocking up what could have been one of the best relationships in the history of forever. No time for running over to Newquay, because today was pasty competition day and the most important afternoon of her mum's year. Every summer Jan was determined — desperate — to win, and like every year it was far more likely that Julie would carry the trophy home again. Her pasties were quite simply unbeatable. She had even won at the World Pasty Championship when it was held at the Eden Project, and if she could beat entrants from five continents it was highly probable she would beat Jan for the umpteenth year.

Several hours, an awful lot of flour, butter, beef skirt, and shooing Tatters away with a tea-towel led to Pippa and Jan standing in the church hall behind a table as the Feast committee were about to begin wandering from table to table tasting each entry. It was so hot and sticky today, she was beginning to worry that the pasties themselves were about to slide off the table and slink sink-wards for a glug of water.

In between waving at everyone already there and wondering how much longer this might take, she spotted Lottie racing through the door with a pasty in hand. Lottie? Baking? Whilst her flatmate could now stuff a stoat one handed (she had improved greatly in recent weeks), the thought of her turning her hand to baking was something that almost didn't bear thinking about. Especially as Pippa knew for a fact that the hand wash in the kitchen had run out at some point last week and neither of them had got around to replacing it yet.

'Am I too late to enter?' Lottie gasped as she fell through the door, a wooden board in her hands with one of Pippa's gingham tea-towels on top

There was a fair bit of tutting from some of the panel and the odd contestant, but Lynne's Dave wasn't having any of that.

'You come share my table, maid. It's a l'il bit of fun. I'm sure no one will mind you turning up a fraction late.'

'Thanks, Dave. How are Lynne and the baby?'

'Yup, both are good. The baby had just fallen asleep as I was leaving so Lynne decided she'd have a quick nap as well. Hopefully she'll pop by later and you can say a quick hello to baby Egbert.'

'Dave!' Pippa reprimanded as she left her mum and came to help Lottie arrange space on Dave's table. 'You know Lynne's going to be really cross if you tell people that the baby is called Egbert!'

Dave grinned quite unrepentantly. 'And how do you know he's not, huh?'

'Cos I was around last week, and Dan nipped in to talk about the christening. At no point did either of them refer to Piran as anything else, and certainly not Egbert.'

'Aye, but she may come around yet.' Pippa couldn't help but laugh at Dave's conviction, as several members of the WI frowned at their rowdiness.

As expected, Julie won hands down, and then the event became more relaxed with everyone wandering around having a taste of all the different pasties on offer. Pippa felt a bit mean, but she wasn't going to risk Lottie's. She sat with her instead, and with Lynne who had just arrived, drinking tea in little cups and saucers the like of which were spotted in every church hall across the land, as Lottie and Lynne pestered her to know what her plans were for the long summer holidays.

'So, this summer I'm going to… oh for goodness sake, I can't keep it quiet any more. Lynne, Lottie already knows about this, but I slept with Kam at half term, and I know I shouldn't have' – Lynne's mouth dropped open but she had the grace to stay silent and let Pippa continue to speak – 'but I did, then afterwards I thought he had lost interest and I've had a bit of a shit last half of term. But it was all just a misunderstanding and pretty much all Sheila's fault and now everything is a mess and I don't know how to fix it. I need to spend my summer making it right and you have to help me! Argggghhh.'

'What do you mean a misunderstanding? How could there be a misunderstanding? You came home on cloud nine, then he froze you out. That's fairly simple. Nothing to misunderstand at all,' Lottie stated, in that tone of someone who had heard it too many times.

Pippa told them all about the letter – her words falling over themselves – desperate to get the story out as quickly and as fairly as possible. Lynne and Lottie listened agog to all that Pippa had to tell.

'This is better than Eastenders,' Lynne, who had miraculously stayed silent during the whole retelling, finally commented.

'This is my life.' Pippa wasn't sure she wanted her life to be more dramatic than a soap opera.

'That poor boy, all term sitting there, having declared his love and waiting for an answer, any answer at all.' Lynne made a aw-bless-him face.

'That's not really helping.'

'Well, the solution is simple. It's not rocket science. You just have to tell him,' Lottie advised.

'I know that, but how?'

'You don't normally need any help to talk,' Lynne chimed in as she hoiked her top up and put Piran onto her breast to feed.

'Cheers.'

'Hey, hey. Look, Pips, that letter sounds pretty lush. You can't change what's passed but you can shape the future. You just have to find the courage, and bearing in mind how you dress' – Lottie quickly nodded at her friend's outfit, which was a definite nod to America's midwest today and matched the tea-towel Lottie had pinched – 'courage is not something you're short off. But just because you found out last night doesn't mean you need to rush over and declare undying love today. He gave that letter some thought and it's a real shame that you didn't get it when he intended but, you know what, a couple of days now shouldn't make too much difference. Let's put our heads together and we'll come up with a plan, a grand gesture, something that makes it clear how important he is to you.'

'Do you think?'

'I do. We'll come up with something, promise.'

'I'm in,' Lynne said before continuing, 'she's right, between us we'll come up with something to rival the letter, or at the very least make it really clear how you feel.'

'Oh, thank you. You're the best friends a girl could have.' The relief was written clear on Pippa's face. She knew this should be an intimate thing, but her head was such a whirl since receiving the letter that she was struggling with rational thought. With her girlfriends to ground her, keep her focused and hopefully stop her making a complete twit of herself, she should be able to right this wrong in the best way possible.

'We are,' Lottie nodded, 'and don't forget you have the best family too. We'll get everyone involved. This is going to be the most romantic Feast Week Penmenna has ever seen. Trust me!'

Chapter Forty-six

The most romantic Feast Week ever was shaping up nicely and Pippa hadn't had a minute to spare, with all the plotting and then the Flora Dance on Wednesday. Now Thursday had arrived and it was carnival day: the day when the traffic in Penmenna was diverted and the schools, local businesses, scout and guides troops, in short anyone with any connection to the community, dressed up in themed costumes and paraded through the streets, finishing up in the school field where there would be judging for the best dressed.

Pippa had lain awake all night trying to work out what she was going to say to Kam when she saw him today, despite Lottie and Lynne's insistence that she say nothing. They argued that the carnival procession was a school related activity and both she and Kam would be there in a professional capacity so she just had to carry on as normal, not slip up by letting him know she now knew about the letter, and then they could do a big romantic reveal on the Saturday. They had also drafted in her mum and dad, which meant Pete and Polly (and Tatters) were now involved, and Pippa had a feeling that the whole village probably now knew the ins and outs of her private life. Lottie's reassurances that they always did anyway was not much succour.

She was going to find it hard to keep this to herself. Words were constantly burbling over the curve of her lips every time she thought of the letter. Words like '*Sorry, I'm an idiot*,' and '*Marry me*'. Those, she needed to keep in; it was just that silence wasn't her natural state of being.

As she approached the school, she saw him wandering down the road towards the building, dressed as Neptune and complete with fork and wavy sea hair made of blue and green crepe paper. Her heart swelled so big with love she didn't know what to do with herself. With any luck she'd lose the power of speech once they came face to face, otherwise she'd blurt out all of the secret plans that her family and friends had already cobbled together.

'Hey, you look great. You were obviously born to be a mermaid,' Kam grinned at her as they reached each other. She had forgotten for a moment that she too was in costume, and up until the revelations on Sea Shanty night she had been really excited about wearing the most beautiful iridescent tail that her mother had managed to make. Today it seemed unimportant and she tried desperately to find her tongue and keep it appropriate, whilst forcing phrases from the letter – now memorised – out of her head.

But it was difficult.

I love the way you light up every room when you enter it.

I love the way you crinkle your nose when you laugh.

Really difficult.

I love the way you have no qualms about being true to yourself and cherish those around you.

'Are you okay?' Kam raised an eyebrow and she realised she hadn't answered him.

'Fine, just mermaid brain I guess. You okay? Right let's go find our babies... um... class. Let's go find the class. They should be milling about on the field.'

She walked beside him, desperate to reach out and grab his hand to give it a little squeeze just so he knew she was here at his side and willing to be so forever. Instead she walked next to him with eyes fixed firmly on the floor, reminding herself that everyone else was on board with the plan and that she should be too.

The children were beyond excited as the two of them walked onto the field and her heart stopped melting over Kam and began to melt a little with pride at how well everyone had done. All of them were in costume: some shopbought, some homemade but all had put in a real effort.

Lottie was darting about the field with her face painting kit adding details to the faces of the children who wanted it, whilst shooting looks at Pippa that very clearly stated, 'Don't you dare spoil the surprise!'

Alice was trying to calm a gaggle of children who were running harum-scarum across the field, toppling each other over, and whose parents had disappeared, a common occurrence with The Smuggler's Curse being so close. Other parents, the ones who had stayed, were taking photos with their phones, and photographers from the local paper and the local news were also swirling around the field snapping images and having mini interviews. Pippa saw Hugo Sweetling from the local news chatting to Rosy in front of the cameras.

The whole field was alive with celebration and, as it had for all the week so far, the sun shone bright with no hint of rain to spoil the fun. A klaxon sounded to request that people got into their groups and lined up in order. The procession was about to begin. It was then that Pippa realised that Marion was nowhere to be seen, not pushing Rosy out of the way to ensure more TV coverage for herself, not sounding the klaxon and shouting orders at anyone in the vicinity, or circling with a scary predatory look trying to see what Neptune had under his scaly tail. This was odd. Where on earth was she?

'Have you seen Marion?' she whispered out of the side of her mouth to Kam as they queued up by the gate ready with the others.

'No. Is she not here? Maybe she had something important on, or they're all on a family holiday.'

'Hmmm, you have met her, right? This is her thing, her biggest event of the year. She's normally reduced at least five children and three sets of parents to tears by now. I'm worried.'

'Well, don't be. There's not a lot you can do right now... Okay, Billy, looking great there... she'll be okay. She's Marion. Maybe she's decided to go sort out Parliament, or Windsor Castle. You know, bigger and better things.'

'I don't know. Maybe I should whizz around and check on her.'

'And leave me here to deal with this great gaggle of monsters? Please, don't. Look the parade is about to begin. If you're really worried I'll come knock on her with you afterwards. But I'm sure she's absolutely fine.'

'Okay, good point. We'll do that.'

Her voice was drowned out by the cheers that erupted from parents and all the visitors who had turned up to celebrate with Penmenna, as the children turned the corner and started off down Fore Street.

There was music blaring from many of the floats. So many community groups had got involved and Pippa thought this year might be the biggest, brashest and most colourful turn out yet. She couldn't stop the beam of pride she was feeling towards her community right now.

Pippa found herself singing along with the float in front, her mouth open wide as she threw herself into the music. She caught Kam watching her out of the corner of her eye and giggled as she said, 'I know, loud and very, very off-key,' and felt the grin cross her face as she said it, and then suddenly wipe clean straight off it as Kam gave her a funny look.

Shit, that was the exact phrasing from the letter. She really hoped the words weren't as etched in his heart as they were in hers, but seeing as they were his words in the first place, she didn't fancy her chances. Good job she never fancied being a spy; she'd be utter rubbish.

She covered her mistake quickly by nodding her head towards the pavement and shouted at him over the noise that surrounded them, 'Look, I've never seen it this busy before. People must have come for miles around.'

The street was lined with people all waving and shouting encouragement. The noise seemed to be rising and it was getting hard to make out any individual words, but looking at Kam's lips (she found it very hard not to) it looked like he had exclaimed, 'No way! How on earth?'

Looking up, she followed his gaze to see his mother, a man she assumed was his father and Nisha, Hema and Anuja lined up along the side of the road next to her own family.

'Oh, that's lovely. Did you not know they were coming?'

'No, no I didn't. They didn't say a word.'

And although Kam didn't look overjoyed to have his family descend, Pippa couldn't help but think their families looked pretty good together.

Chapter Forty-seven

Kam was exhausted. He had never realised walking through a small village wearing a tail and carrying a giant fork would be so draining. Now he was scooting about the field trying to find his parents and sisters. He'd catch a glimpse of them and then, poof, they would disappear again. It was as if they and Pippa's family were playing a game of hide and seek and chase all rolled into one without letting him know he was It.

Besides which, since when had his mum and Pippa's mum become such good friends? That in itself was odd. Surely there was only a limited amount of bonding one could do over a cake stall.

Eventually he tracked them down in one of the marquees at the end of the field which was serving cream teas, and his father – always fond of his mum's sweet treats – looked pretty happy as he rammed a scone topped with jam and a mountainous looking pile of clotted cream into his mouth.

'Hello, boy, these are good. I can see why Cornwall holds some appeal.'

'Ah it's more than a bit of clotted cream that's keeping Kam here,' teased Hema who was instantly rewarded with an evil look, the like of which only an older brother can deliver.

'It's great to see you, a huge surprise. How long are you here for?' Kam was surprised with how genuine he sounded. They were actually really messing with his plans.

'Just until Saturday night. We wanted to come and see the carnival. Jan told us how much work you and Pippa have put into it, so we couldn't miss that. We'll stay for the It's-a-Knockout tournament and the fireworks and then Dad is going to drive us home.'

'That seems silly. Why don't you stay an extra night and head back on the Sunday?'

'No, no, no! This is what we will do, but you are a good boy for asking. Anyway, talking of Pippa…' Kam hadn't realised they had been although it was a subject he could happily chat about for hours, much to Ben's annoyance. 'Where is that darling girl?'

'Um, I think she has just dashed off to check on a friend.' It felt odd calling Marion a friend but it was easier than explaining any further. He felt bad for not going with her but Pippa had insisted he went to find his family and that she would be fine checking in on Marion by herself.

The ice that had seemed to build up between him and Pippa over the last few weeks seemed to be thawing again, and he was pleased about it. It had knocked him for six when she hadn't mentioned his letter at all over the last half term, such behaviour seeming so out of character. She was normally a woman who dealt with things head on and he appreciated that about her. Coy was not a quality he ever thought he could ascribe to Pippa, but then he supposed one lived and learnt. He was hoping that now the thaw had begun they may be able to get their friendship back on track. His feelings may be unrequited but he still missed her company, her easy-going friendship and the silly midnight texting.

He was hoping that, over the course of the next few days, when they would be sort of socialising together without the responsibilities of being at work hanging over their heads, and maybe with a little help from Roger's famed hooch, they may be able to rekindle the friendship and get things back to where they were before they had slept together. He'd just have to try not to look all puppy dog eyes at her and not to mind too much when she did eventually meet someone she wanted a relationship with. Although no matter how noble he wanted to be about it, there was still a real sting when he considered that possibility.

As much as he loved his family, he hoped they weren't going to throw a spanner in the works, and scare Pippa off even more than she was already. The fact that his mother and sisters clearly adored her would have been great if she cared about him as much as he did her, but now that the situation had changed it could be added pressure that they did not need. Argghhh!

Chapter Forty-eight

The big day had arrived and as Pippa walked to her mum's house she was really beginning to doubt the wisdom of what she had agreed to. Doubting the wisdom was a bit of an understatement: she was absolutely terrified. Her feet were so cold they were practically ice-blocks. Somehow, in a matter of a few days, the whole village had got involved and what had seemed like a wild, impractical and unworkable plan now was actually happening. And she was the one in the middle of it, forced to do embarrassing stuff that would no doubt be giggled about for years.

It was no secret that Pippa wasn't easily embarrassed and was pretty game for most things, but this… this was off the scale. She recognised that doing embarrassing stuff meant that Kam would understand how deeply she felt, and she didn't mind doing it for that very reason. She did mind, however, the fact that now she felt pressured into acting the twit because the whole village were expecting it.

Even Rosy had taken the time to let her know that she thought it a sweet idea and that her initial reservations, only caused by professional concerns, were put to one side as time had shown how perfectly matched Pippa and Kam were.

It seemed that the only person who wasn't involved was Marion and that was because she was absent. When Pippa had called at her house after the carnival, she had been met with silence. No lights were on and no sounds were heard. She began to worry even more than she had. Marion would never schedule time away from Feast Week unless it was an emergency and, as the end of term approached, the woman had been looking increasingly frazzled.

Pippa had knocked one last time, when Marion's neighbour popped out and confided that Marion had hightailed it with both boys the minute term had ended, to head off to somewhere hot – Morocco, the neighbour thought – and to stay with an old university friend.

She had also confided that Richard had not appeared to be accompanying them.

With nothing else for Pippa to do, she had returned back to the field and giggled and gossiped with Kam's sisters until the evening was well and truly over. In snatched bits of conversation, held whenever they sent Kam off to fetch something for them, a drink, popcorn, candy floss etc., Pippa had managed to glean that Jan had been in touch with Kam's mum regularly since they had last visited, and the two of them had been concocting a slowly-slowly plan to get their children together romantically. With things not moving as quickly as they had hoped and with Jan letting Geeta know about the Feast Week plan, they had resolved to come down and see how things unfolded.

Geeta had also wanted her husband to see how Kam was a respected member of the local community and that leaving the family business wasn't the most heinous crime imagined, that their son had focus, purpose and respect, although Dev took some persuading that a scaly tail and long coloured hair was the way to do it.

Although it was comic to watch Kam with his parents (both seemed determined to quick fire questions at him without waiting for answers), she could see Kam was getting a bit stressed. Having his family here may not have been part of his plan, but it meant that Pippa got to spend more time with Nisha, Hema and Anuja, which meant a lot of cackling. Later, when Polly had deigned to join them, looking like she perhaps shouldn't have been let loose in the cider tent with her friends, Pippa had invited all three of them to become more involved in the crazy plan that had been hatched. It would appear that whilst some women spend their lives yearning to be bridesmaids or astronauts, Nisha, Hema and Anuja had always wanted to be the Middlesbrough version of Destiny's Child, which worked out rather well.

Now the day itself had dawned. Pippa let herself into her mum's house, her yellow spandex workout gear in a bag as instructed. She couldn't believe she was going ahead with this, or that she had been the one stupid enough to suggest it.

She opened the door and heard even more noise than usual pouring out from all the rooms. Polly was in the living room with Nisha, Hema and Anuja practising a dance routine. Tatters was also taking part and showing great dance potential, skittering about like a gazelle. The kitchen was a-whirr with the sound of Jan's sewing machine and the ever-present smell of baking biscuits.

'Alright, Mum?' Pippa leant down and popped a kiss on the top of her mum's head as she whirred her way at speed through a swathe of red material.

'Yep, good to see, you love. Now, you did bring that yellow thing, the old workout thing of mine you seem so fond of, didn't you?'

'Yes, it's in this bag here. How are they doing?' She jerked her head towards the living room door and the sounds of giggling and music.

'Yep, all seems under control. They're certainly quick learners. Polly is pretty impressed. They've been here for ages, but I think they've got it down pat now. I've just whisked some biscuits in the oven for them. Now, more importantly, I found a solution to cutting up that old yellow thing. When we discussed it, I could see on your face that you really, really didn't want to.'

'Not really, it's irreplaceable. I know you think it should have seen the bin some time ago, but I love it. I don't know how or when or from where we could get another one… but I guess I was prepared to sacrifice it in the name of love. Oh shit, not love. Don't get excited, not love. Um… in the name of romance and potential, then I was prepared to let you hack at it with scissors, although I would have probably just had to wait in the other room so not to witness the act of carnage myself.'

'Well, no hacking required any more. Look, if you pop it on then I can just slide this over the top.' Jan pulled the red fabric from her machine and Pippa saw that her mum had made some kind of coloured sleeve, and that piled next to her were more bits of something fashioned out of the red fabric. 'What are you waiting for, spit spot, chip chop!'

As Pippa came back into the room, once again top to toe in yellow, she reflected that this outfit had had more outings this summer than it had over the past twenty odd years combined! Her mother whirled around her with superhero swiftness, leaving speed trails behind her as she moved, the air punctuated only by the odd 'Uuch!' from Pippa as pins accidentally pricked her. Taking a deep breath, Jan eventually stood back and admired her handiwork.

'Do you know what? It looks fab. I think we've cracked it. I know it's not good to be proud of one's own handiwork, but you know what, love? Your mum is a flipping genius.'

'Hold on, don't let her look yet. I found it. I found it!' Pete ran into the kitchen with a jester's cap held aloft in his hands, also red and yellow complete with multiple fronds and jingling bells. 'Now she can look.' He plonked the cap on her head and pulled it down a little more roughly than was perhaps necessary. Then he too took a step back to admire his work, nodding with satisfaction and sharing we've-smashed-it looks with his mum.

'Come on, then. Let's get you in front of the mirror.' They nudged her into the living room where there was a huge wooden-framed mirror hanging on the wall, surrounded by pictures of the Parkin family, giggling and growing up over the decades.

As Pippa, Pete and Jan entered the room, Polly stopped the music, and she and Kam's three slightly sweaty sisters let out a little cheer and clapped.

'Oh, you look great.'

'I'm sooo happy. I can't believe this is really happening,' Hema added.

'You're not alone.' Pippa quipped back.

What was she thinking?

There reflecting back at her, in bright red and yellow glory, she was dressed like a medieval fool for all the world to see. It had definitely made more sense when it was at the idea's stage as she had chatted with Lynne and Lottie about how she felt like a fool. She took a deep breath, letting it ripple out slowly over her lip as she stared at herself. She supposed if nothing else, and if it all went horribly wrong, there would not be a single person who didn't agree that she had given it her all.

Chapter Forty-nine

Kam wasn't sure what was happening in the world but there was definitely something off kilter. His parents turning up without announcing themselves, whilst odd, could easily be explained: they were just convinced that whatever they did they were the parents so they would always be right. But the fact that his sisters just kept disappearing made no sense at all. One of the biggest joys in their lives was to gang up on him and make him do stupid stuff, but this time they were just – *poof!* – gone. And he didn't know where. When he asked, they became coy and either his mother or father would jump in and change the subject. If he didn't know them all so well, then he probably wouldn't be worried, but he did know them. He knew them better than anyone else, and that was why he was concerned.

Ben had also been a bit weird, calling him last night to say that he'd definitely be coming to Penmenna's Feast Week finale, the It's-a-Knockout tournament and fireworks. Kam didn't remember inviting him, and it was most out of character for Ben to put his hand in his pocket to cover the expenses of an additional member of staff, especially to come half way across the county to a village he didn't really have any links to. It occurred to him his friend might still be trying to sleep with Nisha, but he had received such short shrift last time that Ben couldn't possibly think he was still in with a chance.

There was very definitely something going on. And now, as he was walking to the school field where the competition would be held, dotted with marquees serving typically Cornish refreshments mainly based around cider and clotted cream (Cornwall clearly hadn't gotten to grips with clean eating yet), people were smiling at him. Penmenna had always been friendly, and it was impossible to walk down any street without people smiling and stopping to chat, but today they were not merely smiling but beaming and he wasn't sure he liked it. It was a bit *too* much. He really hoped nothing had happened that would mean that he wouldn't be working in the school next year. In a community like this everyone seemed to know what was happening before the people involved did.

As he entered the field through the big gate, he couldn't believe what he was seeing. The cream teas and light refreshment marquee was still there and, standing on tiptoes, he saw that thankfully, the bar was as well. But between him and these two things was a giant obstacle course. There were huge inflatables and what appeared to be a water wall and a giant slip and slide.

'Come on, come on.' His mum bustled him in, not willing to wait for him to take in all the sights and sounds, but nudging him in the opposite direction to the bar. Not what he had planned.

At one end of the field there was a small wooden stage, and he saw Mickey from the pub, a couple of teenagers and a man in early mediaeval dress tuning guitars and checking amps. There was a drum kit currently unmanned, and Mickey's friend, Andrew, was standing on the edge of the little stage, banging a tambourine against his legs, his eyes closed as he concentrated on counting. Ethel was there with him, in a lace blouse that Kam expected Pippa would have given her eye teeth for, a musical case of some sort down by the side of her with Flynn sat guarding it as she counted with Andrew, bringing her arm down with force on every number. Kam's curiosity was piqued; this looked like it could be quite entertaining.

He scanned the field looking for Pippa or her family, or indeed his own mysteriously vanished sisters. He couldn't see anyone, although there was a shape frantically scurrying around the back of the refreshments tent that looked like it could be the silhouette of Pippa's brother, Pete.

'Mum, could you stop pushing me quite so forcefully. I'd like to look around, maybe go and grab a beer before all the fun starts.'

'I need to get you in pla—'

'Let him go get a drink, Geeta. He might well need it.' It was most unusual for his father to be the voice of reason.

Whilst neither thing either parent had said made much sense to him, at least now his mother was pulling on him, rather than pushing, and in the correct direction.

He saw Lottie scurry past and he called out to her.

'Hi, Kam,' she waved, waved and grinned far too much for it to be normal. 'See you in a bit. I'm just helping the teams get ready. It's gonna blow your mind!'

'They have four teams of four…' His dad launched into an explanation of how the tournament would proceed and Kam didn't have the heart to tell him that he knew. He had been over it with Pippa, who always swore that this was the second best part of Feast Week after the Sea Shanties. '…and then when those first four teams have completed to the course, it's opened up to the rest of the public and everyone can have a turn.'

'So, let me get this straight, the first four teams sort of demonstrate how to follow the course,' Geeta stated as if talking to a small child.

'Yes, indeed.' His father replied.

'And this year the teams are the Parkin family representing their garage, a team from the local church, a team from the TV—'

'I think it's the guy from *Green-Fingered and Gorgeous* and a couple of his friends, one of which used to be on the news.'

'Oh okay, and then the final team represent the Young Farmers, is that right?'

If it wasn't so frustrating, this exchange between his parents would be mildly amusing. Did they think he didn't know how this worked? They suddenly seemed to be founts of local knowledge despite living over four hundred miles away and his father not having visited Cornwall since a family holiday over ten years ago. They were certainly determined to make sure he understood It's-a-Knockout though. A half smile played on his lips as he heard them out. Ben suddenly appeared from nowhere and, with a smirk, handed Kam a drink. His parents apparently having no time for niceties merely bowed their heads at his friend before continuing their lecture.

'So, it's really important we watch very carefully, don't you agree, Dev?'

'I do, now drink up, Kam, and we'll go and get a good spot. Right at the front.'

They both started to pull on him again, dragging him to where they wanted him, his pint sploshing down the side of his glass. What was amusing him a second ago was about to lose its sheen very quickly.

Dragged to the front of the gathering crowd he raised his hand to wave to those taking part: Matt Masters, who was in a team with Sylvie from school, Sylvie's partner, Alex, and some tall blonde man who looked like there was no obstacle he couldn't merely stride over, all Thor-like.

The Parkins, however, were studiously avoiding his eye. Pippa was in some bizarre towelling cloak thing that looked like something a Victorian may have taken to the seaside and failed to respond to his waving. Her brother, though, finally caught his eye and winked before putting his thumb up.

He saw Alice, the teaching assistant in the frightening Mrs Adams' class, who was on the church team along with Dan the vicar – who still looked like he had come straight from Hollywood casting and not like he should be in a dog collar – and a couple of weathered-looking older men. Kam knew that they were the local bell-ringers, so although older than the other teams, they had a strength to their upper arms that would make them a hard group to beat.

Suddenly, there was a screech of white noise that caused everyone's head to turn towards Roger, who stood next to the little stage and was tapping on a microphone.

'Hello, everyone, and welcome to Penmenna's It's-a-Knockout. The last event of Feast Week before you all head back to mine for a taste of the legendary Smuggler's Scuttlebutt.' He delivered this welcome address in a deadpan way that couldn't have been less welcoming. Kam wondered if putting him in charge was an example of Penmenna humour. Roger went on to outline how the course would work before concluding that, unusually, the band would accompany the first part of the course, where the team members would be expected to take turns running through a huge inflatable course climbing, swinging, sliding, jumping and collecting puzzle pieces that they would have to assemble into something that hopefully made sense at the end.

'However, this is Penmenna, so nothing is ever straight-forward and I think you'll find we're going to have a surprise up our sleeve as this plays out. Keep your eyes peeled. You don't want to miss the competition this year.' And with a flourish, most out of character, he motioned to the band, who were still tuning up.

As he waited to see what would happen next, Kam felt his father place his hand on his shoulder. Kam turned a fraction to acknowledge his father, not a man prone to spontaneous displays of affection.

'It suits you here, Kam.'

'Thanks, Dad. I do love it. I can see myself staying for a while.'

'I think you should. You seem to have fitted in well.' Dev squeezed his shoulder and nodded three times. That was his way of saying '*I'm proud of you, son*', and Kam felt pride of his own whoosh over him. He was proud to be part of his family, proud that his father had forgiven him. He gave his dad a pat on the shoulder that he knew would be interpreted as it was meant, as an '*I love you, Dad*'.

He turned back to face the stage, knowing his father wouldn't want this dragged out, to see Rosy walking on stage with a microphone. He knew she could sing, her voice had been outstanding during the Sea Shanties – pure, confident and clean – and now she started to sing into the mic, scanning the crowds as she did so. Then Ethel, brandishing a saxophone, began to play, swiftly followed by the others, Flynn at their heels barking along. He tried to follow the song – he recognised the lyrics – and was just focusing in when the whole band paused, even the dog who appeared to have faultless timing. Roger shouted 'one two three' into the mic and all four teams got on their marks. Nothing unusual so far, apart from Pippa, who appeared to be slipping out of her towel thing – oh my gosh, she was! – to reveal that spandex outfit that had a sweet, sweet spot in his heart. Only now it had been redesigned and patched with bits of red to resemble the costume of an old-fashioned jester. All the teams started to run and Rosy carried on with her song, a song about being a fool in love.

Cogs began to whirr in Kam's brain and as he saw his mum and dad's expectant faces looking at him, he had a feeling something big was about to happen but he had no idea what.

Meanwhile the crowds were cheering. Pete had grabbed Pippa as she completed the course and brought back her part of the puzzle ramming a jester's hat onto her head. By the time Rosy's song finished, the young farmers seemed to be in the lead with three of their pieces assembled, whilst the other teams still only had two apiece, when suddenly the band burst into another song, this one much more recognisable.

Out of nowhere his sisters appeared on the course. They were going to get in the way and cause an accident

349

if they didn't move soon, but Mickey, still tuneful for one missing so many teeth, belted out *Stop! In the name of love* and the whole course froze. The vicar had his leg half over a bit of the inflatable, others were mid run, one with a puzzle piece but they all paused in their positions. Was this usual? Kam couldn't remember seeing this before in any knockout games he had witnessed.

Pippa, the only contestant moving, turned and faced Kam, a look of utter fear on her face. He had never seen her so pale. He still wasn't sure what was happening but he knew the compulsion to race towards her and wrap her up, protect her from whatever was making her look that way was strong. He started to move, but his father gently, silently placed his hand on Kam's arm, keeping him where he was as his sisters moved behind Pippa and gave her the mic Rosy had been using for the previous song. The whole field, which had been murmuring as everyone froze, now stood stock still and silent, waiting to see what would unfold.

This was excruciating, what was happening?

'Stop! In the name of love.' Pippa's voice pierced the silence as she took over singing the song, but with no accompaniment from the band. Her voice started off a little wobbly but soon began to soar, albeit slightly off-key. His sisters launched themselves into some kind of dance routine that would have been funny if it had been a boy band, but was even more hilarious as his sisters did it, although he couldn't help but notice that somehow over the years they had changed from clumsy lumps with no coordination into graceful young women.

But it wasn't upon them that his gaze rested. Instead, he could feel his heart beat faster and faster as Pippa continued to torture the song and the entire field stood there watching her.

He heard a snigger from behind him, and he turned quickly to give the group of small boys, all of whom he recognised from Class Three, a look so stern it would have scared his own mother, who at this moment in time was looking all misty-eyed at Pippa as if she was a fairy queen, granting happiness to all.

He turned back and locked his eyes on Pippa's, holding them there as she butchered the song all the way to the end. He wasn't sure why she was doing this but it was very cute, and yet she didn't seem any less frightened as the song came to a close. He noticed out the corner of his eye that the vicar was trying to get off the inflatable as discreetly as he could, and Matt Masters looked like he might be beginning to have cramps in his leg, yet they all stayed as still as possible.

Pippa stopped singing, and still clutching her microphone started to walk away from her team and from his sisters, and right over towards him.

Oh wow.

What was she about to do?

He didn't know how to react, what to do with his body. Was she really doing this and coming over to him? His breath was increasingly ragged as he looked at this brave, brave woman who had captured his heart all those months ago and then broken it into two after the best day and night of his life. Now she was walking to him with a microphone and for some reason his parents were here, standing behind him and making it quite clear that he wasn't going anywhere. Not that he would. Not that he would ever do anything to upset or embarrass Pippa, who still looked scared but also incredibly determined.

But still this couldn't be real. He was going to wake up any moment now and hear his sisters squabbling in the bathroom, not all standing in a field looking like they were about to cry.

Pippa stopped in front of him. Her eyes hadn't left his as she marched her way across the field towards him, but now they flicked down to her feet and he watched her take a very deep breath before looking up at him again.

'Hello,' he mouthed at her, giving her the biggest smile he could muster.

If anyone had told him he would be standing in a field today having the whole of the Penmenna community and most of the people from all the surrounding villages staring at him he would have been mortified. Normally this would be the sort of thing that his nightmares were made of. *Normally* he would glance down at this point and realise he had no trousers on. But it appeared this was not a dream; he was fully dressed and surrounded by his family whilst the woman who had rejected him – yet he had remained totally infatuated with – was standing in front of him, dressed as a fool, having sung her heart out, loudly and really badly, in front of everyone.

'Hello,' she mouthed back. He watched her give her shoulders a little shake, and knew from that small motion that something else was coming.

'Kam Choudhury, I want to take this opportunity to tell you that I am a fool.' She spoke into the mic, her words loud and clear for all to hear, although there was a little shake to them. She gestured to her costume, slightly shaking her head and with that half smile that he knew was her what-am-I-doing? smile. 'I made a huge misjudgement, ignored my intuition and as a result may have caused you hurt. I need you to know, in front of all these people here today, that I would never ever deliberately hurt you. I think that, with the exception of my own dad, you are the most honourable man I have ever met, and you combine that with being a man I have had so much fun with. We fit, you and I. We may have broken a rule or two while working together, but despite that it's fair to say the whole community are out in force and willing us to sort out our differences.' She nodded at Rosy, who had moved on to the assault course to stand next to her partner Matt, and was beaming over at the both of them, clearly giving her support for whatever this was. And what Kam thought it was, was almost too big for his head and his heart to compute.

Pippa took another deep breath and, still holding his eyes, continued her speech. 'You wrote me a letter, but somehow Sheila got involved and I didn't get it until this week. It made me cry. Everything you said, everything you have written mirrors exactly what I feel. I can't believe how lucky I am to have met you, to spend time with you, and that is something I want to do for as long as you can bear it. Like I said, you and I fit together. It feels like I have found the other half of me, the half that I am meant to be alongside. The half I *want* to be alongside. I want to be able to tell you how much I care for you every single morning for the rest of my life.'

Kam thought his heart was going to power right out of chest, so he took a step forward, and then another. This had to be a dream. There was no way this woman was standing in front of him declaring her heart in front of their whole community. Although right now, he didn't give a fig about anyone in this field apart from Pippa standing in front of him, dressed head to toe in red and yellow, and with bells on. He watched the grin spread across her face, practically ear to ear as he stood opposite her, toe to toe, so close he could feel her breath as she whispered '*Hello*,' again and he whispered it back.

'I haven't finished.'

'You are amazing. This is amazing.' Kam's arm swept to encompass the whole field, but his eyes remained locked on her. 'I certainly have no problem with you telling me every single day how much you want to be with me.'

'I do. I *really* do. You haven't changed your mind, have you?' Their voices, now they were so close, were low, intimate, meant for just the two of them, and the whole field was straining to hear.

'I haven't. I *really* haven't. I cannot tell you how happy this is making me. You've been my everything almost since I first set eyes on you and now, somehow, you are stood in front of me saying everything I ever dreamed of. Pippa Parkin, you are the most wonderful woman I have ever met and I cannot believe my luck.'

Her eyes welled with tears, and he didn't know if they were of relief, happiness or shock, but he did know there was only one thing left for him to do. As he snaked his arm around her waist and pulled her close, he lowered his lips to hers. He felt suffused in the glow of coming home, of the whole world being right, of his love being returned as she kissed him right back, as deeply, as passionately and as committed as he was and the entire field threw up a deafening cheer.

Acknowledgements

I'd like to say a huge thank you to my fabulous agent, Hayley Steed. She is a constant source of support and joy, always making me giggle, calming me down and boosting me up. You are awesome.

Another thank you has to go to my editor, Elizabeth Jenner for being so supportive, particularly when I had a poorly patch and panic earlier this year. And to Laura McCallen for her ever watchful eye. The whole team at Canelo are wonderful and I love working with you all. Keep inviting me to the parties, please.

A huge shout-out and thank you has to go to the very patient Bibek Khanal, who I ran to with concerns and niggles about this book and who guided me straight. Your advice was much needed and I cannot express how grateful I am for all your help.

My friends in teaching will still remain anonymous but much loved. As ever, I am so grateful you answer all my questions. It's been a while since I was in the teaching game, so these updates are much needed.

And of course, the book community – writers, readers, bloggers and my much loved SisterScribes, your enthusiasm and support are invaluable, and I appreciate it more than I can say. A good review or a reader getting in touch are the things that bring the sunshine to the day and make it easier to keep on tapping away at the keyboard. So many of you have been kind, and said the loveliest things – it really means the world, thank you. Do feel free to get in touch with me on Facebook or Twitter, it's always great to hear from you.

Finally, Jack and Katharine – even though you're really old now, I still quite love you. You've remained pretty cute. No-one makes me laugh like you do, and no-one gives me such good, honest advice. You have never steered me wrong and I am so very proud of the adults you have become. Mad love. Namdi, you remain practically perfect in every way (and I remain in vocal denial everywhere but here). And of course, my parents, always having faith, it means the world. x